ECHO POWER

OTHER BOOKS BY ANNA DURAND

ECHO POWER

Echo Power Trilogy, Book One

ANNA DURAND

JACOBSVILLE BOOKS JB MARIETTA, OHIO

ECHO POWER

ISBN: 978-1-949406-88-7 (paperback)
ISBN: 978-1-949406-89-4 (ebook)
ISBN: 978-1-949406-90-0 (audiobook)

Jacobsville Books
www.JacobsvilleBooks.com

Publisher's Cataloging-in-Publication Data
provided by Five Rainbows Cataloging Services

Names: Durand, Anna.
Title: Echo power / Anna Durand.
Description: Marietta, OH : Jacobsville Books, 2022. | Series: Echo power trilogy, bk. 1.
Identifiers: ISBN 978-1-949406-88-7 (paperback) | ISBN 978-1-949406-89-4 (ebook) | ISBN 978-1-949406-90-0 (audiobook)
Subjects: LCSH: Magic--Fiction. | Survival--Fiction. | End of the world--Fiction. | Man-woman relationships--Fiction. | Romance fiction. | Paranormal romance stories. | BISAC: FICTION / Romance / Paranormal / General. | FICTION / Romance / Fantasy. | FICTION / Romance / Suspense. | GSAFD: Love stories. | Occult fiction. | Romantic suspense fiction.
Classification: LCC PS3604.U724 E24 2022 (print) | LCC PS3604.U724 (ebook) | DDC 813/.6--dc23.

CHAPTER ONE

Allison

I CAREEN ACROSS THE GRASS, STUMBLING OVER A HOLE IN THE GROUND, and stagger sideways while my boots bump into things I refuse to look at, things that might be human bodies. I can't stop. Not now. Maybe never. Anyone on the ground is beyond saving, anyway. Overlapping screams pierce the air behind me, but I cannot look back. Green sparks ignite in the unnatural twilight, sizzling and snapping, nipping at my skin. My foot slips in the mud, and my ankle twists sideways, but I keep running. *Don't look down, don't look down. I can't help them.* No one can.

Ahead of me, a hulking figure seizes a smaller one around the neck and jerk its hand. The crack of bones snapping resonates in the air.

The smaller figure crumples to the ground.

Bile surges into my throat. All I can do is gulp it down and keep moving even while my muscles burn.

The ground falls away. I sail through the green-sparked air to smack down hip first. Clawing for a handhold, I lose the remnants of my balance and tumble down a hillside, spinning and spinning as I hurtle sideways down the slope toward where I'd sat to eat my lunch earlier today. The slope that's now drenched in blood. The warm liquid clings to my skin and infiltrates my mouth, its taste tangy and salty with a hint of sweetness that makes me gag. I slam into a barrier. Though I've stopped moving, my head keeps whirling, trapped in an illusion that the world is spinning. I choke back my gorge, but it tastes of blood. *Oh God, no.* I heave myself up onto my hands and knees. There beside me lies the object that halted my fall.

The headless remains of a human being.

I can't focus on anything else, my gaze riveted to the gruesome sight. Pain still throbs inside me from my tumble down the hill. But I just slump here, immobile, my heart pounding so hard my chest hurts while the pressure of nausea thrusts up into my throat. I slant sideways and retch, over and over, until my abdominal muscles ache and my throat burns. When at last the heaving subsides, I struggle to catch my breath.

Out of the corner of my eye, I glimpse the dead man.

So many lifeless bodies litter the area, but I'd managed to avoid looking directly at them until now. This one… Christ, it's impossible to avoid seeing that.

I must keep moving. The beast chasing me will catch up any second.

With an effort that screams agony through my muscles, I hoist myself up and run.

~

THE APOCALYPSE BEGAN AT TWO O'CLOCK ON A SUNNY WEDNESDAY AFternoon, but no one in this city noticed anything unusual at first. We kept going about our business, even when the sky turned a darker, more intense shade of blue like nothing seen on earth before today. I was in the public library shelving books near the front windows when I realized something had changed, something more than the color of the sky. I felt the change deep inside me, and I heard it too. A silence deeper than the void of outer space enveloped the world while an irresistible impulse seized me, luring me outside.

I pushed through the doors and shambled across the portico, past the tall pillars, and out onto the street.

People poured out of vehicles and other buildings, all of us mindlessly drawn down North Main Street toward the viaduct. We crossed the bridge to gather on the grassy hill just past the trail that skirted the river, as if waiting for something to rise up from the water below and land in front of us. We glanced at each other in confusion. Why had we come to this place? Why was the sky a deeper blue than ever before? We didn't speak to each other, but somehow, I knew we were all thinking the same thing.

What on earth is happening?

High above us, the eerie sound of music started up, softly at first, then escalating into the strains of a string symphony like none ever heard in this world. The music surrounded and infiltrated me, the melody beautiful and terrible and mesmerizing, its purpose and meaning beyond comprehension. It vibrated through my soul, wringing tears from my eyes. All around me, people sobbed and dropped to their knees, their gazes glued to the cobalt sky, as hypnotized by the music as I was. I fell to my knees too, helpless to understand what was unfolding around me. Deep inside, though, I sensed the horror hidden beneath the beauty.

If only I had understood a few seconds earlier…

No, nothing would have changed. A power beyond imagining had unleashed itself on the world.

The music froze on a single, discordant note that stretched on and on, making my ears ache and pulsating through my flesh. Then the music stopped—and an unearthly roar erupted, impregnating every molecule of air with its cacophony. I slapped my hands over my ears, but the roar penetrated into me so deeply that I couldn't breathe. And then…

The sky split open.

A rupture in the fabric of the world distended across half the horizon, from high above down to ground level, while a shredding noise grated on my eardrums and reverberated off buildings throughout the city. The hole in the sky disgorged a river of writhing shapes that spilled onto the earth, spreading outward as the amorphous shadows became creatures with arms and legs and heads. They growled and screeched like demons sent up from hell itself.

And then they came for us.

The demons grabbed human beings and tore them to shreds. Screams of agony and terror echoed around me, mingling with the wet sounds of flesh ripping and the cracking of bones. I stood frozen, unable to even blink, witnessing events in mute horror as the creatures ripped men, women, and children asunder. My heart pounded so hard and fast that it robbed me of breath.

A creature raised the severed head of a human being, hoisting it high, and roared in triumph.

Run. Do it now, before those things come for you.

I bolted back down the hill, clinging to the only coherent thought in my mind. *This can't be happening.* But it was. While I fled toward the bridge, fireballs shot out of the rip in the sky and slammed into the earth. The green sparks had snuffed out, and the only light emanated from the meteorites crashing down on the city. But they weren't objects from outer space. They came from another world, from the place on the other side of the rupture in the heavens.

Buildings exploded. Trees burst into flames. Pavement melted. I scrambled up the hill and onto the bridge, heading for…I didn't know where. Anyplace but here.

At the center of the bridge, hunkered a huge beast.

I halted so quickly I almost tripped over my own feet, and a frigid chill iced through me from my skin down to my soul. Behind me, demons rampaged. Ahead of me, this creature blocked my only escape route. He must've stood over six feet tall, a mountain of muscles and wild black hair with a scruffy beard that hid most of his features except for the scar that slashed across his cheek. Every flash of the fireballs lit him up. His long, battered leather coat fluttered around his thighs. It was black, just like his shirt and his worn leather pants that stretched tight over his thighs. I glimpsed hints of tattoos revealed by his partially unbuttoned shirt.

The beast stood there, legs spread, as if he had no intention of allowing me to pass. His gaze landed on me, and his lips peeled back from his teeth, though not in a smile. He sneered at me, fisting his hands at his sides. Jabbing a finger toward me, he growled, "You."

That beast wanted to kill me. I sensed it, though I had no idea what I had done to enrage him. He must have come through the rupture, which made him an alien monster like the others. What could I do? Behind me lay carnage and death. Ahead of me, maybe I could still find a place to hide or a way to escape.

I whirled around, and before he had time to react, I ran back the way I'd come as fast as my battered body could go.

And the beast barreled after me.

~

THAT'S HOW I WIND UP PELTING ACROSS THE VIADUCT YET AGAIN, DODGing other creatures and getting stung by molten fragments of the fireballs that hurtle past overhead. Every explosive impact makes the earth shudder beneath my feet. I need to escape, that's all I know. The hoarse bellows of the beast pursuing me reverberate off the shattered carcasses of the buildings that once formed a city. Now it's a wasteland. Where can I hide? How can I get away from that monster? More creatures, just as terrifying, maraud through the city. I *can't* get away.

But I must try.

My legs tremble, and my ears ring. Any second, I'll pass out. I know this. I have no choice but to stop and rest, though I realize the beast will catch up to me if I do. There must be someplace I can hide, for just a few minutes, long enough to regain my strength and catch my breath. I race past a building I would probably recognize if it weren't reduced to rubble, but up ahead, I see a structure that seems mostly intact. It's a pharmacy. I'd never visited the place, but I drove past it every day on my way to work.

I risk glancing over my shoulder.

The beast is nowhere in sight.

Maybe I've caught a sliver of luck. Veering onto the cracked sidewalk, I leap through a broken window into the pharmacy building. Shelves lie broken and scattered while their contents have sprayed across the blood-spattered floor. I leap over the biggest pile of rubble and drop to my knees, breathing so hard that black spots speckle my vision. I take a long, slow breath. Then another. And another. The ringing in my ears has subsided, and those black spots no longer obscure my sight.

In the gloomy space, I notice a refrigerated case nearby, one that would've held beverages, though its glass front has been smashed. Crawling over the debris, I feel around inside the darkened refrigerator until my fingers close around a plastic bottle. Of what, I don't care. I need to drink something, anything.

When I pull out the bottle, I realize it's water. *Thank heaven.* I unscrew the cap and guzzle the still-cold liquid.

I allow myself a few minutes to finish my drink and rest. Then I know I need to get moving again. As I make my way over the rubble and out the window, I move cautiously so I can scan the vicinity. Just as I step out onto the sidewalk, a solitary fact at last sinks into my brain.

Though it's afternoon, the world is cloaked in twilight. Sure, I'd noticed the semi-darkness before. But the fact the sun had been vanquished didn't hit me until right now. No stars glitter above me, either. Fireballs keep hurtling out of the tear in the sky, seeming to emerge from a black, disk-shaped hole at the center of the rupture. A rim of silvery fire surrounds the disk.

Behind me, footfalls crunch on rubble.

I spin around and yelp as I slam into a manlike creature, stumbling backward.

The beast who had pursued me seizes my upper arms and drags me into his body. His impossibly broad shoulders encompass me. He hoists me off my feet. My boots dangle several inches above the ground. My face is so close to his that I feel his scruffy beard rasping over my chin.

"Everything that's happening"—He snarls his words while spittle peppers my face with every syllable he utters—"it's all your fault."

This brute speaks with a British accent. That's weird, considering where we are, but I have bigger issues to worry about now. It feels like a rock has gotten stuck in my throat, and swallowing hard does nothing to alleviate the constriction. Though I don't want to do it, I force myself to meet his unearthly gaze and not cringe at the brilliance of his golden brown irises. "What are you talking about?"

"This happened because of you."

"No."

He spins me around, my feet touching down on the cracked pavement, and cuffs my wrists behind my back with his much bigger, rougher hands. I try to kick him, but he lashes one leg around both of mine. "Stop fighting. It won't help."

His fingers wriggle as he ties something around my wrists. Rope? Not sure, and it hardly matters. I've been captured by a monster who blames me for the apocalypse unfolding around us.

"Kick me again," he snarls into my ear, "and I'll bind your feet too. Understand?"

I nod.

He shoves me forward while keeping hold of my bindings. "You're coming with me."

"Where?"

"Somewhere else."

"Who are you?"

"If you must have a name, call me Dax." He yanks on my bindings, making me trip over a lump of shattered pavement. "No more talking, Allison, or I'll gag you too."

He knows my name. *He knows.*

I shut up and let the beast haul me down the streets of what used to be a thriving city. It's metamorphosed into a wasteland populated by monsters and whatever survivors remain. The world has died. Whatever is replacing it seems like nowhere any human would want to live.

This used to be Fort Worth, Texas. What will it become now?

Chapter Two

Dax

I GIVE THE GIRL A SHOVE EVERY SO OFTEN TO ENSURE SHE KEEPS MOV-ing, despite the nasty looks she flashes me over her shoulder. Allison Dahl is the reason for all of this. I know it, and she must know it too, though she refuses to admit the truth. This world has been laid waste because of her. And I've been trapped in hell for the same reason. The time has come to extract the truth from her by whatever means necessary.

Screams and unearthly roars echo through the ruins of this metropolis. I have no idea where in the mundane world I've wound up, but the city's name hardly matters now. It no longer exists, not in any form its residents would recognize. I haven't recognized myself for five years. Allison thinks I'm a monster, I'm sure, and she is correct. I have become one of the things mundane humans fear will crawl out from under their beds to devour them.

The only creature I want to devour is Allison Dahl. But she wouldn't like the way I'd fuck her. No, she seems like one of those women who would never allow a man to defile her in filthy ways. I haven't been with a normal woman in far too long, which is the only reason Allison's body intrigues me. Even through the dirt and blood spattered over her from head to toe, I can tell she has a body any man would want to sink his cock into for hours.

I don't have time for that.

Allison stumbles over a chunk of pavement that's been blasted out of the ground and nearly falls flat on her face. She catches herself just in time, despite her bound hands. Her dark hair falls around her face, but I can still see the deep blue of her eyes as she glares up at me.

No, I will not help her. She destroyed the world.

We need a place to hide, a location where I can interrogate her and find out the truth behind what has happened today, and even earlier, when events were set in motion. A safe place? No such thing exists anymore. Fireballs rain down every few minutes, slamming into any remaining structures and igniting whatever they touch, while silver tongues of lightning punch into the ground. Every strike, of lightning or fire, makes the ground tremble beneath our feet.

I don't know this city. But Allison does.

"Where can we hide?" I ask, stabbing a finger into her back, between her shoulder blades.

"How should I know? Everything's destroyed."

"Think of something, or I will break your fingers one by one until you give me the information I need."

"Do you seriously think threats help? I can't focus with all this…" She chokes back a sob. "There's no word for how horrible this is."

"Of course there is. It's an apocalypse. Judgment Day, if you prefer that term."

"Whose judgment?"

Someone screams from high above us, and a dark shape flies off the top of a half-destroyed building. The body smacks down a few feet to our left, hitting with a wet crunch of bones and flesh.

Allison jumps and yelps, then turns her head away, squeezing her eyes shut.

I swallow hard, refusing to glance at the human being who just hit the ground, and shove my prisoner onward. "Keep moving. And think of a place where we can hide. You have two minutes to come up with something, or I will remove your smallest finger with a very dull blade."

She sniffles but keeps trudging forward, sidestepping other bodies and climbing over heaps of rubble. We've just mounted a large pile when she freezes.

"Keep going," I snarl.

"Wait. I think I see a hiding place."

She uses her shoulder to point toward something ahead of us.

From our vantage on the mountain of debris, we have a good view of this section of the city. I have no idea where in the old world I've landed since nothing here resembles anything I remember, and I certainly have no idea how this new world being thrust upon us has changed the topography. But Allison seems to recognize a structure. I squint in the direction that she indicated.

"I don't see anything," I growl. "You're delaying."

"No, I am not. It's an underground place."

"What sort of place?"

She turns toward me, her pale face colored by the glow of a fireball streaking across the sky. "There are tunnels under the city. I guess we'd be relatively safe there, at least for a while."

"If it's underground, how can you see it from here?"

"Can't. But I do see the remnants of the stockyards, and the tunnel is under that, under what was East Exchange Avenue. Don't know what it is now."

I gaze down at the remnants of buildings ahead of us. "What city is this?"

"Used to be Fort Worth, Texas. Why do you care what city this is? You're a monster from another dimension or something."

"Or something, yes." I don't care if she calls me a monster. That belief serves my purposes. I'd never visited America until I was thrown into this city. "Take us to the tunnel."

"I've had enough of you pushing me around. If you want me to take you to a good hiding place, better start being at least marginally polite to me."

"Polite?" I slant toward her, bringing my face to within millimeters of hers. "This is only the beginning of the apocalypse. Etiquette is a bygone concept, you stupid chit. Haven't you noticed the world is being torn apart around us?" I grab her bound hands roughly and force her to bend all the fingers on her right hand except for one, the smallest digit. Then I bring out my knife, holding its long blade to her hand. "Your choice. Do what I say, or lose a finger. Afraid I can't bandage it with clean gauze or disinfect it with alcohol. You will develop an infection and die slowly while in great agony."

"You're evil. Do you know that?"

I chuckle like the beast she thinks I am. "Of course I'm evil. But so are you."

"Me? I—"

A roar erupts behind me, reverberating off the remnants of the buildings. I glance back, searching the darkness but not seeing the source of the animalistic sound.

I seize Allison's arm and start dragging her toward the location she'd indicated a moment ago. "Something is coming. You'd better take us to that underground hideaway now, or we might both wind up as puddles of blood and pulverized bone."

"Please untie my hands. I can't move very fast this way."

She does have a point, though I dislike admitting it. With at least one creature approaching us from behind, we need to find sanctuary, fast. I remove my leather belt from her wrists and stuff it into my pocket. "If you try to run, you lose two fingers."

Though she puckers her lips, and I'm certain she wants to curse at me, she doesn't do it.

I grasp her arm again and urge her to move.

Allison struggles to keep up with my pace as we scramble down the other side of the rubble mound, but she doesn't complain or fight against my hold on her arm. Whatever creature had roared before issues the same noise twice more, sounding closer every time. Soon, we reach a street that has less damage than in the other parts of this city that I've seen. The human carnage seems not to have reached this area yet, since I haven't noticed any bodies, alive or dead. None of the buildings look sturdy enough to qualify as a safe hideaway, so I let Allison lead me toward the place she had called the stockyards.

We pass by structures I can't identify, and I don't ask her what they are because it doesn't matter. She stumbles twice as we navigate more rubble. My hand on her arm is the only reason she doesn't fall, and I keep hold of her strictly because I need her alive to answer my questions, not because I give a toss about her well-being. At last, we come to a place where the ground slopes downward, leading us into a gloomy space beneath the city.

Allison stops near the entrance to the tunnel. "It's dark in there. Don't suppose you have a flashlight or something."

"You think I had time to grab a torch before the Echo thrust me into this world?"

"The Echo? What are you talking about?"

As if she doesn't know. She must. Once I have her in a reasonably secure location, I mean to interrogate her and get the answers I know she must have.

I drag Allison back over the rubble mound we had just scaled and head for a large structure on the other side of what's left of the street she called East Exchange Avenue. The building seems like a shopping mall. Allison trips and crashes to her knees, hissing in a breath when her kneecap strikes a sharp piece of broken asphalt. Her entire face wrenches with pain. I start to reach for her, to help her, but stop. I shouldn't care if she's injured. I don't care. Let the cow get herself up off the ground.

She clambers to her feet, favoring her knee, and glowers at me. "Thanks so much for the assistance."

"Better get used to helping yourself."

I clamp a hand around her upper arm once more and haul her toward the building. One half of it has collapsed, but the other side seems to have minimal damage as far as I can see. One pillar of the portico that leads to the mall's entrance has been shattered, leaving the roof tipped at a precarious angle. We hurry toward the glass doors. Some of the panes have cracked, and the frames have been warped, but I manage to yank one door open.

The lights are still on in here. They flicker but provide just enough illumination to show me the way. I have a feeling the power won't stay on for much longer, not with the impacts of fireballs and lightning shivering through the ground. The sounds grow closer every second.

"We can stay here," Allison says. "Can't we?"

"No. The storm is getting closer, and I doubt this building will survive it."

"Storm? I thought this was an apocalypse."

"It's the same thing."

We pass a restaurant, but the kitchen seems to be on fire, and the flames consume more and more of the dining area. As we hurry through the building in the flickering light, I spot what looks like a shop. I tow Allison along as I search for a torch—a flashlight, she said—or something else I can use to light our way. Finally, I discover an electric lantern.

"That needs batteries," Allison says.

"Obviously," I growl. "Do not speak again unless I ask a question. You are my prisoner. I could kill you—"

"Thought your favorite threat was to cut off my fingers with a dull knife."

"Shut up."

Allison lifts her chin. "Screw you."

The arrogant girl has no idea how much I need to take her up on that unintentional offer. I ignore her comment and hunt among the toppled racks and shelves in the store until I locate what I need—a package of twelve alkaline batteries, double-A size. To insert them into the lantern, though, I'll need to let go of her arm. Unacceptable. If I release her, she will run.

"Open this," I say, handing her the package of batteries.

Despite the fact I'm gripping her arm, she can still use both hands to open the package. And she does that, though she glowers at me first. She keeps flashing me disgusted glances while she struggles to tear open the plastic and cardboard packaging. Once she's completed her task, she thrusts the batteries at me.

I hold out the lantern. "Put them in here."

She puckers her lips, but then snatches the lantern from me and inserts the batteries. She shoves the lantern at me again. "Here. I hope you get electrocuted using the stupid thing."

Every time the chit defies me or insults me, the beast within awakens, and the heat of lust rushes through me. I despise her, but I wouldn't mind shagging her.

I lean in until the whiskers of my beard graze her cheek. "Do not speak to me that way unless you want me to ravage your body for my own pleasure, strictly to silence you."

"If you try that, I'll find a way to slit your throat."

"No, you won't. You're a weakling, not a warrior."

I've never forced myself on a woman, but I can't think of a better threat to intimidate her.

Before she can say anything else, I clamp my hand tighter around her arm and drag her through the store toward the entrance. Allison digs her heels in, pulling with all her strength to stop me. She accomplishes nothing more than to make me growl again. But I stop at the store entrance just long enough to shoot her a dark look.

"We should stay here," she says. "It's a safe place, and we can probably find food in one of the restaurants."

"This is not a safe place. The apocalypse began over the river, but it's coming this way like a plague of insects swarming across the earth. Unlike locusts, this plague will rip you apart in seconds."

"I haven't seen a single living thing since we got to the stockyards district."

Thunder explodes above us as a bolt of lightning punches through the roof right over our heads, plunging deep into the earth beneath the building. Debris and dust choke the air, but through the haze, I see a massive chunk of the ceiling teetering on the verge of tumbling down to crush us. Just as I push Allison, compelling her to run, the ceiling slab crashes down mere feet away from us. We both fall down amid the debris, tripping on the chunks of concrete that once formed the foundation. The lightning tore it apart. Hard, sharp edges slice into our skin, but we have bigger problems right now.

In the corridor outside the store's entrance, figures move around amid the shadows.

Allison is coughing. In the shaft of muted light that shines down through the hole in the ceiling, I can tell she's bleeding from multiple cuts. I'm bleeding too, but I don't care.

Because the real beasts are about to find us.

CHAPTER THREE

Allison

MY SKIN STINGS ALL OVER FROM THE KNIFE-SHARP CUTS THAT FORM A patchwork on my exposed flesh. Maybe I don't have as many cuts as I think, since the blood coating my skin makes it hard to see exactly how much damage has been done. What just happened is impossible. Lightning shouldn't do that. When a bolt hits a building, it can fry electrical stuff and damage the roof, but it can't drill a massive hole through the entire building and the foundation.

My ears ring, thanks to the deafening force of the explosion, but at least I don't think I have any broken bones. I push up until I'm on my knees, surrounded by debris. Dax is kneeling beside me, but he seems focused on something ahead of us, in the direction of the corridor outside the store. Shadows writhe out there, with only the grayish twilight to pierce the darkness. Dark shapes, that's all I can see.

As the ringing in my ears fades away, I start to hear other sounds. Growling. Grunting. Snarling reminiscent of a rabid dog.

"What is that?" I ask.

Dax swivels his head to glare at me. "Monsters, obviously."

"How is that obvious? All I see is shadows moving around out there."

"Those aren't shadows. They're creatures." He seizes my arm and stands, forcing me to scramble to my feet too. "You think I'm a beast, but those things out there make me seem like a sweet little puppy."

Worse beasts than him? I don't want to meet those things.

But I don't have a choice. We can't get out of here unless we go through the corridor.

He reaches inside his leather coat and pulls out a large knife, the one he'd threatened me with earlier. The sharp edge has an elegant curve to it, but the barbs on the opposite edge look like they could shred flesh. He snatches the battery-powered lantern off the shattered floor and seizes my arm again, dragging me toward the store's entrance and the corridor beyond. The corridor full of terrible beasts, according to Dax. Maybe he's just trying to scare me. He seems to enjoy doing that.

The jerk thinks I caused the apocalypse. He's insane and dangerous, but I guess that's what I need in a protector. I have no idea how to defend myself against the creatures that have invaded the city, but Dax at least has a weapon. Maybe he's got more hidden inside his coat. As long as he believes I know what the hell is going on and why, he will keep me alive. Right? My brain isn't running on all thrusters, but I'm pretty sure the beast of a man hauling me away is my only shot at survival.

For now.

I'm a librarian, not a woman warrior. What do I know about combat? Zilch, that's what. I hate feeling helpless.

Just as we step out into the corridor, Dax freezes. He swerves his head left and right, eyes narrowed.

A gang of freakish creatures has gathered in the corridor. I count at least six of them. Each looks different, but every single one of them scares the shit out of me. One has long fangs that protrude from its mouth, extending down its chin. Another has reddish-brown hair all over its body and eyes that flicker with red fire. And those are the nicest ones in the bunch. Every creature growls or snarls or gnashes its teeth, sometimes all three at once.

So this is what hell looks like.

Dax keeps hold of my arm, but pushes me behind his body. He waves his huge knife around like he's showing the monsters what he's got. They don't seem impressed.

"Back away," he growls, though his voice isn't as scary as the animalistic noises coming from the gang of creatures. "Let us pass, or I will be forced to destroy you."

Saliva drips from Fang Boy's mouth. "Give us the woman, and we will let you pass."

The creepy monster speaks? Yeah, this is definitely hell. That hole in the sky must've pulled demons out of the bowels of purgatory and dropped them off here just for fun.

Red Eyes chuckles, trickling a shiver down my spine. "Yes, give her to us."

"No," Dax declares, his voice so commanding and dangerous that another, harder shiver rakes through me. "She belongs to me. Leave now or die."

He brandishes his knife. It glistens in the backlit glow from the hole in the ceiling of the store behind us.

Fang Boy charges us.

Dax shoves me backward and rushes at Fang Boy. He slashes his knife across the monster's throat. Blood pours from the wound, and the creature crumples to his knees, gasping and gurgling.

Red Eyes makes his move next, roaring as he throws himself at Dax.

My sort-of protector dispatches that creature too. He stabs his knife into Red Eyes' gut and yanks it upward, gutting the beast.

I wince and look away. I've seen enough blood and gore today, but I doubt this will be the last.

The other monsters gallop away.

Dax turns toward me with the knife still in his grip. Blood coats his entire hand as well as the blade, and crimson liquid drips onto the floor. He stalks up to me, halting inches away, and wipes his knife off on his shirt. Then he tucks it inside his jacket.

I can't help cringing a little. He just murdered those two creatures without any remorse, without even trying to chase them away. Maybe he had no choice, but I've never witnessed such ferocity.

Breathing hard, he speaks through his clenched teeth. "Let's get back to that tunnel. We can't be above ground when the Echo reaches this section of the city."

He mentioned the Echo before, but he hasn't explained.

I don't get the chance to ask. He plucks up the lantern, then seizes my arm and tows me out of the building. I stumble over debris as we rush across the street, heading for the stockyards tunnel. A new pile of rubble blocks most of the entrance, but Dax tows me through the narrow opening without slowing down. My arm is starting to ache from how tightly he's gripping me. Not that I think he cares about that. Of course he doesn't. He might not be as hideous as those monsters in the mall, but he is a beast just like them.

Terrifying. Merciless. Alien.

A chill ripples through me. I'm the prisoner of a beast from…who knows where. Why hadn't I ever bought a stun gun or at least a can of pepper spray?

Dax halts and switches on the lantern. He sets it down on the cracked terracotta tiles of the floor. "You will stay here while I secure the tunnel at both ends."

He pulls his leather belt out of his pocket.

The creep wants to bind my hands again. Screw that. No more letting him drag me around.

I race for the tunnel's opening, scrambling through the narrow gap in the debris pile.

Large, powerful hands clamp onto my ankles and pull me back into the tunnel. Dax hoists me to my feet and lashes his arms around me, squeezing me to his body. "That was a stupid mistake. You can't outrun me. You can't overpower me. Give up."

"Never."

"Your sudden desire to be feisty will only make your situation worse." He snatches his belt off the floor. "You leave me no choice. Remember, this was your doing, not mine."

He spins me around until my backside is pinned to his front. His thick, musclebound arm restrains me, and I can't get any leverage that I might use to free myself. He's too damn strong. Too damn big. Too damn evil.

Before I realize what he's doing, Dax has bound my wrists with the leather belt. He shoves me against the concrete wall, then kneels in front of me. The jerk uses my own shoelaces to bind my feet. I'd worn my favorite boots today, leather ones with strong, thick laces. If I'd known what would happen today, I would have worn my Velcro tennies instead.

Dax takes a big step backward. "You have no choice now."

He stomps over to the debris that's blocking this end of the tunnel and starts shifting large chunks until he's sealed the entrance.

"What are you doing?" I demand.

He ignores my question and stalks down the tunnel in the other direction, disappearing from my view. Even the sound of his boots clomping fades away. Silence pervades the space, and the smell of blood fills my nostrils. My blood? Most of it probably is. But my boots had crunched on things I couldn't think about when I fled from the epicenter of the apocalypse. Who knows what I've got glued to my body.

I slide down the wall until my butt meets the terracotta floor.

Footfalls clap closer and closer, louder and louder. Dax emerges from the shadows, stopping just inside the circle of light from the lantern.

"You blocked us in, didn't you?" I say. "We're trapped."

"For our protection."

"How are we going to breathe with no ventilation? The air in here won't last forever."

"It will last long enough. I can reopen either entrance as soon as the worst of the Echo has passed through this area."

Time for the cretin to explain a few things. "Why do you keep talking about 'the Echo'? What does it mean?"

"You know as well as I do."

I want to cross my arms, but I can't do that with my wrists bound. So I scowl up at him instead. "Stop telling me I know what's going on. I don't. And I certainly did not cause it."

"That's bollocks." He walks toward me, then crouches close enough that our knees almost touch. "You are responsible for everything that's happening."

"No, I am not. I don't even know what 'the Echo' means."

He studies me for a moment, his expression giving away nothing. "The Echo is the power driving the apocalypse, the power that will merge both worlds."

"There's only one world."

"Wrong. There is this world, the one normal humans live in. Then there is the Echo, the world populated by desecrations of the human form."

"You said the Echo is the power behind what's happening, but now you're calling it a different world." I lean forward. "It can't be both."

"Of course it can. The Echo is the power generating the change, and it is the world that I and the monsters rampaging through this city came from."

I shake my head as I struggle to decide if I should believe him, if I should trust him to tell me the truth about even one thing. "Why do you keep saying I caused what's happening?"

"Because you did."

"No, I did not."

He mutters something that must be a curse, based on his tone. "Enough of this. Tell me about the magics. Tell me the truth or I will torture it out of you."

"Okay, here's the truth." I lean even closer, his breaths reflecting off my face. "I have no fucking idea what you're talking about."

"That's too bad—for you." He brings out his knife, holding its tip to the underside of my chin. "Last chance."

"I can't tell you about 'magics' that I know nothing about."

He presses the knife's tip into my flesh just enough to make his point, but not enough to break the skin. "Tell me about your relationship with Sefton Stainthorpe."

Cold floods through me, raising goosebumps on my arms. "Dr. Stainthorpe? I don't have a relationship with him. I barely know the man."

"Of course you know him. He created the Echo for you, with your help."

"What? You're insane."

Dax draws the knife across my skin, but again without piercing it. "You admit to knowing him. If you won't explain how the two of you did this, then tell me what happened in the days leading up to the merging of the worlds."

I glue my back to the wall, lift my chin, and spit my words at him. "Go to hell."

"We're living in hell already." He touches the knife's wickedly serrated edge to the underside of my ear. "Tell me what I want to I know, or I'll start slicing."

Nothing I can tell him will help because I have no idea how or why the apocalypse came to be. But I might as well share the events that happened before the Echo crashed into my world. Maybe that will satisfy him, though I doubt it.

"I have to start a few weeks ago," I say. "When Dr. Stainthorpe first visited the library."

Chapter Four

Allison
Three Weeks Ago

I'VE GOT THE EVENING SHIFT ON THIS TUESDAY, MANNING THE CHECK-out counter at the public library as I do five days a week, sometimes on Saturdays and sometimes in the evenings, working whatever hours I'm asked to take. While I prepare books for shelving, applying an adhesive plastic covering to paperbacks, I keep glancing at the clock.

Seven forty-two.

My shift ends at nine, closing time. Groaning and rubbing my aching neck, I return to my task. With a ruler, I smooth the bubbles out of the plastic sheath on a Nora Roberts novel. If only real life provided happy endings for everyone, the way these novels always do. Instead it doles out pain far too often and leaves me to slave away at a minimum wage job that doesn't require the master's degree I'd worked so hard to earn. I don't have anyone to go home to either. No parents. No real friends, just work buddies. No loved ones at all, only a long string of bad dates and failed relationships.

I won't tell Dax about that. My past and my private thoughts are none of his damn business. Instead, I get back to my story.

A man pushes through the main doors, stepping off the portico and into the open area in front of the check-out counter. As he walks toward me, I can't help noticing several things about him. He's attractive, with dirty-blond hair cut short and bright blue eyes. The guy has a trim build too, and I can see muscles stretching his suit jacket, though he doesn't seem like he works out obsessively. His suit looks a bit rumpled, just like his hair. He sports a shadow beard too, but based on his unkempt clothes, I suspect he simply hadn't bothered to shave, rather than his stubble being a fashion statement.

I paste on my polite smile as the man shuffles up to the counter, which comes up to waist height. Now I can see his blue eyes are bloodshot and dark circles rim his lower eyelids.

"Good morning," I say. "How may I help you?"

"I am in need of information about alchemy."

He sounds British. I've met quite a few Australians who emigrated to North Texas, but this guy is my first Brit.

"Alchemy?" I say. "Let me check our catalog, but I doubt we have much on that topic. Most people check out novels or kids' books."

The man observes while I type keywords into the search screen on the computer. Just like I thought, we don't have anything about alchemy.

"Sorry," I tell him. "We don't have those kinds of books in our collection, but I could probably get some on interlibrary loan. Or you could try the research databases we have access to. I can show you how to use them."

"That would be brilliant. Thank you, Miss…"

"Allison Dahl."

He offers me his hand to shake. "I am Dr. Sefton Stainthorpe."

"Nice to meet you, Dr. Stainthorpe."

"And you as well, Miss Dahl."

"You can call me Allison."

He tugs at the collar of his shirt and clears his throat. "I prefer formality, if that's acceptable to you."

"Sure. Whatever you want."

I get to work collecting all his info to sign him up with a library card, so I can request books for him via interlibrary loan.

Dax interrupts my story. "Sefton lived in Texas?"

"He gave me a local address, but it could've been fake. The library didn't run background checks on patrons. May I continue?"

"Yes."

Dr. Stainthorpe leaves with my promise to hunt down some books on alchemy. What an odd subject to study. Creating gold from lesser metals? It sounds like nonsense to me. No one can transform one thing into a completely different thing. Can they?

Maybe I don't get the whole alchemy thing, but I always do my job and go the extra mile for my patrons. Two days later, I phone Dr. Stainthorpe to let him know I've found several books for him as well as a ton of articles he can download on his home computer using the library's gateway. He asks me to print them out instead since he "can't understand the internet." Whatever. Printing out weird articles is part of my job.

A week after I'd first met Dr. Stainthorpe, he returns to the library to pick up the stuff I've gathered for him. I'm pushing a cart around while I reshelve books when Dr. Stainthorpe finds me in the stacks.

"How are you this eve, Miss Dahl?" he asks.

I suppress a chuckle. This eve? Nobody talks that way. "Is there any chance I can convince you to call me Allison?"

Shoulders hunched, he averts his gaze. "It seems inappropriate. We aren't well acquainted."

"We can change that." I pat his arm. "Let's be friends, hey?"

I swear his cheeks turn faintly pink, and he still won't look me in the eye. "Perhaps we could be friends. You've gone to a great deal of trouble to find those books for me. Might I take you to dinner?"

"Um…" Not sure if that's ethical or a good idea. But then, I don't have a great track record with men. Dr. Stainthorpe seems nice enough, but I've only met him twice and spoken to him on the phone once. Something about him makes me uneasy, though I can't put my finger on what it is. "Maybe another time. I'm always wiped out after an evening shift."

Yeah, I'm trying to let him down politely.

He looks disappointed and follows me back to the check-out counter in silence. While I scan the barcodes on the books I'd ordered for him, he keeps watching me. When I set the stack on his side of the desk, along with the papers I'd printed out, he scratches the back of his neck and almost winces.

"Do you have any books on quantum physics?" he asks. "I'm particularly interested in string theory and quantum entanglement."

"Uh, let me check." I perform a quick search of our catalog. "Sure. We've got some books on that. If you want in-depth stuff, I can hunt for more ILL books. That means interlibrary loan."

"May I see the books you do have?"

I guide him into the stacks and straight to the science section, then skim the call numbers on the spines until I locate the right ones. I hand them to Dr. Stainthorpe. "Any of these work for you?"

He flips through each of the books, then nods. "Yes, these will do. Though I would appreciate it if you could find more for me."

"Sure. ILL is the best way to get stuff on unusual subjects."

We say goodbye at the desk, and Dr. Stainthorpe leaves.

He returns several times over the next two weeks, always on days when I'm working. We don't chat much, and he doesn't ask me out again. I know nothing about him except his name and that he's British. One day my curiosity gets the better of me, and I search his name on the internet, coming up with only one result—his faculty listing on the Oxford University website, which contains little information about him. He's an associate professor with research interests in physics and the history of science. That's all I learn.

No matter how often I see Dr. Stainthorpe, I can't shake the unease his presence always triggers in me.

Three days before the apocalypse, Dr. Stainthorpe waltzes into the library looking like a different man. The rumpled scientist has put on a crisply pressed navy suit with a white handkerchief in the breast pocket. He has not only combed his hair, but has also brushed it back in a style that accentuates his beautiful face. Wow, he's a hottie. But I still can't muster any interest in him beyond our professional relationship.

He stops at the counter, holding one arm behind his back. Chin raised, he gazes at me with a slight smile on his lips.

"Good morning, Dr. Stainthorpe," I say. "How may I help you today? I hope those books and articles I got you were useful for your research."

"Yes, they have been enormously helpful."

"Glad to hear it."

He whisks his arm out from behind his back, revealing a bouquet of pink roses he holds in his hand. "These are for you, Allison. As thanks for all your hard work."

I accept the bouquet and sniff the flowers, enjoying their sweet scent. "That was very thoughtful, Dr. Stainthorpe."

"Would you call me Sefton?"

"Sure, but I thought you preferred formality."

"I have changed my mind."

"Okay." I set the bouquet on the desk. "Thank you for the roses, Sefton."

"You are the most beautiful woman in the world, Allison."

A shiver lifts the hairs at my nape. I'm not excited by his compliment, though. I feel weird about the whole conversation. The guy who couldn't look me in the eye a week ago is now flirting with me.

Sefton glances around as if he's watching for someone or something. Seeming satisfied with what he saw or didn't see, he zeroes his gaze in on mine. "Have you ever wanted to change the world?"

"Not really. I mean, everybody wishes the world were different, better, but too much is out of our hands."

"What if we could control the world's destiny?"

"That would be fabulous. If I could rule the world, I'd make sure everybody was happy."

He leans forward, arms braced on the desk, and bores his gaze into mine with such intensity that another shiver ripples through me. "I'm not talking about pie-in-the-sky dreams about improving the world. I mean real, tangible change. You and I, we could remake the world together."

"Not sure what you mean."

He lowers his voice to a whisper. "This is no joke, Allison. I want to give you the world, literally. You and I can change everything. I do not speak metaphorically, but in the most literal, concrete sense."

As I stare into his eyes, I realize he's serious. This man believes he can remake the world. "What exactly are you talking about?"

"You will see soon. Then you will understand I've done all of it for you, Allison."

The sound of a cell phone chiming, announcing a new text, emanates from his side of the desk. He pulls out the phone and checks it. His brows furrow, then his eyes light up. His entire expression becomes...excited.

"Please forgive me," he says as he backs away. "The moment is almost upon us. I will come to you when the event is nigh."

Before I can speak, he rushes out of the library.

Alchemy. Quantum entanglement. What do those two things have in common? Nothing that I can see. But clearly, Sefton believes those subjects hold the answers he needs to complete his insane quest to "remake" the world.

The day before the apocalypse, Sefton tracks me down deep in the bowels of the library where I've been shelf reading to make sure all the books are in their correct places. Sefton still dresses like a businessman as he had the last time I saw him. But his eyes are wild, and he seems incapable of standing still, instead bouncing on the balls of his feet.

"Sefton?" I say. "Are you okay?"

"The time is nigh," he announces, his tone and his expression full of excitement. "You must come with me, Allison. I can protect you, but only if we stay together."

"Protect me from what?"

"You will see." He grabs my hand and tugs. "Please. Hurry."

I yank my hand away. "You're scaring me, and I'm not going anywhere with you."

He throws his arms around me, dragging my body into his, and mashes his mouth to mine. I clamp my teeth shut to stop him from pushing his tongue inside and struggle against his hold. He keeps his lips glued to mine as a strange, almost electrical sensation zings into me through our joined mouths. The room spins around me, then settles down, leaving me dazed.

Sefton releases my lips but maintains his hold on my body. "I love you, Allison. And you love me too, I know it."

"No, I don't." I wriggle out of his arms. "I'm sorry, but I just don't feel that way. Please get out of here before I call the police."

He bows his head, knifing his fingers through his hair. "No, no, it wasn't meant to be this way."

"Leave, Sefton. Right now."

"Yes, yes, all right. I will go. You need more time to see, and tomorrow, all will become clear."

He hurries out of the library. I know he exits the building because I trail after him to make sure.

The next morning, I go to work as usual. After reshelving books for an hour, I return to the check-out counter to find someone has left me a note concealed inside an ivory envelope that feels like it's made from high-end paper. My name is scrawled on it in an elegant, sweeping hand.

I cautiously open the envelope and unfold the note.

"Stay in the library until I come for you," the note says. "To change the world, we must first dismantle it."

I stare at the note, at Sefton's elegant signature, and swallow against a tightness in my throat. Then I toss the paper into the trash can.

CHAPTER FIVE

Dax

HOW CAN YOU CLAIM TO BARELY KNOW SEFTON STAINTHORPE when you had a relationship with him?" I grip the belt that binds her wrists and pull her closer. "Stop lying to me. You were deeply involved with Sefton, which means you conspired with him to bring about the merging of worlds."

"I never conspired about anything. And I never really knew Sefton. I thought he was a nice guy—strange, but nice—until I found out he'd been hiding his true self until the day he couldn't hide it any longer." She curls her lip and hisses, "He's a whackjob, just like you."

Does she honestly know nothing? I refuse to believe that because Sefton spoke of her with deep emotion, as if she meant far more to him than a casual acquaintance. And I know she aided him.

"Perhaps he is insane," I say, "but you must have cared for Sefton. Stop lying and tell me how to find him."

"No idea." She yanks her wrists, tearing the belt out of my fingers, and slumps against the wall. "Go on and kill me or rip my fingers off or what-ever you want to do. I don't care. The world has become a nightmare, and we'll both die sooner or later when monsters rip us apart."

"You can't escape me that way." I grasp her chin, forcing her to look at me. "Not yet, at least. I will keep you alive until you tell me where Sefton is."

"For the umpteenth time, I don't know. Are you deaf *and* stupid?"

A boom shivers through the tunnel. Bits of the ceiling tumble to the floor.

The woman who won't tell me the truth snaps her spine straight and peers up at the ceiling, eyes wide. "The ceiling might collapse any second."

"It will hold."

"How do you know? Are you an expert on tunnel construction?" When I don't respond, she huffs. "No, I didn't think so."

Naturally, she's being sarcastic. That makes me want to shag her even more. My cock doesn't care about the apocalypse raging above our heads.

If I want answers from her, I need to take a different approach. "You mentioned Sefton's note urged you to wait in the library until he came for you."

"Yes."

"But you didn't do that."

"I was hypnotized, like everyone else. Duh."

"Hypnotized?" I tilt my head to the side as I study her expression and body language, but I can't find any clues that suggest she's lying. "You weren't mesmerized when I found you. No one was. You were all screaming and running from the beasts."

"Yeah. But before that, the music put us in some kind of trance. We couldn't stop ourselves from going outside and congregating on and around the viaduct."

"That was the bridge across the river."

"Yes." She shuts her eyes, her lips trembling. "The music was almost worse than the monsters that came when the song ended."

"I didn't hear music," I tell her. "It must've happened before I arrived. But I have no doubts it wasn't a normal melody, but something borne of the Echo. That's why I need to find Sefton."

She opens her mouth as if she means to speak, but instead shuts it. Allison scrutinizes me for a long moment, her gaze traveling over me in what seems like an appraisal, though I have no idea what she's attempting to figure out by analyzing me from head to toe. "You know Sefton, don't you? That's why you keep calling him by his first name instead of saying Dr. Stainthorpe like everyone else does. He only asked me to call him Sefton a few days ago."

"Who or what I know is not your concern."

"It damn well is my concern. You're holding me hostage and threatening to dismember me."

"Only your fingers." I squeeze words out through my clenched teeth in a deliberate attempt to cow her. I know she fears me, but she has enough backbone to defy me in spite of that. My only option is to terrify her. "If you keep testing me, I might change my mind. You have many more appendages I can hack to bits."

"Go on and do it. I don't care anymore. The world is ending, and if I have to get hacked up by a beast, it might as well be you."

"The world is not ending. It is transforming."

She stops blinking, her gaze nailed to mine. "What do you mean it's transforming?"

"You'll see. Right now, I need to know where—"

"Gah!" she shouts so loudly that it reverberates through the tunnel. "For the last time, I have no fucking idea where Sefton Stainthorpe is."

Strangely, I believe her. "All right. That means we must wait until the first wave has passed through this part of the city, then we can check the library. Maybe Sefton is waiting there for you."

"Great. A field trip into hell."

I move to the opposite side of the tunnel, directly across from Allison, and sit down on the terracotta floor. All we can do now is wait. The strikes of lightning and fireballs have been lessening in frequency, but even after the skyborne chaos ends, we will need to contend with the monsters that have been dumped here. And we're running out of air in this tunnel, which means we can't wait much longer.

"Are you going to drag me through the city again?" Allison asks.

She can't walk with her feet shackled. But I can't trust her not to try to run away. I'll need to bind her to me somehow, maybe by strapping one of her wrists to one of mine. I have a little time to consider the options. Only when the first wave has passed will I attempt to reopen the tunnel.

Assuming we have enough air to last that long.

Once we venture outside again, we will have other problems. "Is there a shop in this city that sells weapons?"

"Like I'd tell you even if I knew. You probably want to torture me."

All I can do is growl. This woman seems determined to harass me until I snap and do something we will both regret. I'll wind up ravaging her, though not with torture devices.

"Where are you from?" she asks.

"Silence, woman."

"I told you everything I know about Sefton. Time for a little reciprocation, if you want me to cooperate."

Do I believe she will ever cooperate? Of course not. She's trying to wheedle information out of me. So I pretend I didn't hear her question and shut my eyes, listening to the sounds of chaos outside as they dwindle gradually. I swear I can feel Allison glaring at me, her gaze piercing me like a hot, sharp needle thrust into my eye.

She clears her throat. "I don't understand—"

"Silence. There will be no discussion. Do as I say or suffer the consequences."

The infernal woman huffs. "If you want my help, better start giving me some explanations. Otherwise, you can sit there sulking until the next millennium because I will not go anywhere with you."

"You are a fool if you think you'll have a choice. I can force you to do anything I want because I am stronger and larger than you."

"Go ahead and try it, creep. See how far you get."

I can't help it. My lids fly open, and my gaze gravitates to her. The look of sheer defiance on her face makes me want to...do things to her that I should never do. Sex should be the last thing on my mind in the middle of an apocalypse, but maybe this is exactly the time I should indulge my lust. One last shag before we all die.

To claim the woman Sefton coveted… No, jealousy is not the reason I'm behaving this way. It can't be.

Springing to my feet, I stalk up to her and shove my arms under hers. Then I hoist Allison off her feet and pin her to the wall with my body. I'm sure she can feel my cock hardening against her belly. Instead of cringing or struggling to get away from me, she stares into my eyes, not blinking, while her lips turn a deeper shade of pink and her pupils dilate.

Oh yes, she wants me. The woman despises and fears me, but a primal instinct drives this need we both feel. I despise her too, but I haven't been with a woman in so long…

I crush my mouth to hers.

Neither of us moves for a moment, both frozen by the shock of what I've done. Kissing her? It's insanity. I must stop this, despite everything inside me urging me to do the opposite. Not sure I can control myself, not today, not with her. *Back away right now, before you go too far.*

Allison moans low in her throat—and thrusts her tongue between my lips.

I try to pull away, but my body refuses to obey me. Every swipe of her tongue amplifies my hunger until I can no longer hold back. I ravage her with brutal lashes and nips, our teeth clashing and her moans growing more fervent. The scent of her lust makes me drunk, stripping away the vestiges of my control, though I cling to the tatters for as long as possible. Ravenous grunting noises emerge from her as she devours me as wildly as I'm consuming her, our kiss imbued with desperation and fear and something far darker too. With her arms trapped between our torsos, she wriggles against me like she wants to get free and wrap her entire body around mine. Never have I experienced lust like this. It erodes my willpower and propels me to rub my hard length into her belly. I should stop. To do this here and now…

Have I really become the sort of bastard who does a thing like this?

I tear my mouth away from hers, breathing so hard I feel almost light-headed, and set her down on her feet. A matter of inches separates our bodies, and her cheeks have turned pink. Her lips are slightly swollen too, while her gaze has gone glossy and unfocused.

I plant my palms on the wall, bracketing her shoulders, and lean in. "When I fuck you, it will be even more brutal than the way I just kissed you."

"That's never going to happen," she says, though her breathless tone proves less than convincing.

Despite her statement, I know it will happen. Neither of us can fight the overpowering need our kiss inflamed. That's why I must get away from her. Once she takes me to Sefton, I won't need Allison anymore. Can I make myself walk away, leaving her alone in this vicious new world? I'll think about that later.

Perhaps I am starting to believe her story.

No, never.

Her breasts rise and fall with every breath, and her lips are parted as if she wants me to kiss her again.

I slant in more until my lips graze hers. Then I growl, "Remember this the next time you consider harassing me."

"Remember what?"

Ignoring her question, I kneel to untie her bootlaces and unshackle her feet. Then I surge to my full height and liberate one of her hands so I can secure that end of the leather belt to my wrist. This will leave her with one hand free, but she won't get the chance to escape me. If Allison makes the slightest move to do that, I will stop her.

I grab the lantern and drag her down the tunnel to the entrance we had come through earlier. With one boot, I kick at the debris I'd used to seal us in. The chunks of concrete and rock fall away, revealing the twilight outside. I pause and tilt my head to the side to listen. Though I hear distant screams and feral noises, I don't detect any signs of fireballs or lightning.

"Move," I growl as I climb out through the opening, towing her after me.

She clambers over the debris, and I lead her away from the tunnel and onto the street. East Exchange Avenue, she had called it. Not that the name matters anymore.

"Which way to the library?" I demand.

"Um…" She squints and bites her lip. "Not sure."

"No games. Take me there now."

She plants one hand on her hip. "I didn't memorize a map of the city. Give me a minute to think. Everything looks different now."

"You have one minute."

"Until what?"

I tug her into me and lower my head to hers. "Until I walk away and leave you to fend for yourself. Without me, you'll be dead in five minutes."

She spits in my face. "I don't need you. And if you ever try to kiss me again, I'll grab your dick and twist so hard you'll scream like a baby."

"Our kiss was consensual. And you'll beg me to take your body."

"I didn't ask you to kiss me."

"Your desire was unmistakable." I tap her lips with one finger. "And you thrust your tongue into my mouth."

"That was—Ugh, I hate you."

I'm certain she does, but I'm equally as certain that she wants me inside her as much as I need to sink my cock into her soft, willing body. She is beautiful, passionate, fiery, and clever. Of course I hunger for her body. But that's all it will ever be—sex to satiate our mutual needs and numb the fear and pain.

She starts walking, and I let her lead me away. Whether she knows where she's going... I'll find out soon enough.

29

CHAPTER SIX

Allison

I'M TETHERED TO A MONSTER, AND I LET HIM KISS ME. EVEN WORSE, I kissed him back—with tongue. What on earth is wrong with me? I blame the apocalypse and the terror I've experienced ever since chaos descended on the city. How can a girl think clearly when the world is literally falling apart around her? I see no other explanation for my behavior back in the tunnel. Well, maybe I've suddenly developed a taste for crude, mean, obnoxious assholes who treat me like dirt.

No, I don't like that kind of man. So I guess I like grizzled, grimy, unkempt assholes instead. *Ugh.* Worst of all, I liked that kiss. Whatever that says about my mental state, I don't have time to think about it.

We scrabble over mounds of debris, tripping over dead bodies as we rush headlong back toward the epicenter of the destruction. But it doesn't seem as chaotic and terrifying as it had at first, and I'm not sure that's a good thing. I should still be horrified, but maybe I've just gotten numb from the shock.

I still glimpse demonic creatures now and then, but they seem less interested in us than in the corpses that litter the streets. No, I cannot think about that right now. Even if they're feasting on the lifeless remains of human beings, there's nothing I can do about it. No one can help the dead.

Survival. That's my only goal.

Others must have survived, right? Somewhere. Somehow. They would've run just like I did.

My legs burn and ache from trudging who knows how far today, and I feel like I can't catch my breath. Sweat pours down my temples. It must be two or three miles from the stockyards to the library, and I've already walked at least that far today. I haven't eaten since lunch either, when I had yogurt and a banana. How many hours have elapsed since then? Feels like forever.

"Stop," I tell Dax, tugging on our bindings. "I can't walk anymore."

He doesn't stop. He doesn't even slow down or glance at me. His jaw is firmly set while his gaze has narrowed, focused on the path ahead of us. This used to be a street, but I can't recognize enough of it to remember the name.

With all the strength I have left, I yank him hard enough that he stumbles.

Dax glares at me. "What do you think you're doing?"

"Trying to get your attention, obviously." I mop sweat from my forehead with the only part of my shirt's hem that's not soiled with things I refuse to identify. "We have to stop and rest. I'm hungry, exhausted, and probably dehydrated. You've already dragged me miles across the city, and now you're doing it again. I'm not a robot."

He stares at me without expression, though I swear I see a muscle in his jaw ticking.

My knees buckle. I hit the ground hard, slumping my entire body, though my left hand remains bound to his wrist. My arm hangs from his, and it's the only thing that keeps me from collapsing on the ground.

With a growl, Dax squats in front of me. He removes the leather belt that shackles us to each other and shoves it into the pocket of his coat. Then he picks me up and throws me over his shoulders in a fireman's hold. I'd already felt slightly nauseous and dizzy, but with my head upside down, I feel like the world is gyrating around me.

Dax sets off down the street again.

This makes no sense. The man who threatened to cut off my fingers is carrying me because I'm too weak to walk anymore. He terrifies me. I hate him, and he hates me. Yet we kissed, and now he's carrying me, which implies he cares about my welfare.

Minutes tick by, though I have no way to gauge how many. Hazily, I notice when we cross the Paddock Viaduct that spans the West Fork of the Trinity River, though I shut my eyes while we traverse the bridge because I know it must be littered with bodies. I can't take seeing more carnage. After a span of minutes that I can't count, he gently sets me down on what used to be a sidewalk, though the remnants around me only hint at the original purpose. I'm too exhausted to move, and I slip into a restless sleep.

Strong hands shake me. "Wake up, Allison. I found food and water."

I recognize that gruff voice. It's Dax.

"Huh?" I'm gradually rousing, but my head feels like it's full of cotton balls instead of brain cells.

"I have food." He slaps my cheek, though not hard. "Wake up and eat."

I push myself into a more upright position and realize I'm leaning against the brick wall of what used to be a building.

Dax hands me a plastic bag. "Your meal."

I notice he's holding an identical bag in his other hand. I take the one he offered me and pull out the contents—a sub sandwich, a bag of chips, and a bottle of water. He has a backpack slung over his shoulder. It's pooched out like he's filled it with stuff.

"What's that?" I ask, nodding toward the backpack.

"Enough water and food to keep us going for a while." He sits down near me, though not too close, and pulls out his own food. "There was a sandwich shop in a building over there"—He waves toward a semi-ruined structure across the street—"and I took all the food I could find."

"Where did the backpack come from?"

He turns his head to the side, almost as if he's ashamed to tell me. "The person it belonged to no longer needed it."

"Oh."

My throat goes thick when I consider the ramifications of his statement. The original owner of the backpack has no use for it now, but that bag might save our lives.

I dig into my food, wolfing down my sub sandwich faster than I probably should, but I can't help it. Ham and cheese with tomatoes, onions, and fresh spinach never tasted so good in my life. I devour the jalapeno cheddar potato chips too, despite the fact I hate spicy stuff. Can't be choosy when the world is transforming. Into what, I have no clue. Dax doesn't want to tell me.

He studies me while I eat, his eyes flicking this way and that like he's searching for something in my expression. "Why aren't you worried about your family?"

"What?" I say with my mouth crammed full of food. A sliver of lettuce tumbles from my lips, and mayo dribbles down my chin. I swipe it away with the back of my hand.

His mouth twitches, almost like he wants to smile, but the expression fades quickly. "You haven't once expressed concern for your family or your mates."

"Neither have you."

He squints at me, which he seems to think will intimidate me. *Sorry, pal, no dice.* I've been through literal hell today, and I've grown a much thicker skin.

But I decide to be honest. "I don't have a family anymore. My parents died in a plane crash when I was eighteen, and I was an only child. As for friends, those were people I worked with and never saw outside of the library."

"Why don't you have real mates?"

"None of your business." No, I don't want to share my painful past with him. I've given him enough info for now.

After we're done eating, we just sit here for a while. Maybe he's not as indestructible as he seems, because I get the impression he needed rest and sustenance as much as I did.

Finally, I have to ask. "How is the world transforming? All you said before was that I'll see."

"I'm not entirely certain what it is becoming. Only Sefton can answer that question."

He rises, hooking the backpack over his shoulder, and grabs my hand to urge me to stand too. Then we head out again. Despite the destruction, I start to recognize some of the buildings. At last, I spot a street sign that affirms my belief we're going in the right direction. We're on Throckmorton Street, which means we need to get on the next block over to find the Central Branch of the Fort Worth Public Library. We scramble around the remnants of a parking garage and at last reach Taylor Street. Now we stand just behind the library, directly across from the Tarrant County Plaza building.

I spread my arms. "We're here."

"Is this the front entrance?" Dax asks. "If so, we can't get into the building. The facade has collapsed and blocked our way in."

"The main entrance is around the other side."

He follows me down Taylor Street until we reach West Third, then we walk side by side down that street, stopping in front of the portico that shields the main entrance. The four pillars in front have been shattered, and large chunks of them lie scattered around the area. For a moment, I gape at the damage while my brain struggles to come to terms with what I'm seeing. What I keep seeing. Everywhere I look. This can't be real, but it is.

Dax shoves me from behind. "Get moving."

We wend our way through the remains of the columns and step through the shattered glass doors, careful not to get cut. The interior is dark. That means we not only have no lights, but no ventilation either. It's beyond stuffy in here, and I start to sweat just from hopping over freestanding shelving units that have toppled over, spewing books across the floor. When we reach the check-out counter, which is miraculously intact, I stop and face Dax.

Naturally, he glowers at me.

"Well, we're here," I say, waving at our surroundings. "Don't see anything alive in this place except for you and me."

He digs the lantern out of his backpack and switches it on.

I pray there are no bodies in here. My gut twists when I think about that, and I will not go any further into the building to find out. There's no point. The dead can't be saved. I hate that circumstances have forced me to harden myself to the death and destruction around us. Later, I'll feel everything. Won't I?

"Where would Sefton find you whenever he visited the library?" Dax asks.

I shrug. "Wherever I was. Sometimes I'd be at the check-out counter, but other times I might be in the stacks or in a storage room."

"We will check everywhere, then."

"Everywhere? In case it escaped your attention, being a thickheaded lout, this is an enormous building."

He slants toward me. "Better start searching."

The only way I'm getting out of this building is if I find evidence that Sefton was here and left, or if I find a way to disable Dax for long enough that I can escape from him. Option two seems improbable. The bastard is a hulking mass of muscles. So I go for option one and lean over the waist-high check-out counter to rummage through any papers I can find.

"Nothing here," I say.

Dax grasps my ass in both hands, then pushes me up and over the counter. While I crash onto a chair and tumble off it, he watches me with a smug expression. "Look harder."

I scramble to my feet and do what he commanded. What choice do I have? Unless I find a weapon here or suddenly develop superpowers, I'm stuck with the grizzled jerk. He watches me while I root through the papers strewn across the floor, shoving a computer monitor out of the way and avoiding the staples that litter the carpet.

Then I see it. An envelope.

Crawling under the desk, I grab the ivory-colored envelope. It feels and looks like the same fancy paper on which Sefton had written his note that urged me to stay in the library until he came for me. I recognize the elegant handwriting too. "For Allison," it says. Dax will want to see this, I know, but I need to find out what Sefton said before I tell my captor. I kneel under the desk, sitting back on my heels and slouching forward. Then I peel the flap open and pull out the folded sheet of ivory paper tucked inside the envelope.

A shiver tingles over my skin, from my scalp down to my toes.

Whump.

A pair of large, booted feet land in front of me. Dax bends over to seize my arm and drag me out from under the counter. He hoists me off the floor with my feet dangling in the air and our faces aligned. The barely contained fury on his face makes me shiver again.

"You found a note from Sefton," he snarls. "Didn't you? And now you're trying to hide it from me to protect your lover."

"I am not involved with Sefton Stainthorpe. But you're never going to believe me, are you?"

He lets go of me.

My tailbone smacks into the counter's edge. I wince and hiss, but he doesn't pay any attention because my suffering means nothing to him. So what if he scrounged up food and water for me? He wants me alive until he finds Sefton, that's all.

I'm leaning against the counter now with Sefton's note clenched in my hand while the throbbing pain in my tailbone gradually fades.

Dax snatches the note from me. He reads the handwritten text, and his brows knit together. "What does this mean?"

"That Sefton is loony tunes."

"No, it has meaning." He thrusts the note at me. "And you know what it is."

"The only part I understood was 'Dear Allison, sorry I missed you.' The rest is insane."

He throws an arm around me, mashing my body to his, and reads the now-crumpled note. "Through the alchemy of worlds, the alchemy of souls, the Echo shall reveal the true nature of all."

"Crazy talk, like I said."

"No, I don't think so." Dax pins his gaze to mine. "You left out the bit where he vows to find you again."

My best option right now is to say nothing. He won't believe anything I say unless I tell him what he wants to hear, but that would be lying. It's not my fault Sefton became obsessed with me when he tipped over the edge, tumbling headfirst into madness. The alchemy of worlds? What does that mean?

Dax told me the world isn't ending. It's transforming.

The beast clutching me to his body sweeps me up in his arms and climbs over the counter, thumping down on the other side. Then he sets me on my feet and grabs my arm, towing me out of the library.

All those books about alchemy and quantum entanglement... Sefton must have wanted them as part of whatever he did to transform the world. But what is it becoming?

CHAPTER SEVEN

Dax

WHAT DOES THE NOTE MEAN? I ASSUME THE ALCHEMY OF WORLDS HAS already begun, but the alchemy of souls is yet to come. I don't know exactly what Sefton meant by those terms. Still, I'm certain it doesn't herald the beginning of utopia. No, a deranged mind like his would dream up something much worse than what we've seen so far. Sefton always was a master planner.

But I could never have envisioned what he would become—or what he would do. Am I as deranged as he is?

Allison and I exit the library, and I start walking down the pockmarked street for several yards before I realize she is not following me. The bloody-minded woman isn't trying to escape, though. When I turn to look for her, she's sitting on the edge of the pavement in front of the library with her feet on the roadway, holding the wrinkled note. She stares at it with a blank expression.

With a heavy sigh, I stalk back to her. "What are you doing? We need to keep moving."

She holds up the note. "Do you know what this means? Because I don't have a clue."

"Only Sefton knows what it means. That's why we need to find him."

"Told you I don't know where he is." She crumples the note and tosses it away. A breeze latches onto the ball of paper, whisking it across the street. "Might as well start chopping off my fingers."

Why must she keep repeating the threat I'd made earlier? Maybe I should follow through on it, but I don't have time for that right now. I am not delaying because I feel bad for issuing that threat. Her feelings mean nothing to me. Her safety only matters because I need her to take me to Sefton.

I don't care what happens to Allison Dahl. No, I don't.

What I should do is walk away now. Leave her there looking miserable and alone. But I don't do that. For reasons I can't comprehend, I sit down beside her and pull a water bottle out of my backpack, then hand it to her.

Surprise flashes on her face, but only for a second. She accepts the bottle and unscrews the lid, taking a long drink of water. "Thank you."

"Don't thank me. I'm only keeping you fed and hydrated because—"

"Yeah, yeah. I know you hate me. But you're obsessed with the asinine idea that I know how to find Sefton Stainthorpe." She holds the water bottle between her palms, turning it side to side while she studies me. "Why do you hate me? I've never done a damn thing to you."

Not sure I know how to answer that question. From the moment I first saw her, I had been determined to capture and interrogate her, to wrench the truth out of her by whatever means necessary. But do I despise her? Or am I afraid of what she might do to me? She can't hurt me physically. Perhaps I'm afraid of what I might do to *her*. This lust she inflames in me… I don't know what it means or if I can control it.

Since I refuse to answer her question, I change the subject. "Where else might Sefton go in this city?"

"Not a clue."

"That's bollocks. You know him. He left you a note, which must mean he expects you to find him. Sefton needs your help. You are the catalyst, after all."

"I'm the what? If you're implying I conspired with him to start the apocalypse, you're even more wacko than I thought."

She thinks I'm insane, but it's Sefton who deserves that label.

What time of day is it? Hard to tell while the sky still roils with dark energies that all but blot out the heavens. A false twilight had overtaken the city earlier, but sooner or later the real thing will descend on us. True night may prove much deadlier. The city has no electricity which means no lights—except for the battery-powered lantern I nicked from that store. I have no idea how long its batteries will last.

Allison snaps her fingers in front of my face. "Hello? Are you awake?"

I swat her hand away. "I was not asleep."

"Good. Then you can tell me what the hell you meant when you said I'm the catalyst."

Telling her seems like a bad idea. Then again, she might be more cooperative if she understands what precisely is going on since she claims to have no knowledge of what's happened.

"Do you honestly know nothing about the Echo?" I ask.

She groans and rolls her eyes at me. "For the umpteenth time, I do not know anything about any of this. "

I pull out another water bottle and swig half its contents, only in part to delay answering her question. "I told you before that the Echo is the driving force behind the apocalypse and that it will transform both worlds. The Echo is a magical construct. It requires dark energies of such power and scale that no one can comprehend its vastness."

"Ditch the hyperbole and explain."

"It's not hyperbole. Magics of that scale require both a catalyst and an anchor. Otherwise, the construct would crumble."

She swivels toward me and smacks her water bottle down on the pavement. "I am not a catalyst. Whatever Sefton might've done, it's not my fault."

"In his warped mind, he believes he loves you. The magnitude of his obsession fuels the Echo, but he needed you to set the machine in motion."

Her eyes narrow, and her lips flatten. "I had nothing to do with any of that. If Sefton is obsessed with me, that's his problem. I never agreed to become his catalyst."

I believe her, though I can't imagine why. Might Sefton have used Allison as his catalyst without her knowledge? I'm hardly an expert on magical constructs or dark energies, though I learned enough during my time in the Echo to comprehend what my brother has done. But Sefton is a scientist who has spent years learning about and experimenting with things most people think are utter rubbish.

"Perhaps you didn't willingly or knowingly help Sefton," I say. "But he used you to trigger the process. You are the catalyst, and I am the anchor."

"Does that mean you're holding the Echo together?"

"I'm not sure. That's why I need Sefton. Only he understands the intricacies of what he's done."

"Can he stop the worlds from transforming and merging?"

"That's a question for the man who created the Echo."

Allison glances up at the sky, at the dark, seething maelstrom that marks the opening into the Echo. "If you stop threatening to dismember me, I'll go with you."

"You're going with me either way."

"Try saying 'thank you.' It wouldn't actually kill you to be a little bit nice."

I can't help growling softly. "We are not friends. You are still my prisoner, and I still do not trust you."

"Ditto." She offers me her hand. "No dismemberment, and I won't run away without just cause. Do we have a deal?"

She gave herself a way out by including "without just cause" in her statement. But she will regret it if she tries to escape. The situation is too dire for me to be even "a little bit nice" to her.

I shake her hand. "Yes, we have a deal. Now, tell me where else Sefton might have gone."

"I don't know."

"Think, Allison. There must be another place that has meaning for him, something related to you."

She closes her eyes as if she's racking her brain for an answer. Her entire face becomes slightly pinched.

Roars and screeching sounds erupt in the distance.

Her eyes flare wide. She flaps her head left and right as if searching for the source of those noises.

"They're blocks away," I tell her, though I'm not certain of that. "Concentrate on where Sefton might have gone."

She drops her forehead into her palms.

Human screams reverberate from elsewhere in the city, and she flinches. Neither of us can help the poor sods out there. Even I am not strong enough to defeat an army of Echo creatures, and I'm positive Sefton limited my strength on purpose.

Allison lifts her head. "The Kimbell. I told him about it, and later he mentioned he'd gone there."

"What is the Kimbell?"

"It's an art museum. I mentioned to Sefton it was my favorite place in the city." She drinks the last of her water and tosses the empty bottle away. "I told him about a painting I've loved ever since the first time I saw it. Sometimes I go to the Kimbell just to look at that painting again."

"He knows how much that artwork means to you."

"Yes."

I jump up. "Then we should go there."

"The Kimbell is a couple miles away, at least. Maybe you're an invincible caveman, but I can't keep trudging through the city. I'm in good shape, but I never trained for long-distance hiking through post-apocalyptic rubble."

Her mention of being in good shape spurs me to skim my gaze over her body, and I can't resist paying special attention to her breasts. Yes, she is in fine physical condition. Fucking her will be incredible. But she does have a point about hiking through the city anymore today. Even I'm starting to feel knackered. Maybe that explains why I've been...somewhat less nasty to her. I'm too exhausted to snarl and shout at the woman.

I survey the area.

Allison clambers to her feet. "What are you looking for?"

Rather than responding, I amble down the pavement so I can get a better look at the car park across the street. Shattered asphalt and lumps of debris from the buildings nearby obstruct my view. So I jog across the street and climb atop a mound of rubbish to survey the vehicles parked there.

Allison races to catch me up. "Are you thinking maybe we can use one of these cars?"

"Yes."

"Do you know how to hot-wire a car?"

"No, but I'm hoping someone might have left their keys in one of these vehicles or hidden a spare one on the underside."

"Good idea. Maybe we'll get lucky."

I shuffle down the sloping mound of debris and start to search the cars. Most are locked, and I'd never learned how to break into a vehicle. Allison searches too, and she's the first to locate an unlocked car. We don't find a key inside it or hidden anywhere on its exterior. After several more minutes of searching, we find a vehicle that's unlocked and has a key stashed under the sun visor.

Allison doesn't complain when I take the driver's seat. It feels odd to sit on the left side. I'm having trouble adjusting to the change since I literally dropped into this country with no idea where I was. It hardly matters if I accidentally drive on the wrong side of the road. There are no other cars in sight, no movement visible anywhere, no sign of life other than the distant screams and roars.

Luckily, we find a way out of the car park that doesn't require driving over the rubble heap. I doubt this vehicle could handle that. But Allison suggests I should drive onto the rubble because it's a "shortcut" and we need to "scram" as fast as possible.

"This is an older saloon, not an SUV," I tell her. "It isn't built for that."

"A saloon? I guess that's the British word for a sedan, huh?"

"Yes."

"So it doesn't mean there's a wet bar in the backseat."

"No."

She sighs. "Darn. I could use a stiff drink."

When I glance at her sideways, I catch her smirking. Is she teasing me? Considering my behavior, I can't believe she would do that. But her statement about needing a drink had sounded almost playful. I don't want her to get comfortable with me. Her fear of what I might do to her assures her compliance.

"Don't get used to riding in a car," I say, making sure to growl the words while I veer the car around a corner. "Once I get what I want, you will be of no further use to me."

"Gee, you sure know how to sweet-talk a girl."

"Why would I bother with that?" I swerve around a pile of debris, and the headlights flash across the ruined facade of a building, revealing several creatures hunkered there. "You would do well to stop harassing me, unless you want me to finish what we started in the tunnel. I won't be nice to you when I take your body. It will be—"

"Mean and nasty, blah-blah-blah. I've memorized your little speech, so you can shut the hell up about it now."

Allison looks annoyed again, and she's hugging herself too.

Maybe I feel uneasy about upsetting her, but I can't let her see that. I force myself to relax into my seat. "Tell me how to find the Kimbell."

Chapter Eight

Allison

WE DON'T SPEAK FOR THE REST OF THE JOURNEY TO THE MUSEUM, EX-cept when I give him directions. The streets look so different now, and the darkness doesn't help matters, but I manage to get us there. Dax drives too fast, but I don't bother telling him to slow down. He'll do whatever he wants no matter what I say. Maybe I had, for a brief time, thought he might be turning into a semi-normal person. But then he snapped at me again and said nasty things to me again, and I remembered he's nothing but a brute.

I cannot trust him. Not ever.

The drive to the museum is a bumpy one, and Dax has to zig-zag around small groups of monsters from the Echo, all of whom look far more danger-ous than he does. I don't see any normal humans. They can't all be dead, can they? Some must have survived the "first wave," as Dax called it. I don't want to think about what the second wave will be like. Maybe the people who lived in this city have hunkered down to hide from the beasts. Maybe they aren't all dead.

I survived only because Dax captured me and spirited me away from the worst of the madness.

We make a detour when I spot a sign for the street Sefton gave as his address, but he doesn't live there. It's an empty lot. Where did Sefton live? Solving that mystery can wait.

Our journey takes longer than it would have pre-apocalypse, but that's no surprise. We pass by buildings that have been reduced to rubble with no evidence of what they were before the destruction began. Just glimpsing the damage as we rush through the darkened city makes me feel nauseous. My eyes start to burn too, and my throat thickens. I can't help teetering on the verge of tears. Who wouldn't get choked up under these circumstances?

Dax, that's who. He doesn't seem to care about anyone or anything except getting what he wants.

Miraculously, we reach the cultural district. Some of the buildings have survived with moderate damage rather than total devastation, while the Kimbell Art Museum seems to have remained mostly intact. Right across the street, the parking lots have suffered major wounds. Yet the museum has survived with cosmetic injuries, though a small section of the roof has caved in. How is that possible? Dax claims Sefton Stainthorpe created the apocalypse, and he seems to think Sefton did that because of me. Could he have spared the museum because he knows I love it?

No. This can't have anything to do with me.

Dax parks in the driveway of the museum, right next to the huge modern art sculpture that marks the entrance. We head for the glass doors that access the building and find them intact and unlocked, as if everyone fled in such a hurry that they didn't bother to secure the premises. As much as I love art, protecting the collection wouldn't have been my priority either. Getting the hell away from the lightning and fireballs, not to mention the monsters, matters more.

As we make our way into the building, Dax turns on the battery-powered lantern. It provides a surprising amount of light considering how small it is, and we have no trouble navigating through the building. Artworks lie scattered on the floor or hang askew on the walls, as if the place has been looted. But nobody took the paintings or sculptures. Whoever did this rampaged through the building in search of something else. There's a restaurant in here and a gift shop too, so maybe they looted those for supplies.

I trip over a small object on the floor. As I reach down to pick it up, I recognize the item. It's an ancient Mesoamerican statue from the Olmec culture. The six-inch-tall figurine depicts a broad-shouldered man with a large, rounded head and a mouth that curves down in a partial frown. Something about his eyes has always struck me as sad. The whole sculpture feels that way, more today than ever before. This poor little guy survived the end of his civilization thousands of years ago only to experience a genuine apocalypse today. He deserves better than to lie on the floor like a discarded toy. So I gently set him on an empty display pedestal.

"What are you doing?" Dax demands.

"Showing a little respect."

"For what? It's a stone statue." He stalks toward me. The jerk had gone halfway across the room before he noticed I wasn't right behind him.

"Excuse me for wanting to preserve one little thing when the world is ending or transforming or whatever." The start of tears burns in my eyes, but I do not want to cry in front of him. I suck in a breath and will the tears to go away. As if that ever works. "If you want to threaten me some more, go ahead. I don't care. Showing emotion is not a crime."

"Perhaps not, but it will get you killed."

"By you? Go on and try it." I throw my arms wide. "Rip me to pieces."

He stares at me for several seconds, breathing hard, his teeth bared. Then he whirls away from me. "Get moving. We need to find that bloody painting and hope Sefton is there or that he at least left you another note."

Naturally, he speaks those words in a vicious tone like the beast he is.

With only the light of Dax's lantern to guide us, I lead the way as we navigate around the debris and hop over artworks that have fallen onto the floor. Maybe it's a dumb reaction, but I can't help feeling a little sad when I see those beautiful works of art strewn across the floor, damaged and abandoned. I'd visited this museum more times than I can count, and coming here had always given me a sense of peace. Now, it's a war zone.

I almost walk past the painting I'm looking for, but then Dax raises his lantern, dispelling the shadows—and the picture we've been searching for comes into view. I stop six feet away from it, entranced as always by the stark beauty of the image. It's a not a scene of war, though. The painting evokes the perils of the sea while a storm rages around a jetty and a beacon meant to guide ships to port. Two men struggle to aid a boat as its occupants make way for the harbor. The drama and starkness of the imagery has always fascinated me.

"This is it?" Dax says. "The painting you love is of a storm at sea?"

"Yes."

"And you told Sefton about this painting."

"That's right. But I don't see him anywhere around here. Do you?"

Dax peers into the shadows at the edges of the room where the lantern's light peters out. "We should wait here for a while to see if he shows up."

"How long do you plan on waiting?"

"Overnight." He glances at the collapsed ceiling, then scans his gaze over the room again. "If Sefton hasn't turned up by morning, we will move on."

"To where, exactly? If Sefton is still in town, he could be anywhere. Assuming those monsters haven't killed him."

Dax grunts. "They won't. He created them."

"It's time you explained yourself. Tell me how you know so much about Sefton, how you know he created the Echo, and what the hell all these creatures are that apparently came out of the other world." I round on him, stabbing a finger into his chest. "Cough up some answers. No more sidestepping."

"What gives you the idea that you have leverage to make me do anything?" He leans in to glare into my eyes. "I have the power, not you. When and if I feel like explaining myself, I'll tell you."

He's wrong. I have leverage, because he believes he can't find Sefton without me. So I lift my chin and march past the jackass.

Dax grabs my arm. "Where do you think you're going?"

"To the cafe." I shake off his hand. "There might be edible food there, and what you've got in your backpack won't last long. Might as well gobble up whatever's available here."

He squints at me.

I start walking.

The clomping of footsteps behind me lets me know Dax is following. I'm getting damn sick of his behavior, and if he tries to grab me again, I'll sink my teeth into his nose.

In the cafe, we find both food that still seems edible and paper bags to store it in, so we gather as much of the food as we can. We put the bags in a plastic tub we discover in the kitchen. This part of the building suffered minimal damage, but it's getting awfully warm in here thanks to no central air and the Texas summer heat.

Dax takes us back to the South Gallery, where the painting we came to see resides. He thought Sefton would leave a clue for me here, but we found nothing.

On our way back to the gallery, Dax ripped the cushions off a pair of benches and hauled them in here, carrying both under one arm. Each cushion is as long as I am tall. Yeah, the jerk is very strong. He lays the cushions down on the floor after clearing an area, creating a space where we can sleep in relative comfort. A breeze wafts down to us through the hole in the ceiling and makes this room a lot more tolerable, temperature-wise, than the cafe had been.

Maybe I should appreciate the fact he tried to make our sleeping spot comfortable. I can't feel gratitude, though, not for the man who abducted me. Besides, he positioned his makeshift bed in front of mine, essentially trapping me against the wall. I promised him I wouldn't run away as long as he stopped threatening to dismember me, but he clearly doesn't believe I'll stick to my oath. Somehow, I manage to fall asleep. After a day of trudging back and forth across the city, I'm exhausted. But still, it seems like a miracle that I can get any rest when I hear unearthly screams and roars reverberating through the night outside our little sanctuary.

In the morning, Dax announces we need to get moving again. When I ask where he thinks we're going, he just grunts and orders me to move my "arse." We find our borrowed car again, and of course, he insists on driving. I've decided to think of this vehicle as borrowed rather than stolen since the person who owns it is probably dead. The thought gives me a shiver.

Dax has no idea where he's going, but he drives like he has a plan, his gaze fixated on the road and his jaw tight. He makes turn after turn, his choices clearly random. But I've given up on trying to convince him to let me take the wheel. Every time I suggested it, he snarled one sexist statement or another, all related to the idea women are too silly and stupid to be trusted to drive.

I can't believe I kissed the jackass. Can't believe I had a dirty dream about him last night either. Maybe he is hot, in a scruffy caveman way, but I will never do the things I fantasized about in my dreams.

When he turns onto River Drive, I can't stop myself. I need to speak up. "Do you have any idea where you're going?"

"Away from where we were."

"Fabulous plan."

We're approaching the railroad trestle that spans the Trinity River, but he veers off the road mere feet from the bridge and heads across the grassy expanse of Trinity Park.

"You really have no clue what you're doing," I say. "Randomly swerving around doesn't help anything."

He stares straight ahead as we bounce across the walking paths, then he swerves right to duck under the trestle. I'm about to say something when he slams on the brakes, making the car fishtail briefly, and we jerk to a halt at the edge of the grassy riverbank. Dax flings his door open and leaps out.

"What are you doing now?" I ask.

He slams the door shut.

While I watch, probably with my mouth gaping, he traipses down a rocky path that leads to the water. What on earth is he up to? We can't drive across the river or swim to safety. Well, I suppose we could drive over the railroad bridge, but it would be a very bumpy ride. And where would we go, anyway? He still hasn't answered that question.

I climb out of the car and stumble along the rocky path, jogging to catch up as he stomps down the shore. I assume he wants to get away from the lumpy area and avoid the drop-off where the water dives into a swirling cascade. He finds a calmer part of the river and halts.

Then he kicks off his boots and starts to remove his clothing.

I stop a dozen feet from him, suddenly frozen. He's not going to undress all the way. Is he? No, he must want to get rid of his coat, that's all. But the idea he might strip naked gives me a strange fluttery sensation in my tummy. I watch in mute fascination, glued to this spot, while he removes every stitch of his clothing.

Dax now stands buck naked on the shore.

Swallowing hard, I try to look away. But my eyes have other ideas. I drink in the sight of his nude body, all muscles and sinews, from his thick biceps to his taut ass and those powerful thighs. When we met, I'd noticed hints of tattoos peeking out from under his shirt, but now I can see the sweeping designs that cover one arm and half of his torso. Though I want to ask him about his tattoos, I get distracted when he turns halfway toward me.

And I get a good look at his dick.

The long, thick length of it is impressive even though he's not aroused. I can't imagine how big he is when he gets an erection. Well, yeah, I kind of can imagine. But I wish I couldn't. That fluttery sensation grows stronger, and a sultry tingle sweeps over my skin, awakening a deep, wet throbbing inside my sex. No, I cannot want a jerk like Dax.

But heaven help me, I *do* want him.

Dax wades into the river. Then he turns around and looks straight at me. "Come in, Allison. Join me."

CHAPTER NINE

Dax

ALLISON STARES AT ME WITH WIDE EYES, BUT SHE'S NOT GAWPING AT my face. Her attention is fixated on my body. She can see everything since I've waded in only up to my knees. I need to shag that woman. Right now. I'll take her in the water or on the grass or anyplace she wants as long as I can have her this instant. It's been too bloody long since I felt a woman's body wrapped around me. Even longer since I had a girl who wasn't from the Echo.

I wade in deeper, glancing over my shoulder at Allison.

She's rubbing her arms and biting her lip. She wants me, and she wants to disrobe in my presence. I can tell. Understanding a woman's amorous responses had been the key to my success in the bedroom before the Echo.

Allison edges closer to the water.

I drop to my knees and fall backward into the current. My whole body sinks under the surface, and I whisk my fingers through my hair to cleanse the filth from it. When I emerge from the water, I see Allison has removed her boots. She just tossed them onto the grass, and now she pulls her shirt off over her head and lets it flutter down to join her boots on the ground. Her gaze locks on to mine as she shimmies out of her jeans.

The sight of her almost naked transfixes me. Her pale blue bra reveals the inner slopes of her breasts, and her skimpy knickers barely cover the hairs at the apex of her thighs. My breathing grows labored as I watch and wait for her to strip off the rest of her clothing. But she doesn't do it. Allison wades into the water in her underwear, and once she's in up to her knees, she whirls around and flops into the water backward, unleashing a miniature geyser around her.

The splash rains down on me.

She sinks under the surface, then shoots back up, smiling at the sky.

Christ, she's beautiful.

Allison tips her head back to rinse her hair in the water. The movement pushes her breasts up, and her wet bra reveals the hard peaks of her nipples.

Movement catches my attention out of the corner of my eye. Though I turn my head to look, I can't see anything. But I know there had been motion. I slowly scan the river until I see it—an odd ripple in the water that seems to be traveling toward us, fast. The ripple reminds me of when I'd once seen a shark racing through the water, but its dorsal fin had protruded above the surface. Still, whatever is causing the ripple seems to be moving just as fast and creating a similar profile in the water.

The beast is heading straight for Allison.

"Get out of the water!" I shout.

She freezes with both hands in her hair and stares at me.

"Out of the water!" I roar.

I swim for the submerged object that's still racing toward us, placing myself in the path of the beast.

Allison swims toward the shore.

I dive under the water just as the mystery object collides with me. Teeth nip at my flesh, but I grasp what feels like the head of the beast and yank it hard, feeling cervical bones crack. I've snapped the creature's neck. Its limp body floats to the surface.

"What the hell is that?" Allison calls out to me. She's standing at the edge of the water, clutching her clothes.

The beast I've just killed has a humanoid body, but its skin consists of flesh-colored scales, and I see gills on its torso. It's brown eyes look disturbingly human, though now they are vacant.

I stalk back to the shore, halting beside Allison. "Get dressed."

"What was that thing?"

"A creature from the Echo." I'm breathing hard from my struggle with the beast, and water dribbles down my body. "It wanted you."

"Me? Why?"

"You tell me."

She scowls and starts reassembling her clothes. "How many times do I have to say the same thing? I have no idea what's going on."

I seize her arm. "I'm beginning to wonder if the creatures that confronted us in the shopping mall were there for you, just like this beast."

"What? That's crazy."

"Really." I drag her closer. "Sefton left you a note. He planned to come for you, but he reached the library before you could find your way back to it. Whether you want to admit it or not, you are the key to everything that's happening. You are the catalyst."

"And you're the anchor. That's what you said." She wrenches free of my grasp, though only because I let her. "That means you're in this up to your eyeballs too."

"So you admit you are an integral part of what's going on."

"No. I admit you're an asshole and a murderer, and I should never have agreed to go anywhere with you."

My gaze flicks to the dead creature floating down the river, headed for the drop-off and the swirling current below it. "You continue to refuse to cooperate, even though I killed that beast to protect you."

"I came with you. That's cooperation." She combs her fingers through her wet hair to push it away from her face. "Gee, I would've thought you'd want that thing to get me, since you hate me so much."

Why had I intervened? If the creature had wanted her, as I believe, then I doubt it would have harmed her. "You aren't telling me everything. Don't deny it."

She crouches to tie her shoelaces. "I know nothing about the apocalypse, and I am not a catalyst for anything."

"If that's true, then you are of no further use to me." I don't believe for one second that she's not the catalyst, or that she knows nothing. Maybe the truth is buried inside her memory. Either way, I will get what I need from her.

Allison straightens. Her attention flicks down to my cock. She clears her throat and focuses on my face.

But her cheeks have turned faintly pink, and I don't think it's embarrassment. I'd seen the way she admired my body earlier. We dislike each other, but we both suffer from the same overpowering lust. Perhaps I can use that to my advantage and get more out of her than answers. I need something else, something that has no bearing on the apocalypse. I need it badly.

I sling an arm around her waist and haul her into my body, lifting her feet off the ground just enough that we now gaze into each other's eyes head-on. "If you want my protection, you need to do more than simply come with me while we search for Sefton."

"Listen good this time. I know nothing—"

"Stop talking." I slide my free hand onto her arse and shove my fingers between her legs. When she gasps, a bolt of white-hot need shoots through me. My voice grows even rougher, even deeper. "Here's the new arrangement. I will protect you from whatever beasts hunt you and ensure you have enough food and water, as well as safe shelter. In return, you will give me your body to do with as I please, whenever I please, as often as I please."

"No way."

"Accept my terms, or I'll toss you back into the water and let the next creature rip you apart."

I can't believe I'm suggesting such an arrangement. What would my mother think of me now? I glance at the heavens and pray Mum can't see or hear me. I have never been so desperate to get a leg over that I'll do anything to make that happen. But I am now. Perhaps it has been far too long since

I had sex, but I don't want just any woman. I want Allison—only Allison. I need to have her.

No excuse, you sodding arsehole.

Allison glowers at me. But her pupils have dilated, and her breasts heave against my chest. "I hate you."

"I don't care." While she wriggles, with little conviction, I slip my hand inside the waist of her jeans and thrust it down until my fingers push between her arse cheeks. Her wetness teases the tips of my fingers. "Don't deny you want me. I can feel how much you do. Agree to my terms, and I will do more than protect you. I will give you pleasure that will make your eyes roll back in your head."

She's breathing so hard now that she's almost gasping. "I can't—This is wrong."

Whether she means her lust for me or my demand that she give me her body, I don't care which it is. I need to be inside her soon or I will go mad. So I push my hand further between her arse cheeks until my fingertips slide between the soft, slick flesh of her folds. "Yes or no. Tell me your answer in the next five seconds. Four, three, two—"

"Yes. I'll do it."

I flip her legs out from under her and lay her down on the grass, kneeling over her. "Remember, you wanted this as much as I do."

She unzips her jeans.

An explosion detonates in the sky, the shock wave spiraling outward and ricocheting off the buildings as the force of the concussion generates a violent wind that rushes toward us. The tempest generates an animalistic roar. Some structures that had been almost destroyed in the first wave now crumble. Iridescent green ripples of energy pulsate within the gateway to the Echo.

And winged beasts flood out.

"Back to the car," I shout.

Allison doesn't hesitate this time. We both bolt for the car and get inside, slamming the doors shut just as the hellish invasion hits. Winged beasts overrun the city, spewing fire from their mouths. As they draw closer, I can see the humanoid bodies attached to those gigantic wings.

Allison cranes her neck to peer up at the sky through the windscreen. "What are those? Dragons?"

I start the engine and floor the accelerator. The car rockets away, throwing dirt and grass up around us. "Those aren't dragons, not in the traditional sense. They are creatures from the Echo."

Perhaps I've left out significant information, but I won't tell her more until she gives me Sefton. Do I still believe she knows how to find him? The angry part of me, which dominates my behavior, says yes she knows—and I need to force her to confess. But the part of me that I've sublimated, for good reason, has begun to wonder about Allison. She might be telling the truth.

I can't worry about her intentions right now.

"We need to hide somewhere," I say as the car jounces onto the road. "The second wave has begun, and the last place anyone should be is out in the open. We should go back to the tunnel."

"That's too far away. I know of another tunnel, but to get there we'd have to double back to get across the river."

"Why?" I slam on the brakes. "We can reach the other side from the place where we swam in the river."

"That's a railroad bridge. And besides, it's elevated above the road. You can't drive onto it."

"I'm not talking about the bridge." No more explaining. It's time to take action, whether she likes it or not. "Buckle up your seatbelt and hold on."

Yanking the wheel, I jam the accelerator down to the floor and swerve the car back around to go the other direction. Allison yelps, but I don't give a stuff about that. Flames erupt in the sky as more dragon-like creatures emerge from the Echo, heading in this direction. We have minutes at most to get to a relatively safe place. I grip the steering wheel tighter as the car rockets off the road and across the grass, barreling toward my destination.

The rock outcropping beside the railroad bridge.

We swam near that manmade pile of rocks, which has an opening at its center. That's where the water becomes turbulent. I'd seen it when I was washing off in the river. Now, we're racing across the landscape alongside the railroad bridge.

"Stop!" Allison screams. "You'll crash in the river."

Instead of slowing down, I aim straight for the rocks.

The car hits the boulders, bouncing up and thumping down over and over, jerking sideways so I need to grip the wheel even harder until my knuckles ache from the effort.

When we reach the gap in the rock barrier, Allison shrieks.

And the car flies across the gap, slamming back down on the other side. I yank the wheel to veer onto a path that leads up, away from the river.

"You're insane," she snaps. "We could've died."

"If we had crashed in the river, I would've survived."

"But you don't give a shit if I die."

Do I care about her safety? Only until I get everything I want from her. That's what I keep telling myself.

She bars her arms over her chest and turns her head away to stare out the window. "I'm reconsidering the deal we made earlier. Don't want to have sex with an asshole who's also a lunatic."

"You won't renege. You want me too much."

Allison flashes me a nasty look. "I hate you."

"But we both know you want me to fuck you. That's how I can be certain you'll keep up your end of our arrangement." I turn onto a street, the car jouncing over holes in the asphalt. "But right now, I need you to give me directions to the tunnel you know of."

"Fine."

She provides the information, guiding us through the streets to a building that I recognize as a hospital only because the sign is still visible, though it has suffered some damage. The building itself is completely destroyed. Even if we could find the tunnel, I wouldn't trust the structure to hold, not when I'm looking at its battered remains.

"What now?" Allison asks.

"I don't know." For a moment, I stare at the ruined building while my entire body sags. But I don't have the luxury of feeling sorry for myself, so I turn the car around and head back the way we'd come.

The engine sputters and dies.

As the car rolls to a stop, I turn the key in the ignition several times, but the engine won't start up again. Then I see why. The gauges on the dashboard make it clear.

"Why did you stop?" Allison asks.

"Because we're out of petrol."

"I guess that means gas."

"Yes." I smack my fist on the steering wheel. "We're not going anywhere, except on foot. Unless you know of a place within walking distance where we can fill up the tank."

"Even if I did know of a gas station, I doubt there's anyplace that has power of any kind, even from generators. No electricity, no gas pumps."

She's right, of course. And I'm a bloody moron.

I grab the backpack and swing my door open. "We walk, then. And pray we'll find a safe place to hide."

Chapter Ten

Allison

WHILE I WALK ALONGSIDE DAX, AS WE MAKE OUR WAY THROUGH THE remnants of the hospital district, I can't stop thinking about what I agreed to do with him. He demanded I have sex with him and swore he won't protect me anymore unless I do it. I could've said no to his devil's deal. Instead, I agreed.

More proof that I've lost my mind.

That's the only excuse I have for agreeing to give my body to a stranger who treats me like dirt and snarls at me. It's his fault I'm making horrible decisions. Dax makes me so angry, and I fight the constant urge to slug him, fight it only because I'm sure I'd break my hand if I tried to punch his granite jaw or his rock-hard abs.

It doesn't help that I've seen him naked.

The man might be an evil prick, but he has a body any woman would drool over, with hard muscles flexing under every inch of his flesh and a dick of jaw-dropping size. I should not want him to touch me. But every time he pulls me close, whether it's to growl at me or say crude things, I want to rip his clothes off and ride him until we're both slicked with sweat and we come so hard we can't speak afterward.

He doesn't always treat me like dirt. Maybe that's the real reason I agreed to let him fuck me—because I've seen his softer side too. Well, not softer. More like his less prickly and snarly side.

We've just passed a street corner, one I might've recognized if the world hadn't exploded. The street signs are gone, probably buried under a mountain of rubble. Dax has stopped us here, though I don't know why. When I start to ask, he holds up a hand in the universal gesture for "shut up." He tilts his head to the side.

Since he doesn't want me to speak, I mouth, "What?"

"We are not alone," he mouths back.

Then I hear it. Scrabbling sounds. Faint grunting. Whimpering.

Dax claims my hand, leading me toward the noises, which seems like a horrible idea to me. When I kick his shin to get his attention and mouth "no," he ignores me. The brute drags me down the side street, forcing me to climb over a mound of debris in the process, and we don't stop until we've come within view of whoever or whatever is making those noises.

A gang of four creatures has surrounded a young woman at the entrance to an alley. Two more creatures hang back, holding on to a young man who struggles against their grip. The girl keeps trying to get away from the four demons, but they've got her penned. She whimpers and keeps calling out to the young man, but he can't get free to help her.

I look at Dax just as he looks at me. When I open my mouth to suggest we should do something, he rolls his eyes and growls.

Then he whips out his knife and charges across the street.

Since I've gone crazy, I race after him and grab a battered length of pipe from the ground, wielding it like a baseball bat.

"Let her go," Dax commands. "Or you will regret it."

The creatures give up on harassing the girl and rotate their gazes to Dax and me. Every demon in the gang has scaly skin, though two have fangs, one has long talons on its fingers, and the fourth sports spikes on its back. The two holding on to the young man boast spikes on their heads.

"What's this?" one creature says. "Snow White and the Wolfman came out to play. She's juicier meat than this scrawny little thing." The beast nods toward the young woman. "We'll have her for dessert. Snow White looks like an entrée for sure."

Dax widens his stance, brandishing the knife. "Last chance. Run away or die."

"We ain't running. This is our territory."

"Not anymore." Dax glances at me sideways and whispers out of the corner of his mouth, "Get the girl."

Then he charges at the creatures, roaring and slashing his knife in such quick strokes that I can't see what he's doing. I run to the girl, but now it's the young man who needs help. Dax is keeping the other creatures busy, so I summon all the fury and fear I've held in since this morning and unleash it on the two creatures who hold the man. I slam the pipe into the side of one beast's head, and it staggers sideways, releasing the man's arm. Now held by only one creature, he slugs the monster in the gut. That knocks the beast off balance. The man mutters "thank you" as he rushes past me to grab the girl.

They disappear into the night.

I don't blame them for running without trying to help me or Dax. He doesn't need help. And I know he won't let anything happen to me, at least until we find Sefton. When I turn around, I see Dax encircled by four dead creatures. His clothes, hands, and face are spattered with blood.

He goes perfectly still, his gaze riveted to something behind me. "Don't move."

Then he bolts past me.

I spin around just in time to see him gut the other two creatures. A strange thrill shivers through me, and my nipples go hard. I don't enjoy violence. But there is something darkly erotic about watching Dax neutralize those monsters.

Dax brushes past me. "Let's go."

He pauses to let me catch up. Well, that's new.

As we trek down the street, we see figures lurking in the shadows here and there, but we don't stop to investigate. Nothing good ever lurks in darkness. We pass by a broken fire hydrant that's spurting its contents five feet into the air, and Dax stops to rinse off the blood from his fight with those creatures.

He grasps my hand as we continue on our journey.

I suppress my shock as much as I can. He wants to hold my hand? Maybe he worries I'll run away. He can't feel protective of me.

Four creatures jump out of an alley to block our path.

Jeez, won't these demons ever give up? Though the preternatural darkness has gotten darker, a strange yellowish glow emanates from the hole in the sky.

The creatures in front of us look more human than the other beasts I've seen, but still not human enough to ease the anxiety trickling through me. Two of them seem female, and two male. They might pass for human if not for their fangs and red eyes.

"Look what we found," a male creature says. "Bigfoot and his hot girlfriend. Maybe I'll screw your girl to show her what a real monster can do."

Dax's hand tightens around mine. "You will not touch her."

The fanged cretin glances around with fake surprise. "Wow, a tough guy. I'm so totally terrified right now. I mean, there's only eight of us and two of you. But your threat was wicked scary."

He cackles. His friends laugh too.

"Eight?" Dax says. "I see only four of you."

Several more monsters traipse out from behind a trashed SUV.

"Well, ten counting those guys," the cackling creep says. He waves toward the other side of the street. "They're almost done with their dinner. Then we'll have ten of us against two of you."

A female emerges from the group that just appeared.

I recognize her. I mean, she looks very different now. But yeah, I know her. "Sherry? Is that you?"

The green-haired woman with a smattering of scales on her face smiles at me. "Ally, imagine bumping into you out here."

"Are you okay?" I don't see how the answer could be yes.

"Sure, hon, never better." Her gaze shifts to Dax, and she smiles with a strange hunger. "Damn, the apocalypse has been good to you, Ally."

Dax clamps a hand around my upper arm, bending to hiss into my ear, "She is not your friend."

"What? Something's happened to her, but—"

"You don't understand. She is *not* your friend."

"How would you know? I worked with Sherry at the library for more than a year, and you met her thirty seconds ago."

Dax mashes his mouth to my ear. "That creature is not Sherry. It's her Echo."

I don't know what that means because Dax has refused to explain much of anything. Sherry looks different, but I still recognize her. What does "it's her Echo" mean?

A roaring sound, like a massive gale, sweeps by overhead while streams of fire streak across the sky. The chaos above distracts both me and Dax. He releases my hand, turning sideways to observe the heavens.

Arms lash around me, hauling me backward while a rough, lumpy hand seals over my mouth.

Dax is still staring up at the sky to watch humanoid dragons that soar past us. I can't scream with my mouth covered up, and clawing at my captor's arms doesn't help. Neither does kicking. Sherry joins the beast who's dragging me away, but their pals rush at Dax.

He sees me too late. The other beasts have surrounded him, fangs bared, claws at the ready.

My captor slides his hand up just enough to cover my nostrils. I struggle to suck in air as my ears start to ring and black spots pop up in my vision. Can't move. Can't think. The entire world fades away, and everything goes black and silent. When I regain consciousness, I'm lying on my back in a dark place that stinks of blood and rotting flesh. Voices murmur, but I can't see the creatures who are speaking or understand their words. Pushing up on my elbows, I blink rapidly to clear my vision.

This is an alley. I'm lying on a concrete surface near a dumpster, but I doubt the stench comes from there. No, the fetid odor clearly emanates from the decaying corpses piled up against the giant trash receptacle. The bodies are so mangled that I can't identify them as human, though an instinct warns me they are. The creatures who abducted me must have murdered these people. Though I don't want to do it, I force myself to stand up and walk over to the pile of human refuse to get a closer look at the damage done to the bodies. I swear those are tooth marks. Fang marks, I assume. Something ripped these poor souls to shreds.

Shadows obscure the figures gathered at the alley's entrance. But I hear growling and demonic chuckles.

I need to get out of here. Fast. Before I become another corpse tossed away like garbage.

Though I glance around, I don't see a way out. The buildings on either side look solid, less damaged than elsewhere in the city, with only a few small windows high above my head. The concrete block walls would be impossible to scale even if I climbed on top of the dumpster.

Two of the beasts turn away from their buddies and saunter toward me.

I have no means of defending myself. Nothing but my fingernails and my teeth.

As the creatures draw closer, I can tell one of them is Sherry—or the Echo version of her. I didn't get the chance to make Dax explain what that means. The being who resembles Sherry halts an arm's length away, and her male pal stops beside her.

"Mm, aren't you scrumptious?" she purrs. "Your flesh will taste like filet mignon, I bet."

"What are you?"

"Does it matter? Might as well think of me as Sherry."

I fist my hands and grit my teeth. "You are not my friend. You're from the Echo."

"Your big hunk of man candy told you that, didn't he?" She licks her lips, flicking her forked tongue. "Maybe I'll eat him next."

"You'll never catch him."

"Won't we? He might be big and tough, but we're stronger." Anti-Sherry aims a feral smile at her companion. "Time to show her."

Her cohort sniggers. "Yeah. It'll be a shocker."

She sashays over to the heap of corpses and uses the heel of her stiletto shoe to push some of the bodies aside. Then she steps back. "Take a look, hon."

I inch toward the pile and peer down between the bodies she just moved. There, I see the unmarred face of a woman. A human. The woman I'd worked with for more than a year—the real Sherry.

Just yesterday, I would've been horrified at the sight. Today, I feel nothing but a vacant coldness inside me, though only for a moment. Then I fist my hands again, grit my teeth, and seethe at the realization of what these beasts did to Sherry. The world shouldn't be like this. It was far from perfect before, but now it's a demonic fun house that chews up and spits out good people who got trapped in this nightmare. The anger burning inside me grows stronger, hotter, a boiling but hidden rage that I can't release and certainly can't reveal to these beasts.

I want to murder every last member of this gang of monsters. But I'd get myself killed that way, which wouldn't solve a thing. Yes, I want to live. Despite the horrors the Echo has unleashed, despite the fact I have nowhere to go and no one to comfort me, I do not want to die.

But I still need to figure out how to get away from Anti-Sherry and her carnivorous buddies. *Think, Ally, think.* Can't overpower them. Can't climb up the walls of these buildings. Can't fly away either. Distraction seems like my only option. But how can I distract these creatures so I can run away?

Anti-Sherry comes up beside me again, gazing down at the real Sherry with mock wistfulness. "I just couldn't wreck that pretty face. Ruined every other part of her body. Tanner had his fun with her too."

Fun? I grit my teeth and clench my fists, forcing myself to suppress the seething, boiling rage.

In the distance, an engine rumbles. Not a car. Something else. It's probably another member of this monster gang coming to join the party.

"She was pretty, but I'm way stronger," Anti-Sherry says. Then she grins at me, her jagged fangs glistening. "And now I'm hungry again."

The engine roar gets louder and louder, zooming closer every second. The roar has a growling quality to it, but I'm still not sure what kind of vehicle it is.

Voices cry out in surprise, and someone shouts, "Watch where you're going, moron!"

Anti-Sherry and her pals shout and scatter, getting out of the way of the big black motorcycle that just swerved into the alley, heading straight toward…me. The rider brakes hard, tires squealing, the motorcycle angled sideways. It has stopped three feet away from me.

Dax sits astride the big, black machine with his backpack secured to a metal luggage rack at the rear. "Get on."

I jump on behind him and strap my arms around him.

He guns the engine, and we rocket back down the alley, out onto the street, racing away from the monsters.

A tingle rushes over my skin. Dax came for me. He rescued me. I know he only did it because he thinks I can find Sefton for him and because he wants to screw me. But still, he came. No one has ever done that for me. I know I can't trust him. For now, though, I can at least count on him to keep me alive.

Until I learn how to protect myself.

Chapter Eleven

Dax

THE MOTORCYCLE'S ENGINE SNARLS WHEN I GIVE IT MORE POWER, AND we barrel through the streets in a blur of motion. I have no idea what possessed me, but I didn't think about what I was doing. I dispatched the creature that had attacked me, though my victory came too late. The others had already taken Allison. Finding her became my only goal and the sole focus of my thoughts. Get to her. Save her. Why? I shouldn't care what happens to the woman. I don't care, except for the fact that she has a connection to Sefton and I need to find him. Without Allison, I can't do that.

But I'd experienced a strange sense of relief when I'd tracked her down, and when I saw she wasn't injured.

Where are we going? Somewhere else. That's the extent of my plan. I'll keep driving until this machine runs out of petrol or I spot a place that looks like a promising hideout. We do need to hide, now more than ever. The second wave is underway and will complete itself soon. That means the next phase won't be far behind. How many waves will ravage this world? Only Sefton knows.

Allison has her body glued to mine and her cheek pasted to my shoulder. Her delicate hands are linked over my belly. I swear I can feel the heat of her flesh even through my leather jacket. The wind created by our flight whips her hair against my face as I grip the handlebars more tightly and veer around another corner. We seem to have reached an industrial zone where factories and warehouses once occupied the area. Most of them have been destroyed now. All I need is one mostly intact structure, even a small one, that I can easily defend and where we will be relatively safe.

Nothing is for certain anymore. Everything is relative.

The feel of her body wrapped around mine gives me a feeling of…safety. That's bollocks. I haven't felt safe in years, and I might never again experience a sense of security.

Because of Sefton.

I hit the brakes and plant one foot on the ground to hold the bike up while I survey the area. One building had caught my eye as we approached this area. It looks like the remnants of a warehouse. Half of it has been destroyed, but the remainder seems intact. Since a wall separates the halves, the undamaged section should provide enough shelter. I check the petrol gauge. We're down to a quarter of a tank, and I don't want to waste what's left in case we need this bike to save our lives again.

I drive up to the door of the half-ruined warehouse and stop, setting one foot on the ground. Then I glance over my shoulder at Allison. "Open the door."

"What? Why?"

"I don't want to leave this bike out here where anyone might see it."

"Oh. Yeah, I guess that makes sense."

She slides off the motorcycle and trots to the warehouse door. Getting it open takes a moment, since it seems to be stuck. Maybe I should help Allison, but I can't have her thinking I give a damn about her. My only leverage is her belief that I will let her die if she doesn't cooperate. Whether I might do that or not is irrelevant. The unease I feel while watching her struggle with the door does not change anything.

Allison finally yanks the door open, then steps aside to hold it for me.

I drive the motorcycle through the opening, parking it just past the threshold, and dismount the bike.

She closes the door with a thunk, stumbling from the effort. "Thanks for not helping. It was so much easier doing that by myself."

"You managed."

"Wow, I'm so lucky to have a knight in shining armor on my side."

"I saved you from a horde of ravenous beasts. You could try thanking me. I didn't have to do that."

She stalks up to me, tipping her head back to give me a nasty look. "You only rescued me because you want to fuck me."

"No, I also mean to drag the truth out of you by whatever means necessary."

The insolent woman rolls her eyes and huffs. "Oh yeah, I'm so frigging grateful you saved me. Thanks a whole bunch, caveman. I might've been better off with the cannibal freaks."

I lash an arm around her waist and tug her into my body. "If you want to be devoured, we can skip straight to me fucking you. Right here. On the concrete floor."

Her chest heaves with every breath, crushing her breasts to my torso, and their rigid tips prod my chest. "Do it."

My cock jerks, but I can't move. Might've stopped breathing too. She wants me to ravish her. Right here, right now, on the grease-stained floor of a half-demolished warehouse while fire-breathing monsters set the city ablaze. But Allison doesn't want *me*. She agreed to let me shag her only because I vowed I would not protect her otherwise. I shouldn't care if she really wants this. But thoughts of our deal trigger an itch deep under my skin.

I glance around the space, then shove her away. "I need to surveil the area first."

Her mouth kinks up at one corner. "Surveil? Nobody talks like that."

Grunting, I push past her and tear the door open.

"Don't worry about me," she says. "I'll be fine here all by myself. Might eat all the food while you're gone, but you probably don't need to eat, anyway. You're a monster from another world, after all."

Why does she insist on harassing me? The woman ought to know better after spending two days with me. Yet I haven't forced myself on her. I haven't even taped her mouth shut to silence her. Perhaps she has reason to believe I won't harm her, not the way those creatures back in the alley would have done. Allison knows this, which means I've lost my leverage with her.

My surveillance of the area surrounding the warehouse reveals nothing of consequence. I do find a half-full can of petrol, so I carry that back to the building in which I left Allison. When I kick the door open, she leaps up from where she'd been sitting on the floor.

"Oh, there you are," she says, in a casual tone that I'm sure is an act. "Did you 'surveil' the area thoroughly with your monster senses?"

"I am not a monster." Perhaps I am. I don't know anymore. But I do not like her calling me that.

"What are you, then? *Who* are you?"

To avoid looking at her, I pour the petrol into the motorcycle's tank. "You know who I am."

She shakes her head as she ambles up to me, her hips swaying and her gaze locked on mine. "When I asked who you are, you told me that if I needed a name, I could call you Dax."

"We can discuss that after."

"After what?"

Oh, she knows exactly what I meant. The way her pupils are dilating, darkening her eyes, attests to that fact.

I drop the petrol can and take off my leather jacket, tossing it onto the floor. "Strip."

"You could at least say please."

"Why? You want me the way I am, so I have no need to seduce you with honeyed words." I remove my boots and shed my socks, then start to unbutton my shirt. "Strip, Allison. Do it now, or I'll rip the clothes off your body."

She kicks off her boots and begins unhooking her shirt buttons one by one.

My cock throbs. I want her body, but that cannot explain why I'm breathing harder and my pulse is racing. I've shagged more women than I could count, and none of them made me feel this way. It must be the intensity of the circumstances affecting me, not the appeal of the woman.

Allison drops her shirt on the floor and shimmies out of her jeans, leaving only her bra and knickers. But she just stands there, half-naked, with her hard nipples pushing against the fabric of her bra.

"Take off the rest," I growl.

"You first."

I strip off my shirt, then unzip my trousers and let them fall down to my ankles. The vision of Allison's almost naked body distracts me, though, and I stumble when I try to kick my trousers away. I throw out a hand to stop myself from hitting the floor. My palm smacks onto the wall.

And she smirks. "Kind of excited, huh?"

Finally rid of my trousers, I stalk up to her. "Don't think it has anything to do with you. I haven't gotten a leg over with anyone in a long time, that's all."

"Why haven't you—"

I sling my arms around Allison and crush my mouth to hers, trying to convince myself I do it only because I couldn't think of another way to make her stop talking. But the truth is that I need to taste her again. She opens for me and teases my lips with her tongue, all but begging me to kiss her deeply. I can't stop myself. I plunge my tongue deep and ravage her like the beast she thinks I am. I might not like hearing her call me a monster, but it is what I've become. The Echo made me this way. She will never understand that, because I will never explain it to her.

She responds to the lashes of my tongue with hungry swipes of her own, and we consume each other like the world is exploding around us and this is the last time we will ever experience passion. The Echo hasn't destroyed the entire world, not just yet. But the apocalypse has begun. If this is the last time I will ever feel a woman's body wrapped around me, then I need to make this last as long as possible.

Without giving up her lips, I unhook her bra and tear it off. She moans with such intensity that the ravenous sound steals my breath. I grasp her knickers and rip them off too, flinging them away. The hairs on her mound brush against my flesh, and her soft skin is plastered to my body while the scent of her envelops me and inundates my senses. I grip her arse with both hands, hoisting her off the floor, and stagger toward the nearest wall. I crack one eye open, though I can barely keep track of where I'm going. I know only that I need to fuck this woman now, take her hard, brand her body the way I've done to her mouth.

Her back hits the wall.

I growl like a ruddy animal, but I don't care.

She lifts one leg to latch it around my hip, then raises the other and locks her ankles behind my arse. She pulls her head back, severing our kiss. "Do it, Dax. Right now. Take me any way you want."

Can't speak anymore. Can barely breathe.

I thrust into her hard, but I freeze with our bodies joined. My heart pounds so fiercely that I feel like I might pass out, which is bollocks. But I can't think about that, not with her silky flesh enveloping me and her gaze nailed to mine. I punch into her even harder, every thrust driving me deeper inside her and making her body bounce. She throws her head back and lets out a hoarse cry that reverberates through the building. Her cream dribbles onto my balls, which only spurs me to fuck her harder and faster while my grunts and her sharp cries fill the air along with the wet slapping of our bodies colliding.

Every muscle in her body goes rigid, and I know she's about to come.

But I'm not done with her yet. I lift her off my cock and set her down, taking a step back. Though my breaths have become harsh gasps, I manage to speak two words. "Not yet."

"What?" she breathes, gaping at me.

"I said not yet." I need a few more quick breaths before I can say anything else. "You won't come until I let you. And I won't do that until I've satisfied my needs."

She smacks my chest. "You asshole."

"Call me whatever you like." I grasp her chin. "But your body belongs to me."

CHAPTER TWELVE

Allison

HE OWNS MY BODY? LIKE HELL. I MIGHT'VE AGREED TO LET HIM HAVE sex with me, but no part of me belongs to him. Maybe I have to let him do whatever he wants to me, so he'll protect me from the monsters outside. That doesn't make me his property. I should tell him to go to hell, then get out of here as quickly as I can. He thinks I need him. I thought that too, but I can find another way to protect myself.

So what if my body is throbbing with the need to come? I'm not a slave to lust, and I'm definitely not his property.

He palms my ass, then massages it with sensual movements of his strong fingers.

I can't stop myself from sagging into him just a little. When he lowers his head to my neck and nips my flesh, I suck in a sharp breath. I try to steel myself to his seduction, but somehow he knows exactly which buttons to push inside me, exactly how to touch me and arouse me until I'm panting for him. He clamps a hand over one breast, then closes his mouth over the tip and the areola, suckling it so hard that a sharp electric shock fires down my nerves and straight into my sex.

Maybe I am a slave to my lust for Dax, because I sag against him even more. Without his body propping me up, I'd collapse into a heap on the floor.

Dax flips me around so I'm facing away from him, his callused hands rough against my skin.

"Hands on the wall," he says, his voice as rough as his palms.

I slap my hands on the cold concrete.

With one knee, he shoves my thighs apart. Then he takes hold of my hips and thrusts his cock between my legs, though he doesn't push inside me. He pumps his hips while keeping his length nestled between my thighs, rasping it up and down my cleft while alternately hissing in breaths and groaning with what sounds like agony. I feel that way too as my body ramps up toward orgasm again, second by second, every movement of his cock spreading my slickness over his skin.

I grit my teeth and claw at the wall with my fingertips while the pressure inside me intensifies. "Dax, please."

He pistons his hips faster and faster, grunting like a rutting animal while his balls smack into my ass.

Suddenly, he pulls away.

I'm on fire, dammit, so close to climax that I swear I can taste it. But he stopped. Again. I glance over my shoulder, and the bastard is just standing there with his erection jutting straight out from his body in a way I've never seen with any other man. The head is bright red, and his flesh glistens from the tip straight down to the base, coated with my cream and the beads of moisture poised on his crown. I can't catch my breath, overwhelmed by the need to turn around and take him into my mouth just so I can taste him.

But damn, I need to come so badly. I can't stop myself from reaching down to slip my fingers between my folds, where my juices have made my flesh so slick and hot.

Dax seizes my wrist, yanking my hand away from my body. "No."

"I can't stand it anymore."

"You will stand it for as long as I want you to."

He drops to his knees, gripping my ass with both hands, and shoves his face between my thighs. In one long, sensuous lick, he drags his tongue up my cleft from my opening to the rigid head of my clitoris. I cry out, the sound half whimper and half demand. But I don't come. He won't let me. And heaven help me, I don't want him to set me off yet.

He scrapes his teeth down my inner thigh and back up to my mound. With a hungry groan, he sinks his teeth into the flesh there while breaths bluster out of his nostrils to tease the hairs.

I clutch his head and let out a long, guttural moan.

Dax lifts his head to look at me. "Beg me to do it."

"What?"

"Beg me to fuck you until you come."

I'm breathing so hard I can barely understand his command, and I don't have the willpower to resist. "Please, Dax, fuck me until we both come."

His nostrils flare as he rises and rakes his gaze over me from head to toe. With one hand, he strokes his length. "Lie on the floor, facedown."

Why argue? I want this, and I'll consider the consequences of that need later. Can't focus on anything except his dick and what he'll do to me next.

I lie down on the floor with my arms folded under my head. The position grants me a peripheral view of his naked body.

He kneels over my legs, skimming his hands up and down my thighs. While I moan and squirm, he grasps my ankles and pushes until my knees bend, lifting my ass into the air.

"Please, Dax, please," I moan.

He pushes my knees apart and roughly rubs his hand along my folds. "You will scream my name when I finally let you come."

"I'll scream your name right now if that'll make you do it."

He seizes my wrist and bends my arm behind my back, gripping my hip with his other hand. His hold is solid but also gentle, as if he's taking care not to hurt me. When he punches into my body hard and deep, I let out a sharp cry that echoes inside the building. He pummels my body with punishing thrusts while I teeter on the edge, about to plummet over it, and the second he shifts his hand off my hip to reach down and pinch my clit, I come so hard and fast that I can't scream or move or even breathe. My ears start to ring, and black spots appear in my vision. The orgasm goes on and on, the muscles inside me clenching his cock in fierce waves, though the rest of my body has gone stiff, frozen in the throes of ecstasy.

Dax bellows, thrusting a few more times while I feel his release erupting deep inside me.

While he pulls out of my body, I lie flat on the floor, unable to do anything except struggle to regain my breath. Did that really happen? Did I let a beast of a man use my body for his pleasure? Yeah, I did. I agreed to give myself to him, then begged him to take me without caring what he might do to me. And I loved it. Dax made me feel things I've never experienced before, an intensity of sensations that overwhelmed me. If he ordered me to give in to him again, I'd succumb. Not sure if I can reasonably blame the apocalypse for this. I made the decision to surrender my body and soul to a man who hates me and terrifies me.

Does he still scare me? My wits haven't recovered enough for me to answer that question.

I push up off the floor, my arms quivering slightly, and sit back on my heels.

Dax lies beside me, his entire body slack, his eyes closed and his lips curling into the faintest of smiles. A smug one, naturally.

I punch his arm. "Wake up."

He cracks one lid open. "I am not asleep."

"Good. Then you can answer my question now."

"No."

He shuts his eye and links his hands over his belly. His dick is still semi-firm, but he doesn't seem inclined to take possession of my body again. Can't decide if I want him to do that. I stifle a pathetic moan. Of course I want it. I shouldn't, and I hate that I do, but Dax knows every secret way to stoke my deepest, darkest desires until I'm on fire for him. My willpower can't withstand it.

But I need answers, and he will give them to me now. No more passive Allison. No more cowering Allison either. Maybe it's hormones influencing me, but I don't care. If I can handle sex with a man like Dax, I can absolutely tap into my inner warrior—if nothing else, to make the man lying beside me at last tell me everything.

"I want answers," I say. "No more sidestepping my questions. I let you get your rocks off with my body, so it's time you confessed."

"You let me fuck you so I would defend you from the rampaging horde. No part of our arrangement included an exchange of information."

"Fine. Have it your way." I get up and start hunting for my clothes. My panties are trashed, thanks to him. So I crumple them in my hand and toss them away, then pull on my jeans. "I'll take my chances with the horde."

Yeah, I'm playing a dangerous game. But I have no choice. I need answers from Dax, and he thinks I know more about Sefton than I've told him. I don't, though maybe I can use his belief to get what I want.

Dax springs to his feet and stomps over to me.

I've just done up my bra, and now I'm shrugging into my shirt. Despite the way he's glowering at me, I keep my demeanor casual while I fasten the buttons.

"You are going nowhere," Dax snarls, "unless I tell you so. You wouldn't last five minutes out there."

He wants to goad me into snapping at him, so I do the opposite. I stay silent and calm while I tug my socks on and tie my boots.

Dax grabs my arm. "Have you gone deaf? You are going nowhere."

I shake my arm free of his grip and march toward the door.

"Stop." His barked command resounds through the warehouse. In a softer tone, he adds, "All right, have it your way."

Did he just offer to answer my questions? Since his statement was a tad vague, I turn around to get clarification. "Are you going to tell me everything I want to know?"

He fists his hands, then loosens them. "Yes."

I walk straight to him. "Maybe I should tie you up to make sure you can't ditch me."

"That won't be necessary." He shuffles a little closer. "Before I answer your questions, tell me one thing. Why don't you have real mates? You told me it was none of my business the last time I asked. I'd like to know the answer now."

Oh, what the hell. "I was in the plane crash with my parents. They died, but I survived—with serious injuries. Took me months to recover, physically. Not sure I ever fully recovered from the mental damage. Survivor's guilt or whatever. I guess I avoided getting too close to anyone after that because I was afraid another disaster might ruin my life. I've dated, but I steered clear of serious relationships. Guys can be such dicks, anyway. God, I can't believe I just told you all of that."

Because I've never told anyone. Why am I confiding in Dax? Maybe I sense a similar pain in him, or maybe I'm suffering from apocalypse shock.

"I'm sorry, Allison. You've been through hell, even before the Echo."

"Um, thanks. I guess." When he starts to ask another question, I wag a finger at him. "Uh-uh-uh. I answered one of your questions. It's your turn to cough up some info."

"All right." He winces, though only for a second, and rubs his forehead. "What do you want to know?"

"Everything. But we can start with an easy question." I inch closer, and despite my determination not to notice that he's still naked, I can't stop myself from glancing down at his dick. "Um, don't you want to get dressed?"

"Suddenly, it bothers you that I'm naked." He cups my chin with his hand, brushing one finger over the sensitive underside. "You didn't mind a few minutes ago."

"Stop trying to distract me. It won't work."

But yeah, it kind of is working. What we just did, on that floor, makes it impossible for me to ignore the luscious warmth that sweeps through me simply from the touch of his hand. If I live to be ninety, I'll still remember every second of how it felt to have him buried inside me. I wish he'd let me face him while we had sex, but I'm not that surprised he preferred to avoid looking me in the eye.

"Get dressed," I say. "Please."

He gathers his clothes and reassembles them. If I'd thought Dax clothed would eradicate my desire for him, I was a damn idiot. Of course it doesn't. He's still...visible. That's all it takes.

I clear my throat and focus on his face instead of his groin. "What's your name? Your full name, I mean, not just the three-letter version. Who are you?"

He scrubs a hand over his mouth and bows his head briefly. Then he looks straight into my eyes. "I am Daxton Stainthorpe. Sefton is my twin brother."

CHAPTER THIRTEEN

Dax

I'VE TOLD HER WHO I AM. WHY DID I DO THAT? SHE DEMANDED I EX-plain myself, and I gave in. Perhaps I can blame sex for relaxing me so much that I lost control of my mind and my mouth. But no, that's not the reason. Allison told me about her family, that she's alone in this world much like I'd been alone in the Echo, and I felt...connected to her.

Which is rubbish.

She stares at me without blinking. "You're not identical twins, obviously."

"We *are* identical twins. Or we used to be."

"I don't understand. How can you not be identical anymore?"

She wants to understand. And after what we did moments ago, I feel a strange need to explain. I've treated her like my enemy. She shouldn't have stayed with me, and she should not have let me claim her body, yet she has done both. The least I can do is answer her questions.

"Sefton and I were born identical twins," I say. "But the magics he used to create the Echo and anchor me to it had...consequences. I was changed. I no longer resemble my brother or sound like him."

"You aren't from the Echo."

"No. I was born in England."

"I was born in Wisconsin, but I've lived in several places around the country. Guess that doesn't really compare to being thrown into a different world."

Are we having a civil conversation? Not sure. Either I'm hallucinating or we are chatting to each other like normal people.

"Did you volunteer to be the anchor for Sefton's magic?" she asks. "Or did he force it on you?"

"My brother tricked me." I can't help grinding my teeth when I remember how it happened. But I force myself to relax my jaw and exhale a long sigh. "This will take time to explain."

"Well, I guess I better cancel my manicure and the appointment with my hair stylist."

"Don't get comfortable with me. I'm still the monster who ruthlessly pursued you, took you hostage, and forced you to give me your body."

"I haven't forgotten that." She leans against the wall, hands jammed into her trouser pockets. "But I need to know how all of this happened and what might come next. You mentioned a first wave and a second wave. I assume you meant the two events we've experienced since the sky split open—the fireballs and lightning, then the fire-breathing dragon-people. Will there be a third wave? Seems like you're the one who knows what Sefton has planned."

"Whatever you think of me, if I knew what would happen next, I would tell you."

"Are you still convinced I'm responsible for everything?"

That's a tricky question. Lying seems ill-advised, but honesty might prove even worse. I may need to bind her hands again to keep her from fleeing. I'd rather not do that, but I will take whatever measures are necessary to uncover the truth.

"Sefton is clearly obsessed with you," I tell her. "He sent his beasts to find you—and to bring you to him, I assume. That's why he left a note encouraging you to wait in the library. But he cocked it up and forgot to exclude you from whatever trance he cast over the people in this city. That's why he needs his minions."

"Only one creature tried to get to me—the fish-beast. And the only evidence I have to support that theory is your claim that it was aiming for me and not you."

"It was." Growling at her won't help matters, but I can't stop myself. The woman is so bloody-minded. "That beast wanted you. So did the creatures in the alley, the ones who abducted you. And I've begun to suspect the beasts in the shopping mall wanted you too."

"Based on what evidence? The fact that you want everything to be my fault?"

Perhaps I am biased. But I know she is the key to understanding what's happened and to finding my brother. Only he knows how to stop the worlds from merging.

I slap a hand on the wall beside her shoulder. "If you knew what Sefton did to me, you wouldn't think I'm the monster. You'd know he is. I had a normal life once, with family and friends, but my own brother stole that from me and threw me into a nightmare world he created."

"Why did he do all of this? I don't understand. Why would anyone want to destroy the world and remake it into hell on earth?"

I doubt she expects a response. Her questions are rhetorical. Even if she genuinely wants to know, I can't explain why my brother has done any of this.

Allison spears me with her gaze. "I want some answers. Here are the questions. You said the Echo is a world populated with desecrations of the human form. What does that mean?"

"They are twisted copies of the beings who inhabit this world. I doubt Sefton planned for them to be that way. It must be an unintended side effect of creating the Echo."

"So when you said Sherry wasn't the woman I knew, you meant that literally."

"Yes."

"But Anti-Sherry knew me."

I try not to groan and end up hissing out a sigh instead. Anti-Sherry? I suppose that's an accurate description of what the Echo creatures are. "I don't know why Sefton's magics caused everyone in this world to be duplicated, with distortions. But my brother called the other world the Echo for a reason. I doubt he chose the name at random. It probably refers to the fact he created twisted copies of everyone on earth and populated his parallel world with them."

The ground beneath my feet begins to vibrate, as if a giant machine has been switched on somewhere nearby. The vibrations bring with them the grumbling, grinding racket of a machine too.

Allison stiffens. "What's that?"

"Not sure."

I walk toward the door, trying not to make noise with my footsteps, and carefully crack the door open to peer outside.

Behind me, Allison gasps.

Yes, I would gasp too if I hadn't lost the ability to move or breathe. What I'm seeing can't be. What Sefton has done so far unleashed horrific terror on the world, but this...

The disk-like opening where the Echo tore through the fabric of this world is expanding. The grinding cacophony seems to emanate from the ever-growing rift in the two worlds. As the opening spreads across the sky, glistening darkness roils outward in its wake like the trail of an obsidian comet.

Allison grips my forearm. "If it keeps going like that, it will—"

"Consume the sky, then the earth."

Her fingers press harder into my flesh. "What should we do? Run?"

"I doubt that would help. Perhaps the best thing we can do right now is to stay here and wait—and hope Sefton isn't about to destroy the entire universe."

She huddles closer to me as we both stare up at the sky, helpless to stop the onrushing blackness. Nothing will stop what my brother has set in motion. The darkness sweeps across the heavens while the mechanical grinding and grumbling becomes almost deafening, vibrating my eardrums until I have no choice but to slap my hands over my ears. Allison does the same, grimacing and squinting her eyes until they're almost shut.

An explosion detonates overhead.

The warehouse shudders. And the doorway to the Echo vanishes.

"What just happened?" Allison asks. "The portal or whatever… It's gone."

"I know."

The sky shimmers with shades of obsidian and darkest crimson, while pinpoints of purple stars glitter there. I can't explain why, but I slip my arm around Allison's shoulders and pull her close. I feel something is coming, something unspeakable, something that my brother has dispatched. To do what? I believe everything I told Allison earlier—that Sefton wants her—but my conviction about his goal does not explain this wriggling unease.

"Do you feel that?" Allison whispers. "It's like the air is electrified or something."

The hairs at my nape go stiff, and awareness tingles over my skin. I grab her wrist and drag her toward the motorcycle. "We need to go. Now."

"Why? Where are we going?"

"Anywhere that's not here."

I throw open the door and jump onto the motorcycle, twisting the key in the ignition. The machine roars to life.

Allison just stands there, her brows furrowed, and bites her bottom lip.

"Get on," I snarl.

She hops on behind me. We rocket out of the warehouse, past the ruins of other buildings, and onto the asphalt street.

Whump. Whump.

The purposeful pounding of footfalls shakes the earth and rattles my eardrums. No creature borne of this earth or the Echo could create a sound like that with its feet. The thing approaching us from behind must be like nothing else in the universe.

Whump. Whump.

Allison wraps her arms around my midsection, clutching me as if she thinks she might fly off into the sky. I doubt that's what Sefton has in mind. The motorcycle wobbles faintly with every footfall of the pursuing monster.

"Dax!"

Allison's cry makes me glance back to see what she's gaping at, and I halt the bike so fast that the tires squeal. Then I plant one foot on the ground to keep the machine upright.

The monstrosity pursuing us towers above every building in the city, its monstrous form a combination of living thing and machine, with metal plates fused into its flesh and eyes that burn with an electric red gleam. Those twin beams sweep side to side as they scan the city. The creature's massive, metal-encased feet pulverize the asphalt with every step.

Whump. Whump.

"What is that thing?" Allison whispers.

"It must be a golem. A creature created by magic to do its master's bidding."

The golem stops moving and swerves its gaze in our direction. Though the monstrosity is at least four blocks away, its attention zeroes in on Allison.

I press my lips to her ear. "Still think Sefton didn't send those other creatures for you?"

"Oh please," she hisses. "You can't tell which one of us that golem's looking at. Maybe he's got a crush on you."

"That thing wants *you*."

"Just get us the hell out of here."

The golem's eyes pulse once.

I get us the hell out of there, pushing the motorcycle to the limits of its capabilities as we roar down the battered streets. The golem starts walking again, one gigantic step at a time, but I have a feeling it's not as ponderous as it seems. The thing had been searching for Allison, so it took its time. But now…

Though I shouldn't do it, I can't stop myself. I glance back at the golem.

Its mouth cranks open with a mechanical ratcheting noise. A spark of light flashes deep inside its maw.

Oh no. That spark…

The golem bends its knees and breaks into a run, barreling straight for us. A stream of fire erupts from its mouth, spewing the golem's molten breath over our heads, past where we rush down the street.

And the asphalt melts.

I slam on the brakes, tires squealing, and struggle to keep the bike from flipping onto its side. We come to a stop inches from the seething pool of asphalt. The only way past the barrier is to turn around and go back the way we'd come.

Straight into the arms of the golem.

"Fuck," I growl.

"We need a weapon," Allison says. "Something really big."

"Unless you have a missile in your bra, we have nothing big enough to defeat that thing."

Since we've stopped sideways in the street, we both have a good view of the approaching golem. Does it have a weak spot? If it does, I have no sodding clue how to find, much less exploit, its weakness.

Whump. Whump. The creature keeps barreling toward us.

Allison jumps off the bike and jogs toward the golem.

I leap off the machine, not caring that it tumbles onto its side on the ground, and reach Allison in three long strides. I seize her arm to halt her. "What the bloody hell are you doing?"

"That thing is coming for me. I'm giving it what it wants, to stop it from doing any more damage."

"Have you lost your mind? You can't surrender to Sefton's monstrosity."

She flaps her arms. "I have no choice. If I don't go to Sefton, that thing will kill—" She stares straight into my eyes while hers shimmer with the start of tears. "It will hurt people, I know it."

For a moment, I thought she was about to say she's worried the golem will kill me. No, she wouldn't be upset about that. Not after the way I've treated her.

The golem halts half a block away.

Allison raises her hands and shouts, "I surrender."

She can't—I need to do something. Anything.

The golem slowly raises an arm and points a finger at the building to our left.

"I think it wants us to go in there," Allison says.

That is the last thing I want to do. Sit in an abandoned, partially ruined building and wait for my brother to appear? I assume that's what the golem is directing us to do. But it's insanity. I need to find an escape route so I can—

I glance at Allison, my throat suddenly tight. I need to protect her, though not because I promised I would if she had sex with me. I don't want any harm to come to her.

But we're trapped. So I take her hand and lead her into the building.

Chapter Fourteen

Allison

I CAN'T TELL WHAT THIS BUILDING USED TO BE, THANKS TO THE DAMAGE from the apocalypse and the fact it seems to be a vacant structure. It doesn't look like a warehouse. The building was constructed with bricks. But it hardly matters what this place used to be. Today, it's a prison for me and Dax.

The golem has taken up a position in the street, right in front of this building. Through the shattered windows, I can see that hulking monster, and I know we won't get away unless we can take that thing down.

Yeah, sure. Piece of cake.

We're standing maybe twenty feet from the windows. No point in moving deeper into the building. We have nowhere to go. Rubble blocks the back of the structure, spilling down onto the concrete floor. I think I see the remnants of a countertop inside that mound of debris, so maybe this had been a store.

My palm feels warm. When I glance down, I realize Dax is still holding my hand. His palm is warming mine. Why does he want to hold hands? I guess it's an unconscious action, not a sign that he likes me. I'd be good with him just accepting that I'm not in league with the devil, aka Sefton Stainthorpe—his brother.

"How long do you think we'll have to wait?" I ask.

Dax grunts. "Until Sefton feels like showing himself."

A good, specific estimate.

The man I'd labeled a monster releases my hand, then shuffles up to the broken windows to peer out at the golem.

Dax might be a cretin a lot of the time, but he's not a monster. That thing outside is. The Echo creatures are too. But I think the man himself, Dr. Sefton Stainthorpe, might be the worst monster of all. I should've known, shouldn't I? Right, because alchemy and quantum physics inevitably lead to an apocalypse.

I come up beside Dax and gaze out at the monstrosity that guards us. The golem hasn't moved since it took up that position. Its eyes glow steady red. Just looking at the thing makes my skin crawl because it's a nightmare come to life.

Movement draws my attention to street level.

In a spot near the golem's left foot, the atmosphere begins to shimmer, the way hot air can do on a sultry summer's day. But it isn't that hot today. The darkness enveloping the world creates a cool, yet humid, atmosphere. A pinpoint of what looks like sunshine pierces the shimmering air, the light telescoping out until it fills the oval area.

A figure steps through the opening.

It's a portal. From where, I have no clue.

The figure walks toward the building, limping slightly, and the portal winks out of existence.

Sefton Stainthorpe enters the building and halts just inside the doorway. "Good morning. Or is it evening? It's hard to tell today, isn't it?"

He wears a suit with no tie and speaks in a casual tone, like we're all meeting here for lunch.

Dax lunges for his brother, snarling like a wild animal. But when he gets inches away from Sefton, he's thrown backward by an invisible force.

Sefton shakes his head. "Did you think I wouldn't anticipate your reaction? Though, honestly, I think you should be grateful for what I've done. You are now powerful and fearsome."

"Grateful?" Dax snarls. "Your botched magic turned me into a freak. I had no choice."

His brother chuckles. "Botched?"

Dax looks like he might try again to throttle his brother. I need to change the subject. "Where have you been living? The address you gave me was bogus."

"Of course it was." He brushes his hands over his pants and shirt as if he's removing filth. "I dislike visiting any city, but my calculations required me to start the transmutation here. Fortunately, I was able to travel back and forth as needed via portals, rather than living in this place. I prefer England."

"That's, um, interesting."

"All will become clear, eventually." Sefton scuffles toward me, but his brother steps between us. "Really, Dax, it's hopeless. I have more power than any living thing on earth. You needn't worry, though. I have no intention of harming either of you today. In fact, you are both essential to my plans."

I step sideways to get around Dax. "What is your plan, Dr. Stainthorpe?"

His gaze jerks to me. "I told you to call me Sefton."

Could that be a touch of annoyance in his voice? When I'd first met him, he seemed like the kind of guy who would never raise his voice, the kind who was always polite and opened doors for women. Now it turns out he's a lunatic. If I could be that wrong about Sefton, maybe I've been wrong about Dax too. But is he better or worse than I believed?

Time to play along.

I take one step toward the madman. "I'm sorry, Sefton, I forgot. But I really would like to hear what your plan is. And maybe you could explain what your note meant. The part about the alchemy of worlds."

"You should know," Sefton says. "This is my gift to you."

"What is?"

"The alchemy of worlds and of souls, the change that will make everything better." He moves half a step toward me, his expression alight with an excitement that infects his voice too. "I am creating a new and better world, where no one will be able to disguise their true nature because it will be on display for all to see."

"No more crackbrained rubbish," Dax snaps. "What does any of it mean?"

"Why do you think I transmuted you into this"—Sefton waves at Dax's body—"thing that you are now. I did it to reveal your true self. The chancer who shagged every woman he met, took pleasure wherever he wanted without regard for how his actions affected others. *You* are the monster, Dax. I transmuted you to make your inner self show on the outside."

Dax freezes, his face going blank. His voice becomes a harsh whisper. "You did this to me on purpose?"

He had assumed it was an unintended consequence of the magics that Sefton had employed to create the Echo. Now he knows his brother made him this way on purpose.

I want to hug him. But that would be a catastrophically bad idea. Besides, I shouldn't feel sorry for the man who held me hostage and accused me of being Sefton's cohort in creating an apocalypse.

But I can't help it. He looks so...stricken.

Sefton seems oblivious to his brother's reaction. He waves a dismissive hand. "Alchemy is the transmutation of one substance into another, or one being into another. In the classical sense, it's also the quest for eternal life."

"You want to live forever?" I say.

He scuffles closer, now mere inches away. "I want *us* to live forever. Allison, we can rule the world together. Just think, no one will ever look down on us or mistreat us because we will be invincible."

"I don't want to be immortal."

Sefton lifts a hand near my cheek, like he wants to touch me but can't quite do it. "I did all of this for you, pet. We can be together at last, with nothing to stop us. The Echo is my gift to you."

"But I—"

He seizes my hand, gripping it tightly. "I love you, Allison."

Love? He barely knows me. But I don't think it's a good idea to point that out or to tell him I don't feel that way.

My gaze flicks to Dax.

He's still staring at his brother, but his stark expression has hardened into something much darker and angrier. His attention stays nailed to Sefton as he speaks through clenched teeth. "Did you know what would happen to me when you threw me into the Echo?"

"Of course."

Dax lunges for his brother but ricochets off whatever shield Sefton has erected around himself. "We are brothers. How could you do that to me?"

"Because I've never liked you." He rakes his gaze over Dax, his lip curling. "I explained all of this when I gave you the gift of being the anchor." Sefton returns his attention to me. "Come with me, pet, and I will tell you everything."

He holds his hand out to me, palm up.

Go with him? No way. Even before he revealed his madness, I wouldn't have done that. From the start, I'd sensed something off about him, and I'm not going anywhere with Sefton Stainthorpe.

But telling him that seems like a bad, bad, bad idea.

Sefton thrusts his hand out to me again. "Come, Allison."

Come? I am not a dog.

But I need a plan. Can't discuss it with Dax, not when his lunatic brother is standing right in front of me. So I'll need to do this on my own.

Sefton told me the Echo is his gift to me and that we will be invincible together. He also said we would rule the world. Given his personal force field, or whatever it is, I assume he meant magic would give us the power to protect ourselves and control everyone else. He created a frigging golem that could smash a city with one step of its gigantic foot. So yeah, Sefton is very powerful.

But he said "we" would be invincible.

That implies I have power too. I'm the catalyst, that's what Dax said. Without me, Sefton couldn't have created the Echo. I can't prove that, but the evidence suggests it's true. If Sefton has insanely powerful magics, then maybe I do too. Can I use the power he gave me to escape from him and his monsters?

Yeah, if I had any clue how to do that. This is magic, right? Maybe I can just…will it to happen.

Since I don't want to let on that I'm trying to do that, I force myself to focus on Sefton and maintain a neutral expression while I wish with all my mental focus that I were somewhere far away, somewhere Sefton can't find me. While I do that, I need to keep Sefton talking.

"Will there be more waves of beings coming out of the Echo?" I ask.

"No, but there will be waves of…other sorts."

"Like what?" *Get me out of here,* I command the magics. *Get me out of here now, do it, right now, far away from this place, somewhere safe.* "I have to admit what you've done so far is impressive."

"We can discuss that later. Now, it is time to go."

Come on, you stupid magics. Whisk me away.

Peripherally, I see Dax squinting at me. Has he figured out what I'm doing? If Sefton realizes... I am so screwed. He seems a touch annoyed, rather than incensed, so I don't think he's figured it out yet. But I'm pretty sure Dax has. How? I can ask him that later, after we escape from his brother.

My heart stutters. *We.* I thought that word. I want Dax to come with me.

No time to consider the repercussions of that impulse. I keep chanting in my head, keep willing the Echo to do my bidding, though I have no idea if this is how magic works. *Do it, you goddamn magics, do my bidding. I command it. Take me and Dax away right now.*

Sefton squints at me, just like his brother is doing.

A strange sensation sifts through me, like electricity and cool water in my veins. I can't breathe. Can't move. Not because I'm paralyzed, but because I sense the magics heeding my command. It's about to happen.

"No!" Sefton shouts. "You can't—"

He lunges for me just as I lunge for Dax and throw my arms around him.

And we vanish.

CHAPTER FIFTEEN

Dax

THE WORLD SPINS AWAY FROM US, AND WE RUSH THROUGH A VOID deeper and darker than the furthest reaches of outer space. Then we drop down onto a solid surface, swaying for a moment. Allison still has her arms around me. I don't understand what just happened, but I'm certain she is responsible for it. The brightness that engulfs us blinds me for several seconds, but then my vision returns.

I blink swiftly as I try to make sense of our surroundings.

We stand in a meadow filled with wildflowers. The sun shines down on us, warm and soothing. The scent of the outdoors suffuses my senses, and I find myself wrapping my arms around Allison, though I don't know why. It feels…good. That's all I know.

Allison glances around. "Where are we?"

"I should ask you that. This is your doing, isn't it?"

"Well, I tried to use magic to whisk us away. Didn't know if it would work." She takes two steps away from me so she can turn in a circle to inspect the area. "Guess it did work. I wished for us to be far away from Sefton and his apocalypse, in a safe place."

Her statement stops me for a moment as I digest its full meaning. "You wished for me to come with you?"

She faces me, hunching her shoulders and biting her lip. "Yeah. I guess I, um, kind of did."

"Why?"

Yes, I sound stunned. Of course I do. After the way I've treated Allison, she should despise me. But she seems to have stopped hating me and decided to… What? She can't like me. No, she must want me around to protect her from any monsters that might come for us.

She sits down in the grass, closes her eyes, and inhales deeply. Her lips curl into a faint smile. When she looks at me again, she pats the grass beside her. "Sit down. We should talk."

Despite her filthy clothes and disheveled hair, she is beautiful. I can't stop a memory from rushing through me, a replay of our time in the warehouse before Sefton came for us. I remember being inside her, taking her body without mercy, relentless in my need to claim this woman for my own. I hadn't realized that's what I was doing until after we had sex. The act hadn't dulled my hunger for her at all. I still crave her like mad, but now I want to do more than fuck her. I need to make her feel something for me because...I feel something for her.

I drop onto the grass an arm's length from her. "I assume 'talking' involves you demanding information from me."

"Not demanding. Requesting. I'd like it if you volunteered information instead of making me drag it out of you."

The worst part of me insists I should remind her of our arrangement, but I can't speak the words. I need her to want me willingly.

Allison pokes my arm. "Don't you want to remind me that my body is your property?"

"No. Forget our deal."

"Really?" She squeezes my thigh gently. "For the record, you don't need a contract to make me sleep with you. I'll do it anyway."

"Why?"

"Because it feels good. Duh."

I resist the urge to apologize and to explain my behavior. She wants answers now, not my pathetic excuses. "What do you want to know?"

"Tell me what happened between you and Sefton. Why he hates you. Why he made you the anchor for his so-called gift."

"He gave *you* a gift. But he cursed me."

She wriggles her arse to turn toward me. "I'd like to know why Sefton did that. Please."

"We might be twins, but we have never been identical—except in our appearance." I take a deep breath and exhale it slowly. The time has come to tell her everything. "It happened a week ago, back home in England. Sefton asked me to meet him at our ancestral home, in front of the gravestones for our parents."

One Week Ago
Fallenmouth Manor, England

I STRIDE ACROSS THE LAWN, PAST THE SPRAWLING HOME WHERE I ONCE lived with my parents and my brother, heading behind the house toward the family cemetery. Acid roils in my gut, because I never wanted to come back here. This is the property of the Earl of Fallenmouth, not of the Stainthorpe family, not anymore. Without Mum and Dad, I don't want to live here. When the household staff started calling me "my lord," it was too much. I had to leave.

But my brother kept living here. I told him he could. Let Sefton have the place. It holds too many memories for me, too many feelings that I've avoided confronting.

I find Sefton standing at the graves, head down.

"What's going on, Sef?" I ask as I halt beside him. "You made it sound urgent. I rushed here from London, so it had better be good."

"You need to know that I'll be making some changes."

"The estate is your business, not mine. Redecorate all you want."

He lifts his head, aiming his gaze directly at me. "That's not what I meant. The changes I intend to implement are more far-reaching than the upholstery in the house or the shrubs in the garden."

I sigh and shove my hands into my trouser pockets. "Why don't you tell me what it is? I have things to do."

"You mean women to do. Honestly, Dax, Father would be ashamed of you."

No, I won't deny that. It's true.

Sefton's lip curls. "I'm ashamed of you. That's why I've chosen you to be the anchor in my plan to change everything."

A car horn blares three times on the other side of the house.

"Claudia is here," I say. "She's dying to be shagged by an earl. So get on with it, Sef."

"That girl won't want you anymore once I'm done."

"Are you threatening to steal my lover?" I laugh and slug his arm. "Good one, Sef. You almost had me."

"Of course you assume I could never seduce a woman. I'm the quiet one who no one understands, the boy who has no mates." He fists his hands and faces the graves again. "I'll show Mum and Dad. I'll show you too. Soon, everyone will know."

"Know what?" I hold up a hand to stop him from speaking. "Never mind. I'm going to spend the weekend shagging Claudia in the earl's bedroom. She loves that idea. Do what you want, Sef."

As I walk away from him, I hear his voice. "I will, Dax. I will."

I return to the house and do exactly what I told Sefton I would do. I spend the afternoon fucking a woman I sort of like but have no intention of dating, much less marrying. That's who I am. A chancer of an earl who doesn't care about anyone else. My brother can brood by our parents' graves all he wants. They're dead, and I prefer the living.

Especially when the living person with me is a sexy little thing who can't get enough of me.

Just as the sun begins to set, I'm lying in bed with Claudia. We've just shagged, and she is gazing at me with soft eyes warmed by desire. Her body feels warm against me, for sure, and I can't resist gliding a hand up her arm in a teasing caress.

She shivers faintly. "I'm hungry, Dax."

"For food? Or do you mean…"

"I'm hungry for your body." She snuggles up to me. "One more time before we go downstairs for dinner."

Someone knocks on the door.

"Go away," I shout.

"It's me," Sefton says. "I urgently need to discuss something with you."

"Can't it wait? I'm in the middle of an urgent matter myself."

"No, it can't wait."

I sigh, then slap Claudia's arse. "Stay here, darling. I'm sure this won't take long."

She watches me while licking her lips as I pull my clothes on and walk out of the bedroom. My brother gestures for me to follow him, not saying a word about what urgent matter he needs to discuss. Sefton has always been a bit odd, and I've always indulged him. That's what brothers do, isn't it? I've never had any other siblings. I know only that I was expected to look out for Sefton, and I never saw it as an onerous duty.

But I have noticed something else, something I'd overlooked when I was determined to get Claudia upstairs. "Where's the staff, Sefton? I know they like to stay out of the way, but Fallenmouth seems quieter than usual today."

"I sent the staff away. They are no longer necessary."

My brother leads me outside, back to the cemetery.

I groan. "The graves again? Really, Sef? I don't understand your sudden fascination with our parents' headstones."

"They died thirteen years ago today."

"Yes, I know. It's getting dark and chilly, and I didn't bring a coat. So tell me what the bloody hell we're doing out here."

He leans toward me, his voice hushed yet filled with a strange intensity. "Thirteen is a magical number. It's imbued with the frequencies of metaphysical power, ascension, and oneness. But most importantly, thirteen is indivisible in the mathematical sense, which makes it the essence of incorruptible perfection."

What is he on about? This can't be my brother, the logical scientist, spouting New Age rubbish.

I lay a hand on his shoulder. "I think you need to take a holiday, Sef. You've clearly been working too hard."

He shrugs away from my hand. "I resigned."

"You quit your position at Oxford? Why?"

"Because I realized the truth. Humanity is irredeemably corrupted, and the only salvation is to rewrite everything." He tips his head back to gaze up at the darkening sky where the first pinpoints of stars have emerged. "The power of thirteen is vast, but three is of paramount importance. I need two more to complete the spell."

"What spell? Since when are you interested in magic? You are a physicist, Sef, not a sorcerer."

"You understand so little. Ever since we reached puberty, all you've cared about was chasing a bit of skirt." He stabs a finger into my chest. "Now at least you will serve a higher purpose."

Nothing he's told me makes any sense. He must be off his rocker.

"Let's go back inside," I say. "We can break out the Scotch and talk this through."

"There is nothing to 'talk through,' Dax. I have a plan that must be enacted tonight, under the full moon on the thirteenth day of the month."

"All right, Sef," I say slowly. "Time to go back inside and have that drink."

"Stop patronizing me," he hisses. "Allison will understand, but I knew you lacked the intelligence and sophistication to envision the true scope of my plan."

"Who is Allison? Have you met a girl, Sef? About bloody time."

"You will never meet her." He picks up a bag that had been lying on the ground, though I hadn't noticed it before. The twilight concealed it. "Allison Dahl is mine, and you won't get the chance to steal her away from me."

"I've never stolen a girl from you."

He stares down at the graves. "You will be the anchor, which means you'll remain in the Echo even after the beginning of the end arrives. But Allison… She is the catalyst, the reason for everything I do. She wants what I want, as fervently as I desire it."

"This girl of yours wants…what, exactly?" She must be as insane as he has become. The Echo? The catalyst? It's bollocks. "I'm confused, Sef. What are you trying to do?"

He pulls something out of his bag, though it's concealed by his thigh. My brother sidles up to me, his eyes wild and his voice a harsh whisper. "I'm going to create an apocalypse."

"I see. Well, good luck with that." I assume this is an elaborate practical joke, though I've never known my brother to do something like that. "I'll see you at dinner."

"You arrogant prat." Spittle flies from his lips with every word. "Of course you can't believe I could envision a plan as elegantly conceived as this. But in a matter of moments, you will believe."

I rub my eyes and sigh. "No, I won't. I'm done. You can stand out here howling at the moon, but I'm going back to bed. Claudia's waiting for me."

Though I start to turn away, Sefton seizes my wrist and clamps an object around it. Something cold and metallic. I freeze, glancing down at my hand, where a shiny metal bracelet encircles my wrist so snugly that it pinches my skin. My pulse speeds up as a strange sensation of electricity tingles through me. Unusual symbols engraved on the bracelet begin to flicker with a golden light.

I turn toward my brother, but I don't recognize him anymore. "What are you doing?"

He pulls out his mobile and turns the screen toward me. "Look at this woman. Allison Dahl is mine. You could never win her because you are a callous and selfish wanker. I will win not only her, but the entire world."

My gaze lands on the photograph his mobile displays. A beautiful girl with dark hair. Allison Dahl. In the image, she stands behind a waist-high counter while holding a stack of books. Head down, she seems unaware someone is taking her picture.

Sefton steps away from me and starts to chant in another language, maybe Latin, I don't know. He pulls more items out of his bag, laying them on the ground, though I can't see exactly what they are. Night has taken full control of the world, obscuring everything.

The bracelet vibrates, shooting spikes of pain up my arm and out into my entire body. I cry out as my knees buckle and I slump to the ground.

"Stop this," I shout to Sefton. "Please."

My bones begin to crack and shift, forcing me to collapse onto my side on the ground, directly over my parents' graves. My body convulses as an agony unlike anything I could have imagined shreds me from the inside out and the bracelet melts into my flesh, sinking under the skin to scorch through my veins.

And I scream.

Sefton bends over me, holding a knife. He slices a long cut down my inner arm, then carves out another on my cheek. "This is your just punishment. You were always the golden boy, the darling of Mum and Dad's eyes, the perfect son they loved more than me. Why should you inherit an earldom simply because you were born six minutes and fifteen seconds before me? The Echo will right the wrongs done to me, and I will rule the world with Allison at my side."

The cuts on my arm and face burn like acid. The tang of blood seeps into my mouth as the scorching agony becomes overpowering, and numbness rushes through me. Darkness consumes my vision. My brain stops processing sound and sight and sensation as I drift in an abyss, weightless and free of pain. But the blessed release lasts only for a moment.

Then I'm thrust out into hell.

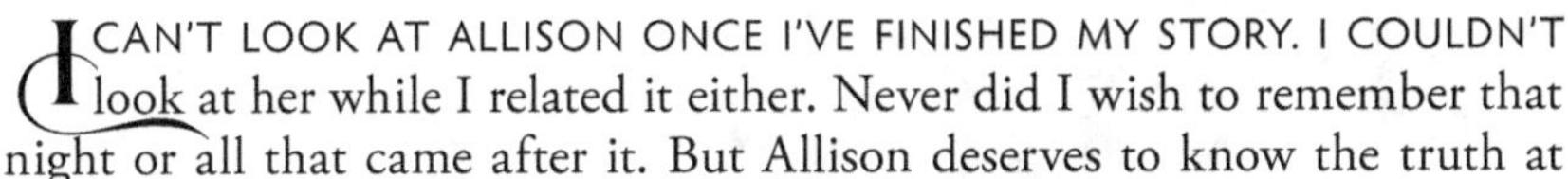

I CAN'T LOOK AT ALLISON ONCE I'VE FINISHED MY STORY. I COULDN'T look at her while I related it either. Never did I wish to remember that night or all that came after it. But Allison deserves to know the truth at last, and so I've told her. My own brother did this to me while I lay atop the graves of our mother and father.

"What was it like in the Echo?" Allison asks, her voice hushed and almost tender. "If you'd rather not talk about it…"

"The Echo is hell. Every depiction of that domain you've ever seen or read about can't come close to the reality." I bend my knees to rest my elbows on them, only so I can hide my face in my raised hands. "I woke up a monster, alone in a brutal world. Gradually, other creatures began to appear, but they were not allies. You've seen what the Echo beings are like. Over the years, I ran into people I recognized, but I quickly realized they were not the men and woman I'd known. They were twisted copies created by my brother."

"Years? Sefton did that to you last week."

I have to look at her now, though I don't want to do it. "Time behaves differently in the Echo. Sefton might have created that world last week, but I lived in it for five years."

She stares at me, not blinking, her lips parted, for a long moment that I don't even try to measure. Though I aim my gaze straight ahead, I can see her peripherally. And I swear I can feel her attention on me, prickling my skin.

At last, she speaks. "I'm so sorry, Dax. I had no idea you'd been in the Echo for so long. Can't imagine how horrific that was."

"Don't feel sorry for me." I swerve my head to glare at her. "Have you forgotten how I treated you until a few hours ago? I abducted you, tied you up, shouted and snarled and accused you of conspiring with Sefton. And let's not overlook the deal I forced you into accepting, the one that requires you to fuck me."

She starts to speak, but I don't let her.

"Remember what I did," I growl. "Sefton was right. I am a monster."

Chapter Sixteen

Allison

Is Dax a monster? Just a few hours ago, I would've said yes. I haven't forgotten the way he treated me, but I also haven't overlooked the glimpses of goodness—or at least not-so-awfulness—in him. Yesterday, when I couldn't walk any further, he picked me up and carried me for two miles. He didn't have to do that. He could've dragged me along with him. Then he got me food and water, and he commandeered a car so I wouldn't have to walk anymore.

Yes, he kidnapped me. Yes, he tied me up and snarled at me. And yes, he vowed he wouldn't protect me unless I had sex with him. The fact I wanted to do that doesn't excuse him. But I'm beginning to understand why he behaved the way he did. Five years in a literal hell world? Yeah, that could turn anyone into a monster.

But Dax isn't a monster. He's a damaged man.

Do I want to save him? Not sure that's a good idea, but then, I have no one else. The most important question seems to be whether he wants to be saved.

I try to lay a hand on his arm, but he scoots sideways to get away from me. I decide not to push. "You are not a monster, but you are traumatized. Even before the apocalypse hit, you were trapped in a horrific place."

He bows his head, hands on his knees. "Sefton was right. I deserve to be in hell."

"No, you do not."

"I don't want to talk about this anymore."

"Tough shit. I *do* want to talk about it." I clamber to my knees and grasp his face with both hands to force him to look at me. "Don't let Sefton mess with your head anymore. He's the demon, not you. I get that you were a player, and you didn't act like an earl or whatever. But that doesn't make you evil."

"Believe what you like."

"Thank you. I will."

Since he won't believe me anytime soon, I stand up and look around. We're in a meadow filled with wildflowers, and rolling hills extend toward the horizon. I recognize this place. It's on the outskirts of Fort Worth, probably twenty miles away, far enough that I can see only the skyline. It's always reminded me of the Emerald City in *The Wizard of Oz*, but not today. The city has become a heap of ruins. Luckily, I'd driven past this rural area before the Echo, so I know where we are.

Too damn close to the epicenter of the apocalypse.

A dark smudge on the horizon draws my attention. What is that? A chill frosts over me from head to toe as I realize the truth. That's the apocalypse, and it's spreading outward, coming this way. In the minute or so while I watch it, the darkness and devastation swarms closer and closer until it overtakes the sun. Clear sky remains above us, but the shadows draw ever nearer.

"We have to go," I say. "Now."

Dax wrinkles his brow. But then he sees what I see, and a muscle jumps in his jaw. He leaps up, grabbing my hand. "Where can we go? It's coming this way. I'm sure anywhere we try to hide, Sefton's apocalypse will find us. He wants to destroy the world and remake it to his liking."

"We need to go someplace that he won't destroy. Got any ideas about that?"

Dax studies the approaching darkness while booms echo in the distance, signs that the fireballs and lightning are coming closer. "I can think of only one place that Sefton might have left untouched."

"Where is it?"

"Our ancestral home. Fallenmouth Manor."

"It's amazing you didn't turn out to be a whackjob like your brother when you both grew up in a house with a weird name like that. Does it have gargoyles on the roof?"

"No." He gives me that squinty-eyed look he always gets right before he's about to snarl something nasty at me. "And I *am* a whackjob. Don't start to think I'm the sort who will cuddle with you and soothe your fears. I'm a monster, just as my brother intended."

"Bullshit." I throw my arms wide. "He's the one who destroyed the freaking world. You've helped me."

He slings his arms around my waist, hauling me into him. "Strictly because I wanted your body."

"Oh please. Your threats no longer impress me, and I'm not scared of you either. Quit trying to tick me off."

He cuffs my wrists behind my back with one hand. "You should be afraid, love. Because I am going to tear my brother limb from limb the next time I see him."

"Can't shock me that way, Dax. Not anymore."

Behind him, the roiling darkness creeps ever closer, and lightning bolts slam into the earth with enough force to make the ground beneath us shiver. Fireballs punch into the earth too, sending volcanoes of dirt and debris pluming into the air. Soon, this beautiful landscape will be a wasteland.

"Sefton might be at Fallenmouth Manor," I say. "Why do you think we'll be safe there?"

"We won't be. But he won't kill you, that much I'm certain of. Sefton believes he loves you, which means he will protect you."

"He hates you."

"But he won't kill me, not yet. He still needs his anchor, or else he would have murdered me already." Dax releases my wrists but keeps his arms around me. "Your body belongs to me. Remember that."

"You just opened up to me in a big way, and now you're feeling weird about it. I get that." I wriggle against him, rubbing against the bulge in his pants. "Your body belongs to me too. But the next time we have sex, I'll be the one who decides when and how it happens."

One corner of his mouth twitches upward the tiniest bit, but only for a split second. "Can you transport us to Fallenmouth Manor?"

"Not sure. I've only done the transporting thing once."

"You are a part of the Echo. You control at least some of its power. Harness that again."

"Don't remember exactly how I did it before."

He releases my wrists and holds me close in a much less obnoxious way. It feels almost tender. "What did you want most of all in that moment, when you took us away from Sefton and his golem?"

"I—" Wanted to save myself, yes. But I also fervently wished to save Dax too. That's probably a sign I've gone crazy, but everything about this new world is bonkers. "I just wanted to escape from Sefton and his creatures. It was too much, and I was afraid of what he might do next."

"Tap into that fervent desire to escape. Use it now."

Wrapping my arms around him, I squeeze my eyes shut and take his advice. I wish with everything I have that we could be at Fallenmouth Manor. I don't even know where that is, but I'm tapping into magics now, not plotting a course on a map. That weird sensation of electricity and cool water rushes through me, and I sense the world shifting around us. The bomb blasts of fireballs and supernatural lightning fall silent as a temperate breeze kisses my cheeks.

I open my eyes. "Is that Fallenmouth Manor?"

"Yes." Dax pushes away from me. "I've come home at last."

He doesn't sound happy about that.

The house squats inside an expansive clearing, its boxy shape a sharp contrast to the almost whimsical way the shrubs and flower beds around it have been sculpted. The gray stone structure features windows with wrought iron sectioning the panes and wrought iron benches in the garden that I can just see to the left of the house. I can't see the cemetery from here, but I imagine that's situated out of sight on purpose.

Dax and I are standing in a circular driveway covered in pea gravel that crunches under our shoes. A concrete fountain hunkers in the middle of the circular drive, and water pours out of the mouth of a leaping stag.

Something about this place creeps me out. Maybe it's the apocalypse doing that, but I think it's this estate too. It feels…haunted. I know we will meet Sefton here. It's inevitable. But I dread the moment when he'll arrive and bring who-knows-what kind of creatures with him. His golem? God, I hope not.

Dax takes my hand to lead me into the house. Wooden double doors block our way, but he twists the knob—and it turns. Nobody locks this place up, I guess. Maybe Sefton has the whole estate surrounded, guarded by his Echo minions. Dax pulls the doors shut as we waltz into the entry-way, and shadows envelop us. But dim light spills out of a room further down the hall.

A chill sweeps over my skin, raising every hair.

Sefton steps out of the room at the end of the hall. "Come inside and join me by the fire. I know it's summer, but a crackling hearth is soothing."

He sounds calm and almost friendly.

Dax doesn't move. Neither do I.

Sefton waves for us to follow him. "Come, join me in the drawing room. We have much to discuss."

Discuss? The man who brought hell to earth wants to sit down by the fire and have a chat.

I glance at Dax.

He shrugs.

We shuffle down the hall to join Sefton in the drawing room. Our host sits in an armchair while Dax and I settle onto padded wooden chairs.

"Thank you for coming," Sefton says. "I assume you, Allison, are respon-sible for getting the two of you here. I hadn't anticipated you would share in the power of the Echo."

"Uh-huh." I squirm in my seat. It's not uncomfortable, but I feel uneasy about everything right now. Especially Sefton Stainthorpe. Considering what Dax told me about his brother, I decide playing nice is my best move. "Didn't mean to horn in on your power. You must be annoyed."

"On the contrary. It's perfectly right that you and I should control the Echo together." Sefton leans forward, his gaze pinned to mine. "But I can't have you defying me."

No, I won't comment on that. Instead, I clear my throat and ask, "Where's your golem?"

"Sleeping. I will rouse him when it becomes necessary." Sefton keeps staring at me with unnerving intensity. "But do not ever run away from me again. If you try, you will wish you hadn't. The world outside this sanctuary will grow even worse as time goes on and the alchemy of worlds reaches its conclusion."

"But your sanctuary will be untouched."

"Precisely." Sefton leans back in his chair, resting one ankle on the opposite knee, wincing slightly. He sets both feet on the floor. "Would you care to join me for dinner? Or are you both too knackered? I can take you straight to your quarters if you prefer."

"Sleep sounds great." I glance at Dax. "What about you?"

"Not hungry. Your idea is best."

Sefton rises, wincing again as he puts weight on his leg, clearly favoring his left knee.

Dax and I both stand up. He eyes his brother with a narrowed gaze and tight lips.

"Come," Sefton says. "Let me show you to your quarters, where you will sleep every night for the rest of your lives."

CHAPTER SEVENTEEN

Dax

MY BROTHER IS INSANE, BEYOND REDEMPTION. BUT THEN, I'M PREJU-diced because he ripped me apart and remade me into a monster, without my permission, without caring what damage his spell would do to me or anyone else caught in the crossfire. Allison was in the crossfire. She might've died, and Sefton did nothing to protect her. He claims to love her, yet he left her alone and defenseless during a catastrophe of biblical proportions.

He created an apocalypse. My brother. Quiet, shy Sefton Stainthorpe has turned the entire world into his own demented experiment.

Sefton mounts the stairs one step at a time, favoring his left leg.

"How did you injure yourself?" I ask.

"During your transformation, you thrashed like a mad beast and kicked me hard in the knee."

I will not apologize for that. He deserved much worse.

We reach the landing, and Sefton pauses to catch his breath. Mounting those stairs seems to have left him winded. That's odd, since he had seemed quite spry earlier, aside from his bad knee. He leads us down the hall toward my old room. I remember this house better than I wish I did, and every room seems filled with the ghosts of the past. I would never have chosen to come back here. This place reminds me that I am not the man I was and never will be again. Isn't a five-year sentence in the Echo enough punishment? Haven't I earned my freedom? But I won't be free, not ever again. Sefton has made certain of that.

At the door to my old room, Sefton halts with his hand resting on the knob of the closed door. "This will be your quarters, Allison. It used to belong to my parents, the Earl and Countess of Fallenmouth."

Allison flicks her gaze to me, then back to Sefton. "Isn't this Dax's room now? He's the Earl of Fallenmouth."

"There are no earls anymore," Sefton hisses. "No dukes, no viscounts, no fucking queen or king. There is only me. I rule over everyone and everything in both worlds, which means I decide which of you sleeps in this room. Do you understand?"

She nods, seeming to have decided speaking is a bad idea.

The best I can do is to partially restrain my anger. I thrust an arm between Allison and Sefton, thumping my palm on the door. "You will not sleep in the same room with her."

"He didn't say he wanted to," Allison tells me while she gently settles a hand on my outstretched arm. "Relax, huh? We're all wiped out. A good night's rest will make us feel better, and then we can have a nice talk in the morning. Okay?"

Nothing about this is okay, but I understand what Allison is really trying to communicate to me. She wants me to placate my mad-as-a-hatter brother so he won't hack off our arms and legs to stop us from escaping.

I lower my arm.

My brother opens the bedroom door. "Your room, Allison."

"Thank you," she says as she steps across the threshold.

"But it will be our room soon."

I glower at Sefton.

He feigns nonchalance fairly well, but the lines tightening around his eyes attest to his true state of mind. "Good night, Allison. You may lock the door if you wish."

He hands her a key.

The wanker had hoped to sleep with her tonight, hadn't he? Sefton changed his mind only when I let my displeasure show.

Allison shuts the door and locks it.

Sefton waves for me to follow him. "You will stay in your old room. The one you slept in until our parents died and you became lord of the manor strictly based on the accident of fate that pushed you out of Mother's arse before me."

"Don't talk about Mum that way. She loved you."

"But she loved you more. Everyone did. I was invisible, drowned out by the sparkling light of your brilliant personality." He stops at the door to my childhood room and hurls it open. "You always looked down on me."

"That's not true. I was proud of you. We might be twins, but I couldn't have hoped to be as clever and accomplished as you. Two PhDs? I didn't try for one." Maybe I'm desperately attempting to convince him that he wasn't invisible all our lives because I don't want my brother to be the maniac who destroyed the world. But since I can't rewind time and stop him from doing that, I lay a hand on his shoulder and try again. "I never hated you, Sef. I loved you. But I can't understand what you've done."

"Of course not. You don't have the vision to comprehend it."

"Sef—"

"I never loved you, Dax. I always despised you, and I always will."

He stalks off down the hall, his footfalls echoing in his wake.

Sefton and I might not have been best mates, but I thought we got on well enough. Now I find out he has always despised me. The dark energy he ingested to become powerful must have emboldened him to become a monster, but he clearly harbored those desires inside him for years, maybe all his life.

I want to go to Allison's room and lose myself inside her body, erase the pain with sex. But I won't use her that way, not anymore. Seeing my brother again, knowing what he has done, I feel like my entire life has been one long dream and now I've woken from it to discover the real world is a nightmare.

Shuffling into my room, I kick the door shut. I had slept in this room until I turned eighteen and went away to university. My parents died two months after my twentieth birthday, and I became the Earl of Fallenmouth. That's another thing Allison and I have in common—losing our parents at a relatively young age—though I had mates and lovers to help me through it while she had no one.

Allison has me now, but that's hardly a blessing.

I kick off my boots and toss my leather coat onto the chair in the corner. Then I drop onto the bed on my back, still clothed, and shut my eyes. Outside the window, far in the distance, creatures scream and shout, but eventually, I manage to sleep.

The sun is just rising when I wake up. Can't believe I slept at all, but exhaustion had overpowered me. I push up into a sitting position and swing my legs off the bed, yawning and stretching. I need to find Allison and make sure she's all right. I pull on my boots, then head for her room.

The door hangs open, and the room is empty.

I take the steps two at a time as I rush downstairs and stop in the foyer. Voices originate from the dining room. I stomp down the hall and through the doorway.

Sefton sits at the head of the long table while Allison occupies the chair beside him.

When she sees me, she smiles—though only for half a second. I'm sure she worries about my brother's reaction if he should notice that she seems rather pleased to see me. I don't blame her for veering her gaze away.

"Good morning, Dax," my brother says, and he sounds almost sincere. "Join us for breakfast. I made this meal myself."

"Because you fired all the staff." I sit down opposite Allison. "When did you learn to cook, Sef?"

"No one taught me. I figured it out on my own."

Oh yes, that makes me want to eat his food. Allison seems to be pushing it around on her plate but not actually consuming any of her meal. Maybe she's afraid Sefton will poison us. He would only risk that with me. Allison is more than a tool for my crackbrained brother to exploit, but right now, my most pressing problem is how to get her to eat. I doubt the food is poisoned, and we both need nourishment. So I spear a piece of blackened sausage with my fork and eat it. "Not bad, Sef. The faint taste of charcoal gives it a distinctive flavor."

"Glad you approve. But that's not charcoal. It's a honey glaze."

"Sure it is. Honey is so often black."

This is bizarre. I'm having a normal conversation with my brother, the madman responsible for the world's ruination, as if we're just two blokes enjoying a morning meal.

Allison still hasn't tasted the food. I consume a mouthful of mashed potatoes and make a noise that implies I like it. Well, the food isn't the worst I've ever had. It's not the best either, but starving refugees from the apocalypse can't be finicky. Allison bites her upper lip, watching me eat. After I've devoured another bite of sausage and two forkfuls of baked beans, she finally starts to eat.

I relax, just a bit. Can't completely relax under the circumstances, but at least Allison won't be malnourished. It seems impossible to believe I kidnapped her a few days ago and treated her like my enemy. Now I'm determined to make sure she has a good breakfast.

After our meal, and more bizarrely mundane conversation, we all walk out into the foyer.

I haven't forgotten what Sefton said last night—that Allison and I will be in this house for the rest of our lives—and it's time to ask him the obvious question. "What do you mean to do with us?"

"I'll share my plans with you when I return."

"Return? From where?"

Sefton shrugs. "I need to survey the areas that have already been transformed. Alchemy on this level is extraordinarily difficult to achieve, and I can't be sure a few things haven't been cocked up in the process. I need to see for myself."

"I'll go with you."

He lets out a harsh laugh. "Are you off your trolley, Dax? I can't let you leave this compound because I can't trust you not to try to escape. Besides, it wouldn't be clever to leave Allison alone here. The entire five-hundred-acre property is warded, magically, to prevent anyone from entering. But the guards... Well, I can't guarantee they'll mind their manners."

"What sort of guards? I haven't seen them."

"No, you wouldn't. They have their orders." He throws a hand up when I start to speak again. "Enough, Dax. I need to say goodbye to Allison."

Sefton clasps her hands, leaning in until their faces hover a hair's breadth apart. "I regret leaving you so soon after our reunion, but it can't be helped. When I return, we will be married. And we shall at last consummate our union."

Consummate? I don't care if he is my flesh and blood. I will murder him if he touches Allison.

"Married?" she says, her jaw dropping. "We hardly know each other. No offense, but I don't love you."

"But you shall." He presses his lips to hers. "We are going to rule the world together, pet."

He shuffles away from us. A portal appears just behind him, and he walks backward through it. The portal vanishes.

"You are not marrying him," I snarl.

"No, I'm not." She bars her arms over her breasts. "But not because you commanded I won't do it. No more growling orders at me. Got it?"

"I can't stand to see him touch you or speak to you as if you're already his."

"He thinks I am." She approaches me, tilting her head back to meet my gaze. "But he is mistaken. Nobody owns me. Not him, not you, not anyone."

"Yes, I know. But I feel…possessive of your body."

"Get over it. If and when I decide to have sex with you again, it will be my choice."

"Of course it will."

She angles her head to the side and squints at me. "Are you being amenable? That can't be right. I must have misheard that, and you really said something nasty."

"I did not. But if you persist in harassing me about it, I might turn back into a beast."

"Don't do that unless I ask you to."

Though I want to know why she might ask me to behave like a beast, I realize we have other matters to discuss.

"Let's go outside," I say. "We could both use some exercise and fresh air. Then we need to discuss our situation."

And figure out how to undo the apocalypse. No, that's not an impossible task at all.

Chapter Eighteen

Allison

I MARCH OUTSIDE, DETERMINED TO…DO SOMETHING. NO IDEA WHAT. I stop in the middle of the yard, or whatever the grassy area around an English mansion is called. I need to do something, anything. Can't just hang out in the ancestral home of Dax and Sefton, sipping tea and nibbling on cucumber sandwiches. Everything seems tranquil and normal here at Fallenmouth Manor, but I know the rest of the world is in ruins or soon will be.

The horror is spreading. I'd watched it rush toward us back in Texas, like a malevolent sandstorm. How many more people have died since then?

Dax hurries to catch up to me. "What are you doing?"

"Gee, I don't know." I throw a scowl his way. "Thought I'd go for a little stroll in the woods to see the wildlife. That's the right thing to do when the entire world, maybe the entire universe, is collapsing around us."

"Sarcasm is not appropriate right now."

"I think it is. But I suppose it would be more appropriate to snarl at you and threaten to kill you or at least tie you up."

The idea of tying Dax up kind of makes me horny. Which is so not helpful right now.

He steps in front of me. "You are behaving irrationally."

"Like you haven't done that too. Does the word kidnapping ring a bell?"

"Why are you in such a foul mood?"

A harsh laugh bursts out of me. "Seriously? Mr. Scowling-Growling Demon from the Echo thinks I'm bitchy."

He grasps my shoulders. "You aren't acting like yourself. What happened?"

What the hell. He'll find out, eventually. "When I woke up this morning, I tested my powers. Tried to whisk myself away like I did yesterday, but it didn't work. I started to feel the tingly electricity thing, then poof. It was gone."

"Perhaps you were too anxious."

"Like I wasn't yesterday when Sefton's golem was hovering behind me?"

His voice and his expression turn gentler. "I'm sorry. Five years in the Echo has made me far less understanding than I used to be. Not that I was a particularly self-aware man before that. But I want to help you, Allison."

For a moment, I can't speak. I gaze into his eyes and wonder how in the world this happened. The beast who had treated me like the enemy has become a man who wants to make me feel better. It's been maybe three days since I met Dax—I've kind of lost count—and I can't process everything I've experienced since then. All I know is that now I trust this man, and I need him.

To help me fix what his brother has done. That's all.

"I appreciate that you want to help," I say. "But if I can't magic us away from here, that means we need to get out the old-fashioned way."

"We used to have several vehicles on the premises. The garage is behind the house."

He clasps my hand, leading me around the backside of the huge mansion where I see the garage he mentioned. It has four big doors in front, but we head for the human-size door on the side. Once we enter the building, he flicks the light switch.

The garage houses super-expensive vehicles. I'm no car expert, but even I can tell the two sedans, one SUV, and one sports car boast price tags so far out of my budget that I couldn't afford to buy a tire for any of these vehicles.

"You're super rich, huh?" I say as I scan the interior of the garage.

"Money hardly matters anymore." Dax approaches the nearest vehicle, a four-door sedan, and opens the driver's door. "I doubt creatures from the Echo accept dollars or pound notes. They want payments in blood."

He finds a key tucked under the visor and tries to start the car. Nothing happens. He pops the hood and gets out to inspect the engine. Screwing his mouth up, he slams the hood shut.

Something I'd almost forgotten springs up in my mind. "I meant to ask you something earlier, but I didn't want to do it in front of Sefton."

"What is it?"

"You said your parents died exactly thirteen years ago on the day Sefton cast his world-destroying spell."

"That's right."

"Well, um..." I hunch my shoulders and avert my gaze, but then force myself to look at him. "My parents died on that day too."

Dax goes completely still, his body rigid, his gaze unblinking. "What?"

"Our parents all died on the same day thirteen years ago. I don't know what that means—"

"I do. Sefton believes the number thirteen is vastly powerful, remember? He somehow discovered the coincidence and used it in his spellcasting."

"Coincidence?" I move closer, tipping my head back to meet his gaze. "Sounds more like fate to me."

"Perhaps it is."

Dax resumes his search, checking the other three vehicles and screwing up his mouth even more with every peek under a hood.

Finally, he returns to me. "Sefton has removed the batteries."

"Of course he has. I knew the garage was too easy. But why can't I teleport or whatever you want to call it?"

"I assume he cast a spell to prevent it."

"Aw, come on. I only got to do that whisking thing twice, and now he's taken it away."

Dax isn't wearing his leather coat today. That fact had escaped my notice for a while, but I don't feel stupid for not realizing it until now. I mean, we're in the middle of an apocalypse, and our host is a lunatic who expects me to marry him and "consummate" our so-called relationship. So yeah, I'm not thinking at the highest level today. Or yesterday. Or the day before.

"Perhaps your 'whisking thing' isn't gone," Dax says. "Not for good, at least."

"Sefton is way more powerful than I am."

"Is he? Sefton keeps talking about sharing the Echo power with you. And you are the catalyst, which must mean all the magics he employed to create the Echo originated from within you."

"That's an awful lot of supposition."

He slides his hands over my shoulders, down my arms, and all the way to my hands. Then he slips his fingers between mine. "Nothing is a certainty anymore. We have to accept that."

"Maybe. But I don't plan to sit around twiddling my thumbs while Sefton is out there doing who knows what."

I like the feel of his fingers threaded with mine a little too much. It feels so good that I want to forget everything and just be here with him. It's crazy. But the whole world has flipped upside down, so maybe I need to stop judging my actions and his based on the way things used to be pre-apocalypse. Yes, he behaved horribly at first. I understand now why he did that. I don't agree with his actions back then, but I get it. He's as scared as the rest of us, though he also needs time to recover from his years in the Echo.

But I cannot, will not, just sit here doing nothing.

Pulling my hands free of his, I march toward the periphery of the woods. The darkness inside that domain gives me a wriggly sensation in my gut, but I won't let fear constrain me anymore.

"Allison, stop!" Dax shouts.

Without looking back, I tell him, "You can come with me or not. Your choice."

"Stop!"

I hear his footfalls pounding behind me, coming closer. But I realize too late why he's running and shouting.

Echo creatures close in around me, emerging from the shadows as if they'd been lying in wait for me.

Oh shit.

I freeze, but the creatures have surrounded me. Everywhere I hear the sounds of gnashing teeth, growling, talons clicking, and even slurping. I don't want to know what these monsters have in mind for me.

Dax crashes through the bushes and stops alongside me, breathing hard. "What the bloody hell did you think you were doing? Running off on your own?"

"Sorry, it was a dumb thing to do. Got any ideas for getting us out of this mess?"

"Afraid not. These creatures were already here on the property, and I doubt Sefton would've left without casting wards around the entire estate, including the forest."

I glance sideways at Dax because moving my head, or even my eyes, strikes me as dangerous right now. "Are you saying these creatures work for him? I wondered if that was the case, but Sefton didn't specify who his guards are."

"The Echo creatures clearly protect the estate. Sefton means to keep us locked in."

Oh, perfect. We're trapped. And what a deceptively beautiful snare it is.

A creature with bronzed skin and hairy flesh moves away from the others as if he's the leader of Sefton's gang of monsters. Yeah, I know for sure the creature is male. He's not wearing any clothes, unless a coat of hair counts.

"You aren't meant to leave," the creature says. "The master forbade it."

I glance at Dax. He has clenched his fists and his jaw too. I've seen that look before. He's about to charge into battle, but he shouldn't do that. We're outnumbered. I close my hand around his fist. "Don't. They aren't going to hurt us. They can't. Sefton wouldn't like it if they did."

Dax grasps my hand. "Turn around slowly."

We rotate in unison, one tiny step at a time, and begin to walk back toward the house. I risk a glance over my shoulder, but the creatures aren't following. They stay in the shadowy confines of the woods, almost as if they can't come any closer to the house. Maybe Sefton created a boundary to keep the creatures where he wants them. He needs us, for now, so I doubt he would give his minions free rein. Too much temptation for vicious beasts.

Dax halts halfway across the lawn, angling sideways to see the woods.

I turn too. The creatures have retreated out of sight. The lawn is off limits to them, apparently, like everything beyond the house and the lawn is off limits to me and Dax.

"What should we do now?" I ask.

"No idea. Wait, I suppose."

"Uh-uh. Told you I won't twiddle my thumbs until His Majesty comes home."

Dax folds his arms over his chest. "What do you suggest we do, then?"

"Oh, I've got an idea. But you won't like it."

"Tell me anyway. Then I'll know whether I need to restrain you again."

I think he's joking. It can be hard to tell with him, but I'm pretty sure he's teasing me.

He arches one brow. "Did you come up with a plan? Or were you having me on?"

"Yes, I have a plan." I square my shoulders and lift my chin. "Teach me how to fight."

"No."

I give him my best stubborn look. "I need to do this."

"You do not need to fight. I will protect you."

"Not good enough. What if you get disabled? Or we get separated?" I poke his chest with my finger. "Teach me how to fight, Dax. I won't give up until you agree to do it. I'll pester and harass and annoy you until—"

"All right." He scrubs a hand over his face and sighs. "What you need to learn is basic self-defense techniques. Once you've mastered that, perhaps we can move on to more advanced maneuvers."

"Great. Let's get started now."

"Not out here. We don't want our watchers to witness everything I teach you."

"Where, then?"

He whirls away and waves for me to follow.

I trot after him only because I need his help to learn how to protect myself. I do not follow because he silently ordered me to do it with his hand-waving. Whether he realizes that or not, I don't care. If he turns all snarly and rude again, he'll get a piece of my mind.

We go inside the house, though calling it a "house" doesn't really describe this enormous structure, and he hurries down the hall. I have to jog to keep up with him. We finally veer into a room at the opposite end of the hall from where the dining room lies. It's a large space with high ceilings and tall windows, though big shrubs block most of the view. The sun shines into the space just enough that it doesn't feel like we're trapped in a box.

I see paintings high up on the walls, each one a depiction of a person—men and women, young and old. Down at eye level, a collection of skinny sword-like implements hangs from hooks on the wall. The floor is wood, but in one section it features a padded mat.

"What is this room?" I ask.

"It's where generations of Stainthorpes learned to fence."

"Fencing is when you play with skinny little pseudo-swords."

He compresses his lips, and I'm sure he wants to growl at me. But he doesn't. "Fencing is a sport. It requires dexterity, control, and skill."

"Don't see how fencing is going to protect me. Besides, it'll take too long for me to learn that."

"I have no intention of teaching you to fence today." He rolls up his sleeves. "I'm going to instruct you in basic self-defense techniques. Just as I told you a few minutes ago."

"Yeah, I remember. I have a brain, you know."

He grunts. "Then act like it."

We're back to Dax the jerk. Maybe he's just scared, which I can understand, but that's no excuse.

I rub my palms together. "I'm ready. Come on, teach me."

Chapter Nineteen

Dax

PERHAPS I SHOULDN'T BOTHER TEACHING ALLISON HOW TO PROtect herself. I can protect her, and the creatures outside are far stronger than any human being in this world. I'm not at all sure any sort of self-defense technique will be enough. But it's all I can offer her.

I saunter up to Allison, halting an arm's length away. "First, you need to learn a few basic principles."

"Go on. I'm ready."

"Avoid the chest. It won't be effective without a weapon. Also avoid the knees. That requires a particular technique, so don't risk it. You're better off sticking to the most vulnerable areas—eyes, nose, throat, and groin."

"Got it."

"When you're in a threatening situation, don't hold back. Make plenty of noise too. Not only will that potentially confuse your attacker, but it will also attract attention that might scare them away." I don't think she fully understands how difficult it will be to ward off an attack, which means I need to make it painfully obvious. "Hit me."

She pulls her head back. "What?"

"I said hit me. Try to knock me down."

"Okay."

Allison bends her knees slightly and raises her fists. Then she just stands there studying me.

"You won't have time to think," I say. "Just do something, or I'll do it for you."

She rushes at me and lunges her knee up to strike me in the groin, but I seize her knee. I push her away, which knocks her off balance, and she tumbles to the floor.

I bend over her. "I wasn't even trying. Imagine what I could do if I really wanted to hurt you. You will never survive an encounter with an Echo creature if you keep holding back. Attack me. Don't think about it. Just do it."

Straightening, I raise my hands, palms up, and wiggle my fingers in a "come and get me" gesture.

Allison scrambles to her feet, planting them wide. Her lips tighten, and her gaze narrows.

Her determination makes me want to kiss her. Hard.

"Remember what I told you," I say. "Or are you so stupid that you can't hold on to a thought for more than five seconds? Maybe you're simply a coward."

She lets out a primal cry as she surges forward to pound her fists on my chest and stomp her foot down on mine.

I catch her wrists and cage her legs by lashing one of mine around both of hers. "Wrong tactic. If I were a murderous beast, you'd be dead."

A frustrated noise erupts out of her as she struggles against my hold.

"Try again," I hiss.

I shove her away with more force, and she tumbles to the mat again. This time she rolls across it and slides off onto the wood floor. Her elbow smacks into the hard surface.

Allison winces and scowls at me. "You asshole."

Stalking over to her, I kneel at her side. "Do you think an assailant will care about your tender feelings? They won't give a toss. Unless you want to be raped and murdered, your body ripped apart, you had better start taking this training seriously."

"How does throwing me across the room help?"

I lean in closer until our noses almost touch. "Now you understand the stakes. I could have killed you without breaking a sweat."

She glares at me for a moment, but gradually, the anger fades from her expression. With a sigh, she struggles to get up off the floor. I offer her my hands, but she scrambles to her feet without my help. When I lead her onto the mat, she faces me with her shoulders back, her chin lifted, and a new resolve evident in her expression.

Now she's ready.

"It's time to teach you," I say. "When an attacker threatens you, grab whatever is to hand—car keys, a brick, anything—then aim for the vulnerable areas."

"Eyes, nose, throat, and groin."

"That's right." I grasp her wrists and hold them between us. "Keep your hands ready and your knees bent."

She bends her knees a bit and keeps her hands raised even after I release her wrists. "Like this?"

"Yes." I back away from her. "First, you're going to try the groin kick. Make sure you've stabilized yourself as much as possible, then lift your leg with the knee bent and swing it upward. Straighten your lower leg just as you make contact with the attacker's groin. This isn't a knee jab. It's your calf doing the damage."

"Think I get it."

"All right. Give it a go, slowly at first." I smirk. "And try not to ram my bollocks. This is training, not an exercise in castration."

"I doubt I can actually whack your balls off with my leg."

"Try the groin kick now."

She rushes toward me, raises her bent knee, and straightens it just as her calf contacts my groin. Luckily, she's restraining herself. I let her try it several more times while I lunge at her and duck side to side while keeping our movements deliberate and painless. Though I'd told her to hold back, now I think that might be the wrong tactic. The only way she'll know for sure she can manage this maneuver is if I let her go all the way.

My balls ache just thinking about it.

"Enough practice," I say. "Time for a live demonstration."

Her eyes widen, and she blinks twice slowly. "You want me to ram your 'bollocks'? A few minutes ago, you told me not to do that."

"I was wrong. We don't have any time to waste. You need to know you can do this, and you need to realize that right now." I wave for her to back away, and I do the same until we're standing at opposite ends of the mat. "I'm going to come at you, but I won't give you any warning."

"You just did warn me."

"I meant I won't warn you when I do it. Understand?"

"Uh-huh. Whatever you say, oh wise master."

I just manage to stifle a growl.

Allison smirks at me, her lips twitching like she's trying not to laugh.

Perfect. She's relaxed and off her guard.

I run at her.

She rushes forward, arms raised in front of her face, and swings her bent knee up, then straightens it to ram her calf into my groin.

Pain slams through me, making me double over and gasp. I look up at her. "That was perfect."

The fact that I'm still gasping and bent over tells me she has mastered that technique.

She grins. "Do I get a gold star?"

I straighten and blow out a breath, cocking one hip to take some of the pressure off my privates, which haven't completely recovered yet. "Next, we'll try the heel palm strike."

Allison bites her lip, eying my groin. "Are you okay? Looked like that really hurt."

"It did, which is a good thing."

"Are you sure you'll be okay? Maybe we should take a breather so you can recover."

"No breaks. With those creatures out there guarding the estate, we both need to be ready for anything."

"Okay. Let's keep going."

I show her the heel palm strike, which involves thrusting a flat palm backward and up into either the attacker's nose or the soft spot under the chin. She masters that technique too. Next, we try the elbow strike—swinging an elbow up crosswise to the attacker to hit the jaw hard. She has no trouble with that move either, even when I have her try performing the elbow strike while I'm behind her. The more we practice, though, the less force she uses, and I have to ask her why.

"Because I'm hitting you, of course," she says. "Don't want to leave you bruised and bloody."

"I can take it. Trust me. I lived in the Echo for five years, and no one in that world pulls their punches." I cup my groin and pretend to grimace. "But I don't think I'll ask you to practice the groin kick again."

Her gaze drops to my cock, and her tone turns husky. "No, I wouldn't want to damage your manly parts."

The way she spoke those words threatens to send all the blood in my body flooding into my "manly parts." I need to change the subject, or I'll be shagging her on the mat.

"Let's try a more advanced technique," I say. Then I crook my finger at her. "Come here. This is a close combat move."

Her lips curve into a sexy smile. "I like the sound of that."

She's flirting with me. I can't imagine why, not after everything I'd done to her before we came to Fallenmouth. Perhaps she thinks I need encouragement to keep up the training since I've been letting her genuinely assault me.

Allison walks up to me, our bodies inches apart.

"Turn around," I tell her.

She obeys my command, which must be a first in our relationship. Or rather, our acquaintance. We don't have the sort of dynamic that the word relationship implies.

I wrap my arms around her midsection, locking my hands and pulling her tight against me. "Now I've got you."

The cheeky woman rubs her arse against me. "Yes, you do."

With every breath I take, I smell our sweat but also the scent of her desire. Christ, she's aroused. How can that be? I'm pushing her hard, testing her limits, forcing her to defend herself against my attacks. Her reaction seems barmy. But I'm getting aroused too. For me, it makes sense. I'm a man, and we blokes don't require much stimulation to get randy. But women aren't meant to like fighting with a man. Are they?

"Break free of my hold," I rumble into her ear. "Do it now."

"Don't know how."

"First, bend forward from the waist." When she follows my instructions, I tell her, "Good. Turn into me and ram your elbow up into my neck, and keep doing that, switching sides every time, until you can get leverage to spin around and execute a groin kick. You can also stomp on the top of my foot."

"Are you sure you want me to do all of that? You said you didn't want me to ram your balls anymore."

"Changed my mind." I tug, crushing my locked hands into her torso hard enough to make her gasp. "Do it now. Don't hold back."

She swings her elbow up, on one side and then the other, striking me in the neck or shoulder every time. When she slams her foot down on mine, my grip loosens a little, just enough to let her spin around and nail me in the groin. I grunt and let go of her, not because I chose to do that. She genuinely outmaneuvered me.

Once I've recovered my ability to breathe and speak, I say, "That's enough for now. You're a quick study, so I doubt it will take many lessons to get you ready to defend yourself. I can't say if these techniques will work on Echo creatures."

"I know. But I feel better just having a few tricks I can use. Being helpless sucks."

"You were never helpless. It takes a strong woman to stand up to a brute like me."

"Inner strength is great." She bumps her hip into me. "But I love being able to beat the crap out of you."

When she says that, while aiming a teasing smile at me, I find myself doing something I haven't done in years. I chuckle. "Yes, you did beat the crap out of me quite well."

Her eyes go wide. "Did you just laugh? Or was I hallucinating?"

I flash her a scowl. "Don't make an issue of it."

Allison raises her hands. "Okay, okay, relax. I'll pretend you never laughed. But for the record, you are not a brute."

"Of course I am."

She studies me for a moment, but then sighs as if she's given up on trying to convert me to her viewpoint. Despite the fact I'm still scowling at her, she walks up to me and splays a hand over my cheek. "Your beard has gotten longer and scratchier. It's kind of like sandpaper, but I might kiss you anyway."

Kiss me? Why on earth would she do that? Yes, I want to fuck her again. But she shouldn't want that, which means she should not want to kiss me either.

I pull away from her. "Let's explore the study for clues to what Sefton has done and what he still plans to do."

Chapter Twenty

Allison

I MUST HAVE EMBARRASSED DAX. WHY ELSE WOULD HE GO ALL CAVE-man again and change the subject so fast I think it caused a minor air disturbance? All I said was that his beard is scratchy and I might kiss him. I'm guessing it was the part about a potential kiss that made him uncomfortable.

He whips his shirt off and uses it to wipe sweat from his brow.

Uh, what? He didn't need to remove his shirt to do that. I wish he were still covered up because the sight of his naked chest makes me flash back to when we got it on in the warehouse. I can't explain why I suggested I might kiss him, but I guess it was the heat of the moment, when we were both sweaty and amped up, that made me say it. I can't deny that sparring with Dax was hot.

Jeez, the world is literally going to hell, and I'm thinking about sex.

"I need a new shirt," Dax announces. "Wait for me in the foyer."

"Sure, because I follow orders when you command me to do something without explaining why."

"I did say why. Should I drop to my knees and beg you to do what I tell you?"

"Yeah, sounds good to me. I beat the crap out of you just now, so maybe you shouldn't try to boss me around."

Rather than snarling at me, he spins around and stalks out of the room.

I follow him into the foyer. Not because he commanded it, but because I need a change of clothes too, which means I have to walk through the foyer to go upstairs. Earlier this morning, I'd found a ton of women's clothes in the closet of the bedroom I'd slept in. A note taped to the closet door had said, "For you, Allison." Sefton bought clothes for me before I set foot in this house.

The creepiest part of all is that Sefton thinks I'm going to marry him.

Dax takes the stairs two at a time, leaving me to scramble after him. The idea of being alone when those creatures are outside makes me uneasy. But Dax goes into his room and shuts the door. Message received. He doesn't want to talk to me or even see me right now. So I retreat into my room and change into clean clothes, despite the fact wearing things a madman chose for me gives me a weird slithery feeling in my gut. Knowing he picked underwear for me is just plain icky. Once I'm dressed in jeans and a T-shirt, I march down to Dax's room and knock on the door.

It swings open.

Dax is wearing nothing but a towel that looks like it's about to fall off his hips.

I shouldn't be ogling him. It's inappropriate when we have important things to do. Things I suddenly can't remember. His hair is wet, and droplets of water trickle down his chest, drawing my focus to the edge of the towel. I can see a few dark hairs poking out above the terry cloth.

"Did you take a shower?" I ask.

"Obviously."

My attention shifts to his face, and I suddenly realize something. "You shaved."

Besides getting rid of his beard, he slicked his wet hair back to tame the wild locks. He looks, um, kind of good clean-shaven. Kind of? *Ugh.* He's hot. Even the scar that slashes across his jaw can't diminish his sex appeal.

Dax frowns. "What is wrong with you?"

"Huh? Nothing." I tear my gaze away from his pecs. "Are you ready to go search the study?"

"Does it look like I'm ready?"

He doesn't wait for my response, instead stomping over to the bed where he's laid out clothes for himself.

I should leave. Wait for him downstairs. But I can't convince my muscles to move. I also can't talk my eyes out of staring at him.

Dax whips the towel off and flings it onto the floor.

Suddenly, I'm breathing harder and my skin feels warm all over—warm and tingly. I can see everything, from his hair down to his toes and all the bits in between. But it's his dick that captivates me. I've seen it before, felt it inside me, so I shouldn't get breathless and tingly from seeing it again. My hand drifts up to my throat, and I can't stop myself from petting my skin while I imagine him touching me.

He stands there for a minute, just gazing down at the clothes he laid out on the bed.

Is he doing that on purpose? To get me horny? If he is... Well, mission accomplished.

Finally, he gets dressed. The charcoal slacks and golden tan dress shirt he chose look damn good on him. He slips on a pair of socks and brown loafers too. I'd chosen casual clothes—jeans, a T-shirt, and tennies—because I assumed we'll be running for our lives again any minute. But he looks like he's heading out to a corporate lunch meeting.

"Did you have a job before Sefton dumped you into the Echo?" I ask.

"I was the CEO of Stainthorpe Limited, our family's marketing firm."

"You made it sound like you were a ladies' man who didn't care about anything but sex."

"Maintaining the company my father started was important to me." He saunters closer, leaving only the barest gap between our bodies. "I admit I was an arse who treated women like toys. But whatever you might think of me, I took my work seriously."

"Never said you didn't. Your brother made it sound that way, though."

"Sefton was jealous when I inherited the title and the business, but I didn't realize how jealous until he…" Dax shuts his eyes briefly and sighs. "Until he destroyed the world."

"It's not your fault he did that."

"Perhaps not. But I should've noticed the signs that something was wrong." He pushes past me. "I'm going to the study. You can follow me or not."

I get that he doesn't like talking about his brother, and I decide to let it go for now. So I hurry down the stairs after him. When we reach the study door, Dax tries to turn the knob, but it won't budge. Sefton keeps his inner sanctum locked.

"You didn't really think he'd leave it open, did you?" I say. "Sefton might be crazy, but he's not stupid."

"But I am. Is that what you're implying?"

"Don't get grumpy with me because your brother locked the study door. You damn well know I never implied you're stupid."

He stares at me, his lips puckered and his body tense.

I stare right back at him, brows raised, arms crossed over my chest.

Dax growls and backs away from the door. Then he runs at it, slamming his large foot into the wood. The door flies open.

He saunters into the study. "Not locked anymore."

"That's just great." I finger the broken lock while I cross the threshold into the room. "Now the lunatic holding us hostage will come home and realize we broke into his study. Good job, Dax."

"I don't give a toss if he knows."

"Start giving 'a toss.' Your brother has an enormous amount of power, and we have no way to stop him."

Dax leans over the big wooden desk that sits in front of a large window and begins to rifle through the papers and notebooks neatly stacked on the desktop. "Let Sefton do what he wants to me. I don't care."

What happened between the moment when I saw him in a towel and the moment we reached the study? I asked what he'd done for a living before the apocalypse, and then he turned into a growling jerk again. He really has some kind of complex about his brother. Jealousy? Guilt? Maybe it's both.

I grab his arm to make him stop and look at me. "Maybe you don't care what happens to you, but I do."

He freezes. His expression goes blank, and he might not be breathing either. "Why would you say that?"

"Because it's true." I grasp his face with both hands. "I don't want you to die, Dax."

"You want me alive to protect you."

"I want you alive, period."

He shuts his eyes, releasing the breath he must've been holding in, and his posture slackens. "You shouldn't care about me."

"Of course I should. I haven't forgotten about the way you treated me at first, but I've seen more sides of you since then." I move closer until my body is brushing against his. "It's too late to tell me not to care about you."

He opens his eyes but doesn't meet my gaze. "We need to search the rest of the study."

Okay, I'll let him get away with pretending he didn't hear what I said. Can't believe I did say it. But I meant every word. Maybe he's right and I shouldn't care about him, but I can't help it. I have seen different sides of him, like earlier when he taught me how to defend myself. That's only the latest in a series of little things he's done that prove he's not a total bastard.

So I help him search the study.

Mostly we find papers on which Sefton wrote down notes that make no sense. I should've gotten a PhD in physics and taken an intensive course in alchemy before walking into this room. Dax is clearly just as confused as I am. If we'd hoped to find the key to stopping the apocalypse inside the study... Well, we were complete idiots.

One of the desk drawers is locked. I don't bother trying to talk Dax out of smashing his way into it because I know that won't do any good. Besides, we've already broken into the room. Sefton will know we invaded his study the second he sees the door.

Dax uses a letter opener to break the lock on the drawer.

We find neatly arranged stacks of cash in there, each block sealed with a strip of thick paper. Empty spaces suggest he spent most of the money, though I can't imagine what he might buy that would help him trigger doomsday.

I shut the drawer.

We give up on the study and search the rest of the house. Dax wants us to split up so we can cover more ground in less time, but I reject that command. Neither of us should be alone, not with those creatures outside and the possibility that Sefton might return at any moment. Safety in numbers, I say, even if the number is only two. None of the many rooms in this mansion provides anything useful. But when we get to the cellar door in the kitchen, it's locked.

"What's down there?" I ask. "I mean, is it usually locked?"

"No, it is not." He takes a large step backward. "And it won't be for long."

I don't even bother trying to stop him. He kicks the door open with a bang that reverberates through the kitchen and hurts my ears. Then we clomp down the stairs into the cellar.

Dax flicks a switch at the top of the stairs, which turns on a light bulb in the space below us.

"Haven't you wondered how this house has electricity when the rest of the world doesn't?" I ask as I follow Dax into the gloom below.

"Sefton used magic to spare the estate from the devastation elsewhere. Why should it surprise you that he ensured his home would have electricity?"

"Fair point."

We've reached the bottom of the stairs when he stops to turn toward me. "Did you just admit I was right? Perhaps I imagined that."

I roll my eyes.

A draft wafts over me, so cold that it raises goosebumps on my arms. I get the strangest feeling that something is in here with us, something dark and strange and intangible. The dank basement is weirding me out, that's all.

The chill teases my skin again.

"Do you feel that?" I ask.

"Yes." Dax walks further into the cellar, fists clenched, scanning the area with his gaze. He halts in the middle of the cramped, shadowy space. "I have felt this before."

"What is it?"

"Dark magics."

"They're just floating around in here?"

He glances at me over his shoulder. "No. I believe Sefton is storing them here."

"You can't know that. Can you?"

"I suspect it, and I can find out for sure."

Dax creeps toward a row of metal shelves that hold various sizes and shapes of boxes, all fashioned from wood or metal and featuring strange symbols etched on their surfaces. He stops inches away from the shelves, scrutinizing them while he just stands there, not even moving his head. Then he stretches out a hand to touch one box.

He jerks and gasps, yanking his hand away.

"What happened?" I ask as I come up beside him.

"It stung me." He rubs his palm. "Felt something like an electrical shock combined with a jellyfish sting."

"Ouch. I guess your brother protected these boxes. That must mean they hold something important, huh?"

"Yes. I suspect they're part of the magics he used to create the Echo and start an apocalypse."

I touch one of the boxes, and my entire body jerks, making me stumble backward half a step. Yeah, that felt a lot like electricity and a wasp sting. I've never been stung by a jellyfish, but wasps have gotten me a time or two.

"Are you all right?" Dax asks.

"I'm fine. I was hoping I'd be able to get into these boxes, but I guess I'm not sharing Sefton's magic anymore."

Which means we're screwed.

Chapter Twenty-One

Dax

I'M NOT CONVINCED THAT THE FACT ALLISON CAN'T ACCESS THOSE BOX-
es means she no longer shares the power Sefton has gathered for himself.
But she believes that, and I have no evidence to the contrary. For once, I keep
my mouth shut. Well, that's what I should do. I've never been good at not
speaking my mind, and I manage to stay silent only until we've gone back
upstairs and stand in the foyer, neither of us having any idea what to do now.

"You might still have the power of the Echo inside you," I say. "Perhaps
the spell Sefton cast to stop you from escaping again is also dampening the
magics you share with him. Or maybe it's not sharing at all."

"What do you mean it's not sharing?"

"Sefton told us you share the Echo power. We don't know if that's true. Your
magics might stem from a different source."

"I guess that could be the case. Doesn't help me now, though."

"When did you first notice something different inside you?"

"Back in the warehouse." She hugs herself and looks away, biting the
inside of her lip. "When we, um…"

"When we what? You need to tell me everything."

"Oh really." She lifts her chin. "Have you told me everything? No, of
course not."

I thought we were past all this rubbish, but of course we're not. Did I
expect her to trust me implicitly just because I fucked her? Yes, I'm that sort
of idiot. And perhaps I've misunderstood her mood right now. She told me
she noticed a change "back in the warehouse." She can't mean… No. It has
nothing to do with me.

Even when I'd been popular with women, I hadn't known a ruddy thing
about intuiting their feelings and needs—other than the sexual kind. I'm

even worse at it now. Allison won't tell me what she wants, and that fact irritates me. Which explains why I resort to growling at her.

"What are you claiming I haven't told you?" I demand. "You know about my past and what Sefton did to me."

She huffs. "You seriously think that's everything? Come on. You were trapped in the Echo for five years."

"I'm aware of that."

"Tell me about it."

"About what?"

She throws her arms out and growls, not unlike the way I often do. "Tell me what happened to you in the Echo."

"You don't want to know."

Allison throws her head back and makes another frustrated growling noise. "You are so pigheaded. I want to know. I need to know. Has it never occurred to you that what happened in the Echo might have some bearing on the current situation?"

"Not what I went through. It was torture, not information gathering."

She stares at me for a moment, lips puckered. Then she exhales a long sigh. "Do what you want. I'm going to the kitchen to get a snack. All that self-defense training made me hungry."

Allison whirls around and marches down the hallway toward the kitchen.

I hurry after her.

Yes, I've now been reduced to trailing after a woman like a lost puppy. In the Echo, I was fearsome. I'd needed to be, thanks to the brutality inherent in that world. I became a monster out of necessity. But the longer I'm with Allison, the less I feel like a beast. I haven't reverted to the old me, but I have begun to feel less like the monster who abducted Allison and more like a human being. Something has shifted inside me, but I can't explain or describe the change.

I find Allison in the kitchen. Though she was only a few seconds ahead of me, she already has the refrigerator open and is grabbing items from inside, then tossing them onto the island. Tossing them with more vigor than seems necessary.

Allison wants to know everything. And I suddenly realize I want to tell her.

She has dumped so many items onto the island that I can't believe she really intends to eat all of it. She's angry with me, and hurling packaged foods is her way of expressing that frustration.

I wrap an arm around her waist and hoist her off her feet, setting her down beside the island. Then I slam the refrigerator door.

Allison leans against the island. "What are you doing?"

"Shut up and listen."

"You shut up. That's what you're best at."

Naturally, I want to growl at her. But I resist the impulse and instead cage her to the island with my hands framing her body. "I grew up in this house. After my parents died, I moved to London and rarely came home unless a bird I was shagging wanted to see Fallenmouth. Hiding out in my London flat was easier than dealing with my brother. He wasn't insane back then, at least visibly, but I knew he felt slighted. So I left him alone."

"What does any of that have to do with the Echo?"

"It should be obvious. He turned me into a monster and threw me into the hell world he had created." I lean in closer. "One minute, I was a normal bloke who loved to shag women. The next, I became a genuine monster and found myself living in a world I didn't understand and could barely cope with. But I had no choice. I had to cope with all of it, and I didn't do that very well."

"Can't imagine what that must've been like."

"Yes, you can. We are both living it. Sefton turned the Echo inside out and brought hell down on the earth." I scrub a hand over my eyes and bow my head. "I killed living creatures. They would have killed me, so I justified it as self-defense. After a while, though, I couldn't tell the difference between benign monsters and the sort who only wanted to destroy anything they came across. I'm not proud of what I did to survive."

"Were there any normal people in the Echo?"

"No. Only beasts like me."

She lays a hand on my cheek. "You are not a beast. Even when we first met, I saw glimpses of who you really are. You are not a creature from the Echo. You're a man who lost his way through no fault of his own."

I'm about to point out that it *was* my fault, but something else she just said finally sinks into my brain. "What do you mean you saw glimpses?"

"At first, I hated you. But even then, I noticed little things you did that contradicted the idea you were nothing but a monster." She slides her hand down to my shoulder. "You found food for me. You carried me when I couldn't walk anymore, and later, you found a car for us for the same reason. You saved my life several times, and I've stopped believing you did that strictly because you wanted to have sex with me."

"I forced you to be with me. Vowed I wouldn't protect you unless you gave me your body."

"Yeah, you did that. But it's bullshit that you 'forced' me to get naked with you. Despite all your snarling and nastiness, you never assaulted me." She seals two fingers over my lips when I try to protest. "You never forced me. I wanted to be with you back in the warehouse. I wanted you, period. Maybe that desire terrified me at first, but not anymore."

I peel her fingers away from my lips. "But you shouldn't want me."

"Stop telling me what I should or shouldn't feel. Without you, I never would've survived the first wave, much less everything that came after."

Bloody hell, she's stubborn. I can't convince her to despise me again, though that would be safer for her.

Allison drums her fingers on the island and studies me. "When you were in the Echo, did you have sex with, um, female creatures?"

"Only a few times, when I first arrived in that world."

"Why not after that?"

I can't help it. I snarl again. "Because they are hideous, vile creatures that may look female, but they are not women."

"Mm-hm." She insists on studying me more, as if she thinks she can ferret out my deeper motivations that way, which is bollocks. "Are you saying you were celibate for the better part of five years?"

"Yes."

"Well, that does explain a few things."

I push away from the island, away from her. "What do you claim it explains? I couldn't stomach shagging monsters anymore, but there's no deeper meaning in that decision."

"Sure there is." She slants toward me. "It means you're a good person underneath all the growling and snarling and generally rude behavior. If you were scum, like you want me to believe, then you would've screwed whatever humanlike monsters you met."

Though I try to respond, to deny her claim, she doesn't give me the chance.

Allison jabs a finger into my chest. "You're not fooling me anymore. I'm on to your game. And I finally understand why you were so desperate to get me naked that you threatened to throw me to the wolves if I didn't have sex with you."

"No, you—"

"Zip it, Dax." She raises onto her tiptoes, leveling our gazes. "You were so pent-up when we first met that you couldn't admit you like me. But here I was, a normal human female, and you needed to let off steam. That's why, when we had sex, it was so explosive."

She's right, of course. I hadn't been with a woman for so long that I couldn't control my lust for her. But it's more than that. I want her because, as she said, I've come to like her. I trust Allison and want to protect her in any way I can. She's the opposite of all the women I used to shag as a normal man, and when I'm with her, I feel things I've never experienced before. But it doesn't mean anything, it can't. We aren't two people navigating a romance. We're an integral part of the apocalypse, and nothing we say or do will change that. I am the anchor. She is the catalyst. What if she wants me only because of the magics that connect us?

Enough talking. I need action.

I push past her. "I'm going to search the entire house. Must be a ruddy clue somewhere in here."

"Think I'll go outside and get some fresh air."

Spinning around, I jab a finger toward her. "You will not leave this house on your own."

"Come with me, then."

"There's no time for relaxation. We have no idea when Sefton might return, and we need to find out how he created the Echo."

"We both know those boxes in the cellar are the key. Since we can't get into them, we might as well stretch our legs and get some sunshine."

"I can't play silly buggers with you while the rest of the world is burning."

She clasps my hands. "You need to relax, or we'll never find what we're looking for. Trust me. Nobody on earth is more pent-up than you. It's time to take a break."

"And do what?"

"Go for a walk."

I see no point in arguing, so I let her lead me outside and onto the lawn. We wander aimlessly while Allison admires the flowers that lie in ground beds or climb up the trellises attached to the house. She holds my hand the entire time. I should pull away from her, to get some necessary distance, but I can't make myself do it. The feel of her hand in mine gives me a strange sense of peace. I wish we could stay here at Fallenmouth forever, safe in the bubble my brother created around the estate, and pretend the apocalypse never happened. Above us, the sun shines. But it's a deception. I know that beyond the perimeter of the estate, human beings are fighting for their lives against impossible odds.

Too many have died already. Many more will die soon.

Allison stops and faces me. "You suck at relaxing, don't you?"

"Yes."

"Let me help."

She takes my face in her hands and kisses me. I should push her away, but I can't do it. I should stop her from deepening the kiss, but I can't manage that either. All my body will allow me to do is reciprocate, coiling my tongue around hers and wrapping my arms around her body to pull her close.

Perhaps, in this one moment, I can forget about the world beyond Fallenmouth.

But only for a moment.

Chapter Twenty-Two

Allison

OUR KISS LASTS ONLY FOR A MINUTE, THEN DAX INSISTS WE RETREAT into the house. I go along with that because I can see those creatures patrolling the perimeter of the lawn, just inside the woods. I can't see their faces, only their shadowy shapes. So yeah, I'm good with going back inside. Fallen-mouth might look like a beautiful and serene place, but that's an illusion. Magic ensures the estate remains as it was before the apocalypse.

Dax insists we need to search every inch of the house, and I decide to go along with that idea. I think it's bullshit. The boxes in the cellar are clearly the source of Sefton's "alchemy of worlds," but Dax needs to do something. It's a guy thing.

Naturally, we find zip after searching the whole house.

By then, it's after dark, and I'm too exhausted to do anything other than eat a sandwich and go to bed. Dax insists I should lock my bedroom door. I bite my tongue instead of pointing out that Sefton could teleport into this room anytime. At least those creatures out there can't storm the house, unless their master removes the invisible boundary around the yard. The beasts are wickedly strong, and Sefton has powerful magics on his side.

Nobody storms the house. Not that night or the next morning.

After breakfast, Dax announces that I need more training so I can learn how to fight instead of only knowing how to fend off an attack. He starts with fencing, which he describes as "a combat sport."

I roll my eyes. "That foil thingy looks like a skinny metal stick that wouldn't hurt a fly."

"The foil is a dangerous weapon," he says. "Especially if the blade breaks. A Ukrainian fencing champion died that way. Perhaps I should demonstrate how dangerous a foil is."

We both wear protective clothing and full-face masks, plus gloves. I've seen this stuff in movies, but never could I have imagined I'd need to learn swordplay.

Dax removes his mask and makes a come-on gesture. "Strike my cheek with the tip of your foil."

"What? If it can hurt you, I'm not doing that."

"You need to know what a foil can do." He sets his weapon down and makes that come-on gesture with both hands. "Cut me."

I thrust my foil out to nick his cheek, drawing a thin trickle of blood. "Are you okay?"

"You'll need to be more aggressive when we're sparring." He plucks his foil off the floor. "Especially if you want to graduate to a larger, deadlier sword."

"You have bigger swords around here? I've only seen the fencing foils."

"That's because you insisted on searching the solarium while I was ransacking the sitting room. My father kept a pair of eighteenth-century cutlasses on the wall above the fireplace mantel, as well as a medieval broadsword."

"You're going to teach me how to use a real sword? Cool. A cutlass sounds like a pirate sword."

He frowns at me, which is a somewhat softer expression than his usual scowl. "You need to take this seriously. Your life may depend on your ability to fight."

"I know. And I do take it seriously. But if I don't crack a joke now and then, I'll go bonkers. Wouldn't kill you to lighten up on occasion."

"To 'lighten up' in the Echo means death."

"Okay, message received." I square my shoulders and raise my foil. "A death match it is, then."

No, I don't kill Dax. I meant that as a dig at his "every moment is a life-or-death event" attitude. An affectionate dig. Because yeah, I've realized I do like him, especially now that I understand more about what he's been through, in and out of the Echo.

Following a morning of sparring with Dax and an afternoon of more self-defense training, I am once again too exhausted to do anything except gobble up a sandwich and go to bed. Dax tries to talk me into waiting while he makes a big dinner for us, complete with vegetables, though he claims he's never been good at cooking. I'm too wiped out. Maybe living on sandwiches and soda pop isn't the healthiest choice, but for crying out loud, there's an apocalypse going on out there. Screw green beans and spinach. I need cheese and chocolate.

For the next three days, Dax teaches me how to fence and graduates me up to a cutlass. Swords are kind of awesome. The cutlass isn't as heavy as a broadsword, so he tells me it's a good weapon for a woman. There were female pirates, after all. If those ladies could handle a cutlass, so can I. Despite his constant admonishments that I need to stop making jokes, I do take my training seriously. The world outside this estate has no electricity, no running water, just devastation. When we go back out into that new world, which I know we will do eventually, I need to be prepared.

Dax's family armory doesn't include guns or explosives. I never used to want stuff like that, but now I wish we had some.

Every day, we both go down to the cellar multiple times and try to open those boxes. Dax gets more frustrated with every attempt. Maybe I should tell him my theory about why I was able to teleport us away from Sefton and the golem, but I don't know how he'll react. My theory isn't scientific. It's very, very personal. I doubt he'll want to consider the idea, much less accept it.

Because I've become convinced that sex with Dax gave me the power to spirit us away.

It's crazy, I know. And sooner or later, I'll have to share my theory with him. But not today. I'm enjoying this time with Dax, learning to fight and taking walks around the lawn. We kiss now and then, but he hasn't even suggested sex. I'm starting to wonder if he's lost interest, but I think it's more likely that he's as tired as I am. A tough guy would never admit to that.

On the fifth day since our mad host left us here, I realize I need a day off from combat lessons. I've gotten a little sore from all the physical activity. I used to exercise, pre-apocalypse, but I didn't do this kind of intensive training.

"I need a break," I tell Dax. "Please. I'm getting sore."

He stares at me for a few seconds. Then he marches over to a door I hadn't realized was a door, since it blends into the wall and has no knob. He pushes on a section of the wall, and the door pops open. He ducks inside what looks like a closet, emerging with a folded-up table under one arm.

"What's that for?" I ask.

Dax being Dax, he grunts instead of speaking. Then he carries the folded-up table over to the windows and sets it up there. He glances at me and pats the padded tabletop. "Lie on this."

I walk over there, but I can't help eying the table with a touch of suspicion. "Why do you want me to do that?"

"You are sore. I'm going to give you a massage."

Pretty sure I'm gaping at him. My hot but grumpy roommate wants to rub me down? The idea both shocks me and turns me on.

Dax scoops me up and deposits me on the table, on my back. "Roll over and cross your arms above your head."

Only now do I notice the bottle of massage oil he has tucked under his arm.

I roll onto my stomach and link my hands above my head.

He pushes my shirt up to expose nearly all of my back, then he unhooks my bra and lets the halves fall to my sides. With one cheek on the table, I can see him sideways. My nipples harden while I watch him pour oil onto his palm and rub his hands together to spread it around. By the time he lays his hands on me, I'm already wet for him. He slides his palms over my back, massaging tight muscles and getting me more turned on every second. When he pulls my sweatpants and underwear down to my ankles, I start breathing harder. To feel his hands on my ass, rubbing while he works his way down my thighs, gets me so hot for him that I want to squirm and moan. I just manage to suppress that response. But damn, this man knows how to touch a woman.

"Turn onto your back," he says, his voice rougher and rumblier, the way he sounded that day in the warehouse when he vowed to fuck me on the concrete floor.

Just as I start to roll over, a scream echoes outside the house.

I jump off the table and yank my clothes back into place. "What was that?"

Dax grabs a cutlass and sprints out of the room.

Another scream pierces the air, followed by the ravenous howls and bellows of the Echo creatures.

I race after Dax, catching up to him just as he flings the front door open and bolts outside. But as he sprints across the lawn, I lag behind him in my pursuit. His legs are longer, and I can't quite catch up.

A girl tumbles out of the woods, crashing through a hydrangea bush, and collapses on the lawn.

Dax reaches her first, but the girl shrieks when he tries to help her up. I get there a few seconds later and drop to my knees beside the girl.

"Are you hurt?" I ask. "What did those creatures do to you?"

Her blue eyes home in on me. She's breathing hard, and her cheeks are pink, but I can't see any wounds on her. She seems like a teenager. The girl bites her lip, glancing back and forth between me and Dax.

"It's okay," I tell her. "He's a good guy. We want to help you, if we can. Will you let us do that?"

She nods.

"Can you walk?" I ask.

"Y-yeah. I think so."

"Good." I offer her my hands. "Let me help you up."

The girl sounds American, and I want to ask where she's from and how she got here. But questions can wait.

Snarling and the snapping of teeth makes me glance at the woods even while the girl takes my hands and we stand up together. The creatures who guard this estate are watching us. Glaring at us. Ravening for blood they know they won't get, not today. No one can penetrate the estate, Sefton had said. It's magically warded. The Echo creatures are allowed to guard the perimeter and the woods, but they can't cross into the yard. So how did this girl get in? I remember Sefton saying he couldn't guarantee the creatures would "mind their manners." I think he was just trying to scare me. It seems like the so-called guards can't step onto the lawn.

I brush leaves out of the girl's hair. "My name is Allison, and that's Dax. What's your name?"

"Willow."

"Are you sure you aren't hurt?"

She nods. "I'm okay. Those monsters didn't chase me until I got almost to the yard."

The creatures are still observing us from a discreet distance, so I lead Willow and Dax back into the house. We go into the sitting room, and I take a seat on the sofa. Willow drops onto the sofa too, with one cushion separating us.

Dax stands nearby, arms barred over his chest.

Willow keeps glancing at him sideways while wringing her hands.

I look at Dax. "Why don't you get some food and water for Willow? She must be hungry."

He narrows his gaze and flattens his lips, which I've come to realize means he's worried. Grumpiness is a cover.

"Please," I say. "Find something for our guest to eat."

Dax lowers his arms and sighs, then walks out the door.

"Is he a monster?" Willow asks.

"No. Dax is a good man, but he can be grumpy when he's worried. Don't let it get to you." I lay my hand over hers. "First, I want you to know you will be safe here. Dax and I will not hurt you. Do you believe me?"

She chews on her lip and nods.

"How old are you, Willow?"

"Fifteen."

Christ, she's so young. I don't want to grill her, but I do need to know more about the girl. Though I hate thinking that way, I can't help worrying Sefton has used this girl to get to me. Not sure how or why he would do that, but I can't shake the worry.

"Where are your parents?" I ask.

She bows her head, wringing her hands more vigorously. "They died in the first wave. Mom and Dad hid me in a sewer drain, but they had to go out to look for food. Monsters got them."

"I'm so sorry, Willow. I lost my parents too, but it was a long time ago. You were very brave to get past those creatures in the woods."

She shrugs. "Heard there was a place in the countryside that hadn't been destroyed. So I came here. Nobody else could get into the woods, but I did."

"Do you know how you did that?"

Willow shakes her head. "The other people I was with kind of bounced off the air or something. They couldn't get in."

"I'm sorry your friends didn't get in too."

She throws me a sidelong look. "I'm not. They weren't my friends, and they weren't nice like you."

Dax returns with food for our guest, and I don't ask any more questions—for now. Willow scarfs down the food and water Dax got for her, then she starts yawning. Though it's late afternoon, we take Willow upstairs and let her choose which bedroom she wants. She picks the one next to mine. I sit on the bed until she falls asleep, then leave the room and shut the door as quietly as possible.

How did this girl get through Sefton's safeguards?

If someone else has the power to breach the wards around Fallen-mouth… Maybe Dax and I aren't the only ones connected to the Echo.

Chapter Twenty-Three

Dax

ALLISON DOESN'T WANT TO GO FAR FROM OUR HOUSEGUEST, SO she stays in her bedroom with the door open in case the girl needs to call out for help. I go into the cellar and try yet again to break into the boxes. No luck, of course. I wonder if the young girl who broke through the wards can help us. I don't want to upset Willow, though. She seems frightened of me, and those creatures outside don't help matters.

Willow trusts Allison. They seem to have forged an instant, if fragile, bond.

Unfortunately, I can imagine what Willow might've gone through since the alchemy of worlds began. I'd rather not envision it, but my mind has other ideas. Maybe she didn't experience the full terror of the Echo, like I did, but the strangers she took up with could have abused her.

After giving up on Sefton's boxes, I go outside to patrol the grounds and make sure none of those creatures managed to pierce the wards the way Willow had done. I see no evidence they have. Just before I left Allison upstairs, she suggested the girl might have a connection to the Echo that allows her to circumvent the magics that bar anyone from getting onto the estate. Is that possible? Given the cataclysmic power my brother has amassed, I can't rule out anything.

I return to the house just as Willow and Allison are coming down the staircase. We all need to eat, and I insist on cooking for the girls. Allison offers to help. We wind up collaborating on a meal while Willow sits on a stool at the island watching us. We bicker over which dishes to make, but it's not a real argument. I think we're teasing each other. It seems odd to do that when the rest of the world is in chaos, but I've decided Allison was right. We both need to relax once in a while and allow ourselves to "lighten up." I'd forgotten how to do that after five years in purgatory.

Our mutual teasing encourages Willow to sit up straighter and almost smile.

When I drop a fish finger on the floor, Allison plucks it up and holds it to my mouth. "Five second rule. You dropped it, you eat it."

"No thank you."

She pulls her hand away, then moves it toward my mouth again while making train whistle noises. "Open up."

I tickle her belly, making her laugh so hard her eyes water. She tosses the fish finger into the sink.

"Are you surrendering?" I ask as I pause in my tickling.

She raises her hands. "Yes, I surrender. That fish stick was my white flag."

"I'm not sure a fish flag is a proper way of surrendering, but I will accept it."

Allison bows deeply. "Thank you, Lord Fallenmouth."

She rises and smiles at me, looking so beautiful that I want to kiss her. But we are not alone.

Willow is grinning at us.

By the time we finish cooking and eating our meal, our guest seems much more relaxed than when we first met her. We all retreat into the sitting room to drink hot cocoa. I would've preferred vodka, but we do have a minor in the house. I feel odd about drinking in front of a teenage girl. Instead, I sit in a large armchair while sipping cocoa.

Allison takes a few sips of her drink, then sets her mug down on the end table. "Willow, do you mind if I ask you a few questions?"

The girl stares down into her cocoa mug. "Okay."

"How did you end up in England? You sound American."

"My parents always wanted to see the UK, so we came over on vacation." She clutches her mug with both hands. "We would've been flying home today."

I assume Allison started with an easy question before she gently prods the girl about other matters.

"You said the people you were with weren't nice," Allison says. "Did they hurt you?"

Willow says nothing, though I can see the movements in her throat every time she swallows hard.

"I should leave so you two can discuss this," I say, half rising from my chair.

"No," Willow says, her head popping up. "You can stay."

"Are you sure?"

"Yeah. You're okay."

I've passed muster with a fifteen-year-old girl. Not sure if that means she trusts me, or if she simply trusts Allison's opinion of me. Maybe my ridiculous behavior in the kitchen convinced the girl I'm not a monster after all. I sit back down.

"They said mean things to me," Willow tells us. "Called me bad names, told me I was dragging them down. When I cried, they would slap me hard. They didn't give me much food, even when they found a big box of granola bars. They decided we should head out this way because other people were saying there's a place in the country where everything is still pretty and nice."

"How did you get here?" Allison asks. "You couldn't have walked the whole way."

"The people I was with found a car that still had gas in it. That got us most of the way here. We walked after that."

Allison nibbles on her lower lip as if she's considering what to say next. "How did you get away from those people?"

"When I saw the woods, I just ran. Not sure why, but I felt like I needed to be here." The girl stares down into her cocoa mug again. "Then those creatures came after me. They didn't hurt me, just made a lot of noise and chased me."

"You're safe now, sweetie." Allison chews her lip again, glancing at me as if she wants my approval. For what, I have no idea. She looks at the girl again. "Willow, do you, um, have any idea how you got here when nobody else has been able to cross into the woods?"

Willow takes a big gulp of cocoa, then sets her mug on the table. "You mean how did I get through the magic barrier or whatever. Don't know. I heard people talking about that, but I have no idea how it works. My parents never believed in supernatural stuff, but now everybody knows it's real. I mean, that's how all of this happened, right? Magic made the world crazy."

Yes, that's exactly what my brother has done. He made the world as crazy as he is.

The girl yawns.

Allison and I escort her upstairs. Though we tell Willow she can lock her bedroom door if she wants, she prefers not to do that. She does close the door, though. I walk Allison to her room, right next door to Willow's.

Allison grasps the doorknob.

"Wait," I say. "I was, ah, wondering if perhaps..."

"Spit it out, Dax." She gives me a teasing smile. "Never heard you hem and haw before. It's cute."

"I was trying to ask if you would, well..." I feel my face tightening into a pinched expression, and for some bloody stupid reason, I scratch the back of my neck. "May I come in?"

"Sure."

We enter the bedroom, where I had slept before Sefton banished me to the Echo and where my parents had once slept. It feels odd to do what I'm about to suggest, and do it in this room, but it also feels right somehow. Not that I've had much experience with doing the right thing.

Not until Allison.

She stops at the foot of the bed. "What did you need to ask me?"

"I want to make love to you."

"That's not a question." She leans into me, spreading her palms over my chest. "But yes, I would love that."

"We should undress, then. Shouldn't we?"

She laughs. "Ya think?"

I can't move, my body seemingly rooted to this spot while Allison strips off her clothes. I hadn't given myself time to appreciate the beauty of her body when we'd shagged in the warehouse. But I can't resist poring over every inch of her as she undresses now, here in my ancestral home, in the bed where I had seduced more women than I care to remember.

Tonight, it's different. *She* is different.

Have I changed? Allison seems to think so, and I trust her judgment.

While I've been admiring the swell of her breasts and the curve of her hips, she got rid of all her clothes. Flipping the covers back, she lies down on the bed. "Your turn."

I strip quickly and crawl up the bed until I'm straddling her body on my hands and knees. Perhaps I should say something, but it feels wrong to interrupt this moment with words, especially since I have no bloody idea what to say. Instead of speaking, I seal my mouth over hers, deepening the kiss until we're devouring each other with our tongues and lips and teeth. She slides her hands up and down my arms, then runs them over my back to grasp my nape.

Peeling my lips away from hers, I open my eyes.

Allison is gazing straight at me with a soft smile tightening her lips.

I press my mouth to hers again, only for a second, while I lower my body until every inch of me touches every inch of her. I drag my mouth across her cheek to her ear, where I pull the lobe into my mouth to suckle and nibble on it. She arches her neck and pushes her fingers into my hair. I shimmy down her body while kissing, nipping, and licking her skin, starting with the delicate curve of her throat and moving down to her chest, inching ever closer to her breasts. Her skin feels so soft, and it smells like sweet, womanly things that I can't describe. I find myself inhaling the scent of her skin, reveling in it, as I keep moving lower until my head rests between those lush mounds. I kiss a path toward her left breast and at last seal my mouth around its rigid peak.

A breathless cry rushes out of her. She grips my head with both hands and spreads her thighs.

She wants me to take her right now, but I won't rush this. Allison deserves better than what I gave her the first time. She deserves to be worshiped. And this time, I need to gaze into her eyes while I push her toward climax.

I tease her nipple with light nips and sweeps of my tongue until she's writhing beneath me and her breathing becomes labored, her chest rising and falling in a faster rhythm. I release her peak and drag my tongue down her belly, pausing to swirl it inside her navel, then slither lower until I reach her hips. The thatch of hairs on her mound tickles my chin and lips, and the scent of her desire suffuses my senses. Fuck, it makes my cock throb.

"Please, Dax," she moans. "Oh God, I need you inside me."

I need that too, but I will not sacrifice her pleasure to satisfy my own needs. Not anymore.

Sliding further down her body, I push my mouth between her folds to latch on to her nub. The flavor of her coats my tongue as I lick and suckle her clit, and she thrusts her hips up as if she needs me to consume her completely. I shove my hands under her arse to angle her body up, giving me deeper access to her slick flesh.

"Dax!" she cries out as her release tightens her entire body, lifting her head off the pillow. More cries of pleasure erupt out of her while she clenches the sheets in her fists.

I lift my head just as she goes limp. "Allison, I have never seen anything as beautiful as you, especially when you come."

"Call me Ally. Please."

"All right—Ally." I love the way those syllables feel on my tongue. She wants me to use her nickname. Part of me relishes that, but another part of me feels unworthy of it. "Have I exhausted you?"

"Oh no, not even close." She smiles and tickles my nose with her fingertips. "Don't stop now. It was just getting good."

"Not stopping. Couldn't if I wanted to. I need to feel your cream all over my cock."

She bends her knees, framing my head with her thighs. "Then make it happen."

I rise to my knees, plant my hands at either side of her shoulders, and plunge into the silky softness of her body, loving the way her flesh molds to mine. We gaze into each other's eyes as if an invisible rope binds us together, while I thrust into her again and again, groaning every time I sink inside and sucking in a breath with every retreat. Her slickness coats my length, and the wet sounds of our bodies merging and separating echoes around us.

Allison grips my wrists and struggles to catch her breath, though she can't seem to do it. I can't control my ragged breathing either. The sensation of her body wrapped around my cock steals my breath and my thoughts. All I know is how good this feels, how beautiful her eyes are, and how much I need to lose myself inside her.

"Oh yes, Dax." Her spine bows up, and she throws her head back.

I punch into her harder and faster, grinding myself into her flesh, rubbing that nub until she stops breathing. Her body curls into itself, and I know she's about to climax. She squeezes her eyes shut, her mouth drops open, and the waves of her orgasm milk me so fiercely that I splutter. But I keep thrusting and marshal all my willpower to hold back my release until she's done. Just as the last spasm of her climax wanes, I let go.

With two more punishing thrusts, I'm done. Spasms fire through my cock so hard and fast that I lose my breath, and I come with such force that I grit my teeth and struggle for breath while my fingers dig into the mattress.

Then I collapse on top of Allison.

She brushes her fingers through my hair and sweetly kisses me.

My cock is still inside her. I should move my arse to pull out, but I have no energy to do that. I'm exhausted in the best way, and besides, I don't want to move when she's gazing at me with tenderness in her eyes.

"Ally, I—"

The door explodes inward.

And my brother storms into the room.

Chapter Twenty-Four

Allison

DAX YANKS THE COVERS OVER ME AND LEAPS OFF THE BED. SEFTON hobbles into the room while Dax stalks up to him without bothering to put any clothes on. The brothers stand an arm's length from each other, both wearing furious expressions. Dax has his hands fisted and his shoulders bunched. Sefton seems to be quivering slightly from the intensity of his rage.

"You bastard," he snarls at Dax. "You had no right to touch her. Allison is mine."

I'm what? Nobody owns me.

Yanking on my shirt and pants, I jump off the bed and move to stand beside Dax.

Sefton's eyes narrow to slits. "You have betrayed me, Allison."

"No, I didn't. You said I was going to marry you, but I never agreed to that."

"You didn't need to agree." He clenches his jaw, baring his teeth when he speaks again. "You belong to me."

I want to tell him to go to hell, but considering the vast power he has amassed, I don't think I should annoy him any further. But I will not marry him or sleep with him. Will I have a choice if he employs magic to get what he wants?

"Sefton, please stop this," Dax says, sounding calmer than I would've expected. "You can't force Allison to love you. Please let her go. You don't need the catalyst anymore."

"Oh really." Sefton leans toward his brother and lowers his voice to a harsh whisper. "You are the one I don't need anymore."

Sefton steps back a few paces, raises his hands, and shoves them toward Dax. He can't touch him, not from several yards away. But a visible wave of energy, like heat rising up from the pavement in the summer, rushes toward Dax and slams into him. He's thrown backward just as a portal opens behind him.

He sails through it. The portal telescopes shut.

I stand paralyzed, my mouth open and my eyes wide, unable to speak or comprehend what just happened. Dax is gone.

"Whuh—" I swing my head toward the spot where Dax had stood, then veer my attention back to Sefton. "What did you do to him? Is he dead?"

"Does it matter?" Sefton seizes my arms, hauling me into him. "The answer is no. You will do as I say, or you will suffer the consequences. Do you understand?"

The fury in his voice and on his face convinces me that I need to play along, at least until I can figure out what to do. Can I do anything? Well, maybe I should test my theory that sex with Dax amps up my Echo power. If I can open those damn boxes...

Willow. The thought blasts through my mind, and I wrench free of Sefton to race past him and get to the girl's room.

She isn't there.

"Did you honestly think I wouldn't know about the sniveling child you brought here?"

I whirl around, coming face to face with Sefton. "What did you do to her?"

"She is irrelevant."

"Where is she?"

"Forget about Dax and the child. You will never see either of them again."

I want to pound my fists on his chest, slug him in the gut, run him through with a cutlass. But I can't be sure that would kill him, or even hurt him. He has that damn force field or whatever that protects him. He also has those creatures outside. *Shit.*

As much as I don't want to do it, I know I must placate him. Play along, at least for a while. He'll have to let his shields down if he wants to have sex with me. That might be my only opening, unless I can access those boxes in the cellar.

Without Dax's help? Yes, I can do it. I must do it.

My chest aches when I think about Dax. Sefton wouldn't have killed him, would he? The use of a portal to get rid of him suggests he sent him away. Don't need teleportation to commit murder. I must believe Dax and Willow are alive, somewhere. To believe the opposite... That would destroy me.

"All right," I say. "No more talk of Willow or Dax."

Sefton's entire demeanor softens, though I sense the tension crackling under the surface.

"Did your trip outside the estate go well?" I ask. Might as well engage in inane conversation in the hopes of learning something useful from him.

"The alchemy of worlds is progressing as expected."

"So that's good news. Right?" Not for me or anyone else on earth, except for Sefton and maybe the Echo creatures. I've become a spy, haven't I? Pretending to be something I'm not, pretending to believe in things I don't subscribe to, all to keep a madman from lashing out at innocent people.

"There is no good or bad news," he says. "Only truth and power."

Whatever that means. "I get what the alchemy of worlds is. But I'm confused about the alchemy of souls."

He clasps his hands behind his back. "You will find out soon enough anyway, so I suppose you might as well know now. The alchemy of souls will transmute the Echo version of every human being, merging the Echo soul with the human one to create a hybrid. Since both souls are entangled at the quantum level, the result should be quite interesting. That is how the Echo shall reveal all—as in the true nature of every person on earth."

He's going to jam our souls into the bodies of Echo creatures and force us to become one with those monsters. How that equates to revealing our true nature is a question only the madman can answer. But since I have no response to his statement that won't enrage him, I change the subject. "What will you do now?"

"It's time for our union."

Oh, how I wish he meant we were joining a labor union. No such luck. I'm sure he's talking about our sham wedding and the sex he expects to get afterward. Do I have the power to stop Sefton from transmuting the souls of every human on earth? Even if my sex theory for teleportation is valid, that doesn't guarantee I can save Dax and Willow. If I bring them back here, Sefton might kill them or send them away again. I have no idea how long my power boost might work.

Better save it for opening those boxes.

Hang on, Dax. Hang on, Willow. I will never forget about you.

I shove my hands into my pants pockets. "What now? You must have more important stuff to keep tabs on."

"Yes, I do." He takes a step toward me. "Why did you let my brother shag you?"

There is no way I can answer that question unless I lie. "Dax threatened to give me to the Echo creatures if I didn't have sex with him."

"You seemed to be enjoying it."

"Did it ever occur to you that I faked it so he wouldn't kill me?"

Sefton studies me with squinted eyes while his fingers twitch. "If you despise him, why were you so upset that I sent him away? You demanded to know what I did with him."

Damn, I suck at lying. *Say something to convince him, do it now.*

I resist the urge to bite my lip and force myself to look him in the eye. "Dax is the anchor. I was afraid all your hard work might be destroyed if he dies."

Sefton slants toward me. "Should I believe you? I'd like to, Allison, but your behavior suggests otherwise. You did escape from me a few days ago. And you fucked my brother. These actions must have consequences."

My throat has gone tight and dry. My pulse beats so fast that I'm starting to feel lightheaded, but I can't give in to the fear. I need to stay calm, at least on the outside.

He grabs my arm and drags me out into the hall, then shoves me into the bedroom where Dax and I had made love a matter of minutes ago. The sheets are still rumpled. Dax's clothes lie on the floor beside my underwear.

Sefton hovers on the threshold, one hand on the knob. He's breathing hard, almost wheezing.

"Are you okay?" I ask. "You seem tired."

"Yes, I am tired—of waiting to get what I want."

I suddenly wonder if he's suffering from power drain. All the magics he keeps tapping into might have weakened his body.

He twists the doorknob in his hand. "You will remain here while I prepare for the ceremony."

Sefton slams the door shut.

I stare at the door, immobilized by shock and fear and so many other emotions that I can't sort them out. Ceremony? He intends to force me to marry him so he can…rape me.

A chill shudders through me, making my teeth chatter. Yeah, I'm terrified of what Sefton might do next. But I can't just stand here waiting for it to happen. Dax taught me how to defend myself—and how to fight.

I hurry to the door and try the knob. It twists freely, but the door will not open. I yank as hard as I can. Nothing happens. Sefton must've sealed the door from the outside via supernatural means.

Should I risk using some of my power to break out of this room? I wish I had a magical power meter that would let me know how much I can afford to use.

The door swings open, forcing me to stumble backward out of its way.

Sefton locks his hand around my upper arm. "Soon we will be wedded, and the power of that union will reinforce the merging of the worlds. You will be one with me."

"But I don't love you. How will a forced union give you what you want?"

"It will. I need only your power." He hauls me out the door. "Our sexual union will cement the bond."

"No, it won't. We have no bond, Sefton. I barely know you, and quite frankly, I don't like you anymore. You are insane."

Yeah, I've thrown the "placate him" plan out the window. I know what he intends to do to me, and I will never let him do it, even if I have to die to stop him.

He tries to drag me down the hall, but I dig my heels in, which forces him to stop. With his bad knee, I don't think he can fight me if I resist, at least not enough to make me go where he wants.

Sefton halts and half turns to look at me, still cuffing my arm with his hand. His lips compress into a hard line, his gaze narrows and sharpens on me, and he hisses words through his gritted teeth. "Give yourself to me willingly, or I will take you by force."

Like hell he will.

I relax as if I'm giving in, and his grip loosens a touch. Seizing the opening, I yank my arm free of his grasp and run for the staircase. Sefton reacts a split second too late. I leap onto the railing and slide down it faster than his bad knee will let him get to the stairs. The instant I reach the bottom, I race through the foyer and rip the front door open to sprint outside into the light of the full moon. Just as my bare feet touch down on the grass, figures jump out to block my way.

The Echo creatures have surrounded me.

I halt so quickly that I stumble and almost hit the ground. I'm gasping for breath, my heart thrashing.

"Did you really think I wouldn't have a backup plan?"

The sound of Sefton's voice right behind me raises every hair on my body.

He lashes his arms around my midsection with his hands over my navel, pinning my arms to my sides. His lips scrape against my ear as he hisses, "You are mine."

Everything Dax had taught me, all the hours I spent practicing with him, suddenly comes crashing through my mind, and I know what I need to do. I lock my hands together, slant forward, and twist sideways to slam my elbow into his throat, then twist the other way to hit him again. His grip falters. I don't need to do the rest of the moves Dax had shown me. I shove away from Sefton and dash through a gap between two of the creatures. Before anyone has time to react, I'm pelting across the lawn toward the woods, crashing through bushes, mere feet from the cover of the trees.

A figure leaps out in front of me, catching me in mid stride and hoisting me off my feet. Powerful, scaly arms bind my body to the creature's.

My face is mashed to the beast's throat while my feet dangle above the ground. I can't get any leverage. This wasn't one of the moves Dax taught me, and this creature is way stronger than any human being. Out of the corner of my eye, I can see the person hobbling toward us now.

Sefton stops inches away. His horde of fiends gathers behind him.

For a moment, he just stands there, his hands trembling and his breathing uneven, until he recovers his composure. Then he traces the backs of his fingers over my cheek. "Why did you do that? Fighting me is useless, and now I'll have to punish you."

"I will never stop fighting, you sick son of a bitch."

"You lied to me, pet." He slants in, our chins almost touching. "You will regret this."

He takes a step back, waving his hand in my face.

And darkness consumes me.

Chapter Twenty-Five

Dax

AM I DEAD? SINCE I'VE NEVER DIED BEFORE, I CAN'T TELL IF THAT'S what happened to me. I can't move and don't feel or hear anything. As my senses gradually rouse, I detect a solid surface beneath me and feel warmth on my face. The sun? Not sure. My muscles still refuse to function, and my brain seems to be having trouble revving up again. Soon, though, I begin to detect sounds—birds chirping, wind rustling, my heart beating.

Not dead after all.

Something nudges my leg. "Are you in a coma?"

That voice. I've heard it before. Peeling my lids apart, which requires an enormous effort, I squint at Willow. "Does it look like I'm in a coma?"

She hugs herself, hunching her shoulders. "Sorry. Glad you're not dead."

"As am I."

"What happened? Where's Allison?"

"Back at Fallenmouth, I assume. That's the house we were in before…" Before my lunatic brother hurled us to somewhere else.

Willow nods. "I remember the house. Allison will be okay there, right?"

"She knows how to take care of herself."

But I have no idea what Sefton might do to her.

I lever myself into a sitting position, my legs stretched out, and take a look at my body. I am no longer naked. Sefton apparently saw fit to clothe me when he discarded me like a broken toy. I'm wearing my old clothes, the things I'd had on when I was thrown out of the Echo. The warmth of the air and the sun make me start to sweat, thanks to my leather coat.

Why did Sefton clothe me? He sacrificed some of his precious power to make sure I was no longer naked. *He did it because he's crackers, you moron.* And of course, he did not send me here with my knife, the one I keep hidden inside my coat.

I clamber to my feet and brush grass and dirt off my clothes.

"Where are we?" Willow asks.

"Not a bloody clue."

I turn in a circle to take in our surroundings, but I still can't say for sure where my brother sent us. Or why he sent us. He could've simply killed us both. We seem to be on the side of a mountain, based on the sloping terrain, though I can't see what lies below us. Trees block the view. If I knew anything about old-school navigation, I could chart our location based on the sun's position in the sky or some such bollocks. I am not versed in navigation techniques. We're in the mountains. That's all I can deduce.

"Are you growling?" Willow asks, her eyes widening. "Are you a bear-man or something?"

"No." I hadn't realized I growled until she said that, but I don't sound like a sodding bear. Do I? Perhaps I have sometimes behaved like a wild animal, but I do not sound like one, and I am not a bear-man. "Have you seen anyone else here?"

Willow shakes her head.

Sefton undoubtedly dropped us in the middle of nowhere, in a place where we would have little chance of running into other humans and potentially finding help. Since he'd been enraged at the time, I can't help speculating, or perhaps hoping, he cocked it up somehow and left us near some sort of civilization.

"We need to get to higher ground," I say. "Someplace where we can see what's around us. If we're lucky, there will be someone nearby."

"Might be the monsters."

I glance at Willow. The girl is still hugging herself. She was terrorized by strangers and Echo creatures, so I can't blame her for being ill at ease. Allison would know what to say to the girl to make her feel better, but I haven't got a ruddy clue. After five years in the Echo, I've forgotten anything I might have known about how to comfort another person.

Especially a child.

Naturally, I react like the prat I am. I pat the girl's shoulder. "I doubt the monsters live here. Besides, if any of them show up, I will rip their heads off."

Her eyes bulge.

Yes, here is proof positive that I know nothing about children. I've terrified the girl, so I try to backpedal. "Ah, well, I meant that metaphorically. I'm sure the monsters are…lovely people deep down."

Willow still stares at me, her face blank.

Then she starts laughing, spluttering so much that she needs to slap a hand over her mouth. When she finally stops laughing at me, she wipes her eyes with her shirt.

"What is so bloody funny?" I snarl.

The girl might not be laughing anymore, but she is smiling. "Lovely people? You're funny, but you're kind of a dork too."

"I'm a what?"

"A dork. It means you're clueless." She pats my arm the way I had patted hers. "You don't know much about kids, do you?"

"No." I squint at the girl. "A matter of hours ago, you were screaming and cowering on the lawn. You would only speak to Allison. Now you're harassing me."

"I was scared because those people-things were after me. But you and Allison are cool."

No one has ever called me "cool" before. I was an earl, so most people referred to me as Lord Fallenmouth, whether I wanted them to or not. But Allison calls me "hot." I like that term best.

A fierce pang stabs into my chest. *Allison.* I abandoned her, though not by choice, and I can't imagine what my brother is doing to her right now. No, that's a lie. I *can* imagine it, though I wish I couldn't. Allison is strong and clever. She knows how to defend herself. I have to hope that's enough.

"If you're about to hurl," Willow says, "could you go behind a bush or something to do it? I might blow chunks if I see that."

Hurl? Blow chunks? I'm suddenly grateful that I don't have any children if that's how they speak. Could Allison and I raise a baby in this new world? No, she wouldn't want that. She can't want it. Not with me.

Willow squeezes her eyes shut and cinches up her entire face. "Okay, go on and do it. I can't see now."

"Go on and do what?"

"Hurl."

"What are you talking about?"

She cracks one lid to peek at me. "Throwing up."

I growl. Can anyone blame me? This child speaks nonsense, but at least I understood that phrase. "I am not about to throw up or 'blow chunks' or 'hurl.' Satisfied?"

Willow opens both eyes, and her features relax. "Sure, yeah. What kind of school did you go to where kids don't talk that way?"

"I attended a prestigious boarding school."

"Rich kids don't barf, huh?"

"We need to get moving."

Together, we hike up the mountainside. I still can't determine where we are in the world, other than on a forested mountain. That's so bloody helpful. I hear birds high up in the boughs, and I see a squirrel racing up a tree. This place, wherever it might be, clearly has not been affected by Sefton's apocalypse yet. Will it be spared?

That's doubtful. My brother won't stop until he has destroyed everything except Fallenmouth. Perhaps he will destroy that too once he's finished with the rest of the world.

"How did we get here?" Willow asks. "I fell asleep in my room. But when I woke up, I was here."

"My brother opened a magical portal and flung us to this place, which I assume is the location furthest from where he is."

"Don't you get along with your brother?"

"No." I clench my fists without meaning to as the memory of Sefton storming into the bedroom replays in my mind. "He is the madman who instigated the apocalypse."

"Seriously?"

"Yes."

"Wow, that's harsh. Why did he keep Allison?"

I grumble out a sigh. Are all children so intrusive? "Sefton is obsessed with Allison. She and I are two sides of the triangle my brother needed to create the Echo and instigate the apocalypse. She is the catalyst, I am the anchor."

"That's freaky."

"Yes, it is." At least I understand what the word freaky means. "Do you know what the Echo is?"

"Uh-huh. I heard people talking about it. I guess those monsters like to tell everybody where they came from."

I grunt.

Mercifully, she does not speak while we cross into a less wooded area. I pause for a moment to take in the view, though not because I feel like doing a bit of sightseeing. I'm hoping to find clues to where we are and if there might be settlements nearby. I see nothing, so we continue up the mountain. When we crest its summit, I turn in a circle to inspect the area and perhaps find a place where we can camp for the night. It's still daylight here, though the sun is sinking toward the horizon.

Below us, on the other side of the mountain we've just hiked up, I see a beach stretching out along the coast of an ocean while waves crash on the shore. This mountain range is high, but small compared to the sort they have in the Himalayas or the Andes.

Where are we? Someplace far from England, that's for certain.

"Bloody hell," I grumble. "I have no idea where we've wound up, or how to get back to Allison."

I hadn't meant to say that out loud, but the words poured out anyway.

Willow slips her hand into mine. "It's okay. We'll find her again."

A child is comforting me. And for some reason, I find myself clasping her hand.

"Maybe we should go down there," Willow says. "Might find a town or something if we walk far enough."

The terrain leading down to the beach is steep, which forces us to take it slow. I keep hold of Willow's hand strictly to ensure she won't tumble off a cliff. Allison would not be happy if I let her new mate die in a terrible accident. I do *not* like the child. She asks annoying questions and uses bizarre words.

At last, we set foot on the beach. The girl immediately rushes into the waves to get herself soaked by the three-foot swells. She laughs and shrieks, splashing around in the water. Though she waves for me to join her, I do not do that. Maybe I had jumped into the river back in Fort Worth, but that had been different. I don't feel like playing in the swells, not when Allison is trapped at Fallenmouth with my mad brother.

Once Willow has grown tired of splashing and shrieking, we head off down the beach, following the coast with steep mountain slopes on one side and the ocean on the other. I wish I could figure out where we are. I wish I had a weapon too. But most of all, I wish I were with Allison.

We've just rounded a corner into a small cove when movement catches my eye. Someone is walking away from us, apparently not having noticed our presence, and the individual carries an armload of what looks like driftwood. I lay a hand on Willow's arm as we halt to observe the other person. It's a man, I think. But with the deepening sunset and the distance between us, it's hard to tell for certain.

I tighten my grip on Willow's hand while we edge along the cliffs, following the stranger.

He turns toward us. "You can stop trying to hide. I saw you two before you came around the cliffs. Might as well come to my house for dinner. Hope you like fish."

Trusting a stranger seems unwise, but I am quite hungry, and Willow must be too. I have no weapons, but I'm bigger and stronger than this man, just as my brother remade me to be. So I let the bloke guide us around an outcropping, where he has a makeshift tent set up using what looks like a vinyl tarpaulin and several pieces of tree branches.

The man drops his load on the sand. "I'll get the fire started. Either of you know how to gut a fish? If not, you can start the fire while I handle dinner."

"I can gut the fish," I say.

Willow wrinkles her nose. "Ew. That's way too icky."

The only reason I know how to prepare a fish for eating is because my father loved fishing. He would take me and Sefton to his favorite river, then show us how to gut the fish he caught. I'd hated the sport, but I wanted to spend time with my father. Sefton always thought it was a ridiculous way to waste time.

The stranger offers his hand to me. "I'm Grant Larson."

I shake his hand. "Daxton Stainthorpe, but I prefer Dax. And this is Willow, ah…"

"Willow Greenwood," the girl says. Then she shakes Grant's hand too. "I don't use a nickname."

"Can't tell you how nice it is to meet both of you," Grant says. "I was beginning to think nobody else had survived."

I glance around. "This area clearly hasn't been touched by the Echo."

Grant's brows rise. "The Echo? Is that what they call it? At first, I thought it was a meteor, but then the crazy lightning started, and the demons flooded out of the hole in the sky."

"Where are we?"

"You're on the Lost Coast. Fitting name, hey? I used to come here to go hiking before… Well, you know."

"I'm afraid we have no idea where the Lost Coast is." And I will not admit to him that the girl and I were thrown into this region by magic. Not until I decide if I trust him.

"Not from around here, huh?" Grant says. "The Lost Coast is in Humboldt County."

"I'm not familiar with that area."

"California, buddy. You're in Northern California."

CHAPTER TWENTY-SIX

Allison

I WAKE UP SLOWLY, LIKE CRAWLING UP A MUDDY SLOPE IN THE PITCH dark. What happened? A fog envelops my mind as if I've been drugged, which slows my progress in rising from sleep. But slowly, I begin to sense things—the rustling of leaves in the wind, the warmth of sunshine on my face, cushy softness beneath me, and the scent of leather. Why would I smell that? With more effort than seems possible, I pry my lids open and try to make sense of my environment.

This is the bedroom I've slept in since coming to Fallenmouth. The window is open, allowing a pleasant breeze to waft through the space. The leaves on the ash tree rustle, though I can only see the top branches. I realize I'm lying on the bed, on top of the covers, but I can't seem to move my arms or legs. Blinking rapidly, I struggle to clear the haze. At last, I understand why I feel immobilized. It's not sleepiness holding me down.

Leather straps tie my hands to the headboard rails and my ankles to the footboard posts. Sefton must've ordered his minions to tie me to the bed. I'm spreadeagled and can't even move enough to scratch my nose.

Where are Dax and Willow? Did Sefton kill them?

I can't worry about that right now. First, I need to get free of these bindings. But if I tap into my Echo power to do that, I have no idea how much energy I'll have left for either zipping myself to wherever Dax and Willow are, or for opening those boxes in the cellar. My teleporting isn't exactly...exact. The first time I'd done it, I dropped us in a random location. The second time, I'd gotten us to Fallenmouth, but I can't be sure that wasn't a fluke. What if I whisk us straight into a war zone where Echo creatures reign?

Suck it up, girl, that's fear talking.

The door swings open, and Sefton approaches the bed. "Good morning, Allison. Today is the most important day of your life. I've given you the night to reconsider your actions yesterday, and I trust you will not attempt to escape again. But whether you've changed your mind is irrelevant. We will be bound in every way after the ceremony this morning."

Never going to happen. I'm with Dax, not this creep.

Sefton leans over to kiss my cheek. "You will be a beautiful bride."

Then he hobbles out of the room, shutting the door.

Screw this. I am not going to lie here and wait for Sefton to "consummate" our so-called union without my consent. If I can free myself and get downstairs to the exercise room, I can grab a cutlass. That's the best weapon available to me, and I've gotten pretty damn good with a blade. That, combined with my self-defense skills, should give me just enough of an advantage. Echo creatures might be wickedly strong and vicious, but they don't seem like the brightest bulbs. And yeah, I've had plenty of time to reconsider my choices. Sefton won't like what I've decided.

No more waiting. It's time to save myself.

I shut my eyes and focus on the leather restraints as I imagine them popping open. I focus so hard that a stabbing pain fires up in my temple, but I don't care. *Open, dammit, set me free.* I grit my teeth, clench my fists, bluster breaths out through my nostrils even as the pain gets sharper and harder. *Open, open, open.*

The instant the restraints break, my arms fall onto the mattress. I sit up and swing my legs off the bed. After hours of lying here tied up, my arms and legs feel a little sore, but I can handle that. The real test is whether I still have the agility to fight.

I slide off the bed until my bare feet touch the floor, then gently settle my weight onto my legs. I'm standing now, and I don't feel wobbly at all. So I take one step. That seems okay, and I take another step, then another, and another, until I've walked past the foot of the bed. Then I kick it up a notch by walking briskly toward the window, pivoting on my heels, and walking briskly to the door. I feel a few minor twinges, but I think those will iron themselves out the more I move.

Time for the final test.

I run to the window, whirl around, and run back to the door.

No twinges, no wobbling, nothing that indicates I can't handle a fight. I want to throw my arms up and shout "woo-hoo," but I don't do it. The noise might alert my captor and his minions. But in my mind, I am fist-pumping and shouting.

Once I find some socks and shoes, not to mention a bra and panties, I'm ready to go. I'd only pulled on my pants and shirt last night. Feels good to be fully dressed again. This is my battle armor.

I turn the doorknob with care to avoid making any noise, and pray the door isn't magically barred anymore. But when I try to open it, the door won't budge. *Dammit.* I risk sending out a small pulse of power. Though I don't hear or see anything, somehow I know I've unsealed the barrier. Yanking the door open, I tiptoe into the hall.

Nobody around. Guess they all assume I can't escape.

Tiptoeing swiftly down the hall, I head to the stairs and pause there to listen and watch. The coast seems clear. I continue down to the foyer, but freeze with my hand on the banister.

Although the sitting room door is shut, I hear voices in there. I want to know what they're talking about, but I have more pressing issues. I skirt around the staircase to scurry down the hall, staying on the opposite side from the sitting room, and make my way to the cellar door. Its lock is still broken from when Dax kicked the door open. Why Sefton doesn't guard it, I have no idea. Maybe he believes no one else has any chance of touching, much less opening, all those boxes. His arrogance is hard to overlook, but I shouldn't assume anything.

I ease the cellar door open and slip inside. The single bulb positioned in the center of the subterranean room can't squelch the shadows that seem to writhe in every corner. A damp odor suffuses the space, and the faint creak of each step sends a shiver down my spine. One step at a time, I slink down the stairs with my pulse beating faster and my breaths growing shallower. I force myself to take deeper breaths and exhale slowly because the last thing I need is to get lightheaded while I'm breaching Sefton's creepy basement lair. As I hop off the last step, the magics inside those boxes slither out to lick at me, though they hadn't done that the other day. Something has changed. I can feel it, but whether the change is good or cataclysmically bad, I need to keep going and find out what Sefton is hiding.

The closer I get to the shelves that hold the boxes, the stronger the magics grow, until they're prickling my skin with electrical currents of energy. Every hair on my body stiffens as a tingling sensation sweeps over my flesh. I raise my hand, inching it ever closer to a metal box on the middle shelf, and focus on utilizing the power within me. I wish magic came with an instruction manual, but I'll have to wing it. As I will the box to let me open it, the tingling becomes stronger and sharper, like a thousand needles pricking my skin, digging in deeper and deeper. I suck in a breath and hold it because I can't breathe anymore, not with a strange pressure bearing down on my chest. When I stretch my arm out to reach for the box, the pressure makes my hand tremble. It's like pushing through quicksand. My entire arm begins to quiver from the effort, and my ears start to ring. Black dots speckle my vision.

The box's lid pops open. The electric tingling vanishes.

Blowing out a breath, I sag against the shelves. The box lies open six inches away, but I need a minute or two to catch my breath and recover from the assault of those magics.

Holy cow, I beat them.

Once the ringing in my ears fades away, I straighten and pick up the box. It's heavy, but not so ponderous that I can't hold it. The sides of the box are half an inch thick, and the exterior is engraved with strange symbols. I'd noticed the symbols before, but now I sense their importance. One looks like a crescent moon. Another appears to show a circle with a dot in the middle. I also note the symbols for male and female, as well as various triangle symbols, some of which have lines drawn through them, and even more symbols with stranger designs.

Within the box lies…nothing. While velvet lines the interior, there's nothing inside it but air. No, it must contain something. I'm not seeing it, that's all. Not seeing or not feeling? I spread my hand over the box and gradually lower it into the vacant space until my palm settles onto the velvet lining.

Symbols on the exterior begin to glow and flash in some kind of sequence, but I have no idea what it means.

"You are very clever, Allison, to find these boxes and open one."

Sefton's voice sends a chill skittering down my spine. I glance over my shoulder and see him standing halfway across the room. "Why don't you guard the boxes the way you guard everything else? A locked door isn't a real fortification. Your creatures protect the estate, but these precious containers of magic are just lying here undefended."

"Are they undefended? I know you and Dax broke into my study and explored the cellar while I was gone. I sensed it every time you two tried to access the boxes." Sefton shuffles closer, coming up alongside me. "Only one who is worthy may open the vessels and access the magics in them."

"That doesn't answer my question. Why don't you protect these boxes?"

"But I did explain. Only the worthy may use the boxes. No further security measures are necessary, and besides, the magics need to roam free."

I had removed my hand from the box when he approached, but now I settle it inside the "vessel," triggering the engraved icons to glow. "What are these symbols? I recognize a few of them, but—"

"They are alchemical symbols." He pulls my hand out of the box and encloses it in his palms. "I needed years to research and uncover the secrets hidden within ancient texts and at last realize that alchemy holds the key to remaking the world. When I met you, I recognized I had found not only the catalyst I needed to begin the transmutation but also a soul mate who would stand beside me while the alchemy of worlds unfolds."

"You never said any of that to me. I'm not your soul mate. I'm just the employee who happened to be manning the check-out counter on the day you showed up at the library."

"I know, and that was fate at work." He moves closer, still clasping my hand. "How many others would have understood what I needed when I asked about alchemy and quantum physics? You knew, and you gathered the information."

"Any librarian could've done that. I found what you asked for by searching a computer system. That's not fate, it's dumb luck."

"Look at the symbols." He releases my hand, then throws an arm around my shoulders to hold me to his side. "*Look* at them. Until today, the symbols had only been activated when I touched them. They obey me—and now you. Notice which symbols activate when you touch the box. Do it."

I do what he says only because I need to know what the symbols mean. Maybe he's going to explain. So I stretch my hand out again and flatten my palm on the box's bottom.

The symbols begin to glow in a repeating sequence.

"Do you see?" Sefton whispers into my ear. "Watch as the sequence restarts. Venus, the symbol for woman and for copper. Jupiter, the king of the gods who represents the chemical element tin. Terra, the earthly embodiment of woman and the symbol for earth itself, the basis upon which all else rests. Ignis, the fire of passion and the burning flame of life that shall turn the world to ash so that it may be reborn anew."

To change the world, we must first dismantle it. One of his notes to me had said that, but I didn't understand what he'd meant until it was too late.

He points to the wooden box adjacent to the one inside which my hand lies. "Open that one and see what its symbols reveal."

Might as well let him tell me everything. I swallow against a constriction in my throat and open the other box. The second my hand touches the velvet interior, the symbols on the exterior begin to activate.

"The sun," he says, "symbol of warmth and life, also associated with the element gold. That is you, Allison. The warm and radiant woman who sparked the alchemical reaction. The moon represents darkness and the metal silver, and it binds me to you."

Sounds like baloney to me. Why would the moon bind me to him?

Three symbols light up in unison.

Sefton plasters his mouth to my ear and whispers, "Tria Prima. The three elements that triggered the original transmutation, the change that created all other matter. That's why I needed the three of us together—to recreate the Tria Prima. In ancient alchemy, three physical elements comprised the triangle, but I needed more than mercury, sulfur, and salt to achieve my goal. Only a trio of humans could accomplish the feat. Well, that and the quintessentia, which is the unknowable essence of everything, the prime catalyst that generated the universe."

Quintessentia? Tria Prima? The scariest part of all this is that I'm beginning to make sense of his lunatic ramblings. Because he's not just rambling anymore. He's telling me how he created the Echo and started the transmutation of two worlds into one.

He pulls me away from the shelves, dragging me backward, and rests his hands on my shoulders. "On that day when Dax and I stood before our parents' graves, I had already planted the seed of the transmutation within you. We are entangled, the three of us, bound at the quantum level."

"You planted the seed when you kissed me."

"Exactly. You didn't need to be present when I triggered the Tria Prima. I already possessed the requisite magics, and all I needed on that day was Dax."

Though I want to push away from him, I know I shouldn't. Not yet. I need more answers. "What did you mean about the three of us being entangled?"

"Quantum entanglement links discrete particles, even across vast distances. What affects one affects the other. That is how we share power. Eventually, I will find a way to sever Dax from the entanglement. But you and I shall forever be entwined."

Bound to him forever? No way.

"Once I achieved the entangled state," Sefton says, "the pieces fell into place. And voila, the apocalypse began. The elegance and beautiful horror of the transmutation is stunning. Don't you agree?"

My God, he really is insane. Nothing can save him now. He's gone too far beyond the edge of sanity, so far that he can no longer see reality as anything but a distant star in another galaxy. If I'd ever thought I might somehow bring him back from the madness, talk sense into him, now I realize that can never happen. He has murdered countless human beings, destroyed entire cities, and created monsters that do his bidding. No one should have that much power, and there's only one way to stop him.

Sefton Stainthorpe must die. And I'm going to kill him.

Chapter Twenty-Seven

Dax

Last night, Willow and Grant slept. I did not. At least, I didn't sleep soundly, but that was on purpose. My years in the Echo taught me the life-threatening consequences of letting my guard down in the presence of strangers. I met Willow less than two days ago, yet I trust the child. Perhaps because Allison trusts her.

Our host, Grant, is another story. He seems amiable and as normal as anyone can be under the circumstances, but I have an intuition that he's keeping something from us. I can't blame him for that. We just met, and I am not the most…friendly person. Everyone in this world has known the Echo for only a matter of days, while I lived in it for five years. Of course I'm a growling, snarling beast.

But I need to know what Grant is hiding.

I stand watch on the shore while Grant and Willow wade out into the water to catch our breakfast. They use sticks with sharpened tips, punching them into the gentle swells whenever they see a fish. While they focus on their task, I scan the shore and the mountains behind us, the sky too.

But my thoughts keep circling back to one question.

What has Sefton done to Allison? If that bastard has hurt her, I will tear him apart. I don't care that he's my brother. He lost the right to expect me to feel sorry for him when he turned the world inside out.

Willow sprints up to me, grinning, and holds up her spear—with a fish impaled on it. "I caught one. Isn't that awesome?"

"Yes, it's awesome." I probably sound less than enthused, but I can't help that. What if Sefton starves Allison to punish her for shagging me? I need to get back to her, but I have no idea how to accomplish that feat.

"You sure worry a lot," Willow says. "Mostly about Allison, right? You're scared about what your brother might do to her."

"I have no way to get back to Allison. So yes, I am deeply concerned."

She nods gravely. "Yeah, not having cars or planes or even scooters really sucks."

"Yes, it certainly does suck."

Maybe I should tell Grant that Sefton created the apocalypse. But our host is within earshot, and I still can't figure him out.

Grant saunters out of the water wearing only a pair of long swim trunks and carrying a spear loaded with two fish. They're both smaller than the one Willow caught. She is a clever child, and a brave one considering that she ran through a crowd of Echo creatures to reach Fallenmouth. She reminds me of Allison in some ways.

Grant leads us back to his campsite along the rim of the mountain. "Dax, why don't you prepare the fish while I get the fire going again?"

"I can do that."

"What about me?" Willow asks. "Don't I get a job?"

"You can help me," I say. "Learning how to gut and clean a fish is a useful skill. But if you still feel it's 'too icky,' I can handle the task alone."

She wrinkles her nose. "Still sounds yucky. But I'm in."

Willow learns quickly, and I only need to demonstrate the techniques for her once, then she takes care of the other two fish on her own. I keep an eye on Grant the entire time. He reignites the fire and creates a makeshift spit for roasting our catch, and soon we're all enjoying a hearty breakfast. Well, "enjoying" might be an overstatement. We're too hungry to care that our meal is slightly burned.

After breakfast, Willow wades out into the waves to hunt for seashells, though I'm not convinced she will find any. I order her to remain within my sight. She rolls her eyes and calls me "such a dork."

Grant excuses himself to find "a boy bush." I decide that's his polite way of saying he needs to relieve himself.

And I take the opportunity to explore his makeshift shelter.

Last night, it had been essentially dark by the time we found Grant and he offered us shelter. The interior of the shelter had been too gloomy for me to see what he keeps inside it, but I need to know more about our host. That requires reconnaissance.

I quickly search the shelter but find nothing of interest—until a spider lands on my boot and I stomp my foot to shake it off. The sole of my boot hits something hard. Metal, I'd say. The object lies buried under the sand alongside the spot where Grant had slept. He *is* hiding something. And I need to know what it is.

Leaning out of the shelter, I check whether Grant is coming back yet. I see only Willow building a sandcastle.

But our host might return at any moment. I need to hurry.

Pulling back Grant's sleeping bag, I dig in the sand to excavate the mystery item, which turns out to be a metal box. I brush the sand away from its top and open the lid.

A gun lies inside the box, nestled on top of a sheaf of folded papers.

"It's a Beretta .9mm semi-auto, in case you were wondering."

When I glance over my shoulder, Grant is hovering just outside the shelter. He's wearing jeans and a T-shirt now, with hiking boots and a denim jacket. I hadn't seen him change clothes, but I did notice he took a pile of clothing with him when he wandered off into the woods.

I rise from my crouch and exit the tent with the box in my hand.

Grant waits while I approach him, his expression as calm as his voice had been.

"Where did you get a gun?" I demand.

"Took it off a dead body. I didn't kill the guy. But I did take his weapon since I figured he didn't need it anymore." Grant taps the box's rim. "Only one bullet in there. Check and you'll see."

I pop the magazine out and see no rounds inside it. Then I check the chamber. One bullet.

"What did you mean to do with a single round?" I ask. "That won't stop an Echo creature."

"I know. But I thought if things got tough..." He raises a hand to his temple with his thumb and forefinger forming a gun-like shape, then snaps his thumb down. "Pow. I'd rather be dead than get tortured by those creatures."

"That's understandable." I pull the papers out from under the gun and set the box down on the sand. Another object tumbles out too—a photograph. I pick it up and study the picture of a blonde woman hugging a sandy-haired toddler. "What is this?"

Grant snatches the photo from me. "It's personal."

"Is this your family?"

He grinds his teeth, making his jaw muscles work. "Yeah. They were."

Clearly, he doesn't want to discuss the matter. If his family died, I have no desire to dredge up his pain. Unfolding the sheaf, I feel my brows rise as I realize what I'm holding. "Scientific papers? These look like they all relate to quantum physics."

"Bingo."

"Are you a scientist?"

"No, I was a deputy sheriff. When the shit hit the universal fan, I was hiking in the mountains just outside Los Angeles." He bows his head and rubs the back of his neck. "Didn't have my service weapon with me, so I couldn't do much when the creatures came. Tried to save people, but..."

"You couldn't fight them. The Echo creatures are incredibly strong and completely focused on destroying anything and anyone they encounter."

I am one of those creatures, at least in part. Sefton's transformation granted me more strength than any normal human could muster. Though I can fight those creatures, it's no easy task to defeat them. For a man like Grant, it must be terrifying to realize that not even his muscular physique, strength, and police training could save him if a horde attacked. So yes, I understand the need for one bullet.

Willow screams.

I drop the papers and run across the beach toward her, where she's been kneeling to create her sandcastle. In the sky above us, a winged Echo creature dives straight down at her.

The beast extends the claws on its hands and feet, preparing to snatch the girl.

My heart pounds so hard and fast that I almost can't breathe. Just as I reach Willow, the beast swoops in for the grab. I latch on to its hind legs, but that only slows it down. The creature is too strong and too determined. It flies up until my feet lift off the ground, and the thing flails its legs to shake me off. Its tail smacks me in the face, and I tumble to the sand.

Willow is running toward the shelter, toward Grant.

The beast swoops down again to grab Willow.

Grant raises the gun and fires at the creature's head. Blood spurts from its forehead. The beast loses its grip on Willow.

I race over to the girl, scooping her up in my arms just as the creature shrieks and soars away over the ridge of the mountain. I carry Willow to the shelter and set her down on her feet. "Are you injured?"

"No, I'm okay." Tears trickle down her cheeks, and her lips tremble. She flings her arms around me, hugging me tightly. "That creature almost got you. Why didn't you run away?"

"I was more concerned with not letting it get you." I caress her hair the way my mother had always done for me when I was a little boy and something scared me. I glance at Grant. "Why did you sacrifice your only bullet?"

"Couldn't let either of you get taken. I've seen what those creatures do to their prisoners." He tosses the gun into the brush behind the shelter. "I was a cop. Saving lives is what I do."

How can I not trust him after this? Maybe I shouldn't, but I feel that I can. "Let's all sit down and talk about things. We should get to know each other a bit more."

"Sounds good."

We sit on the sand just outside the shelter, near the fire that still smolders.

And I tell a stranger everything. Well, almost everything. I will not divulge my connection to the Echo or Allison's link to it, and I leave out the fact that the creator of doomsday is my twin brother. I might trust Grant now, but I have no idea how he might react to those truths. I do tell him about the golem Sefton sent to retrieve Allison, but I omit the fact that she whisked us both away. Keeping that bit of the story somewhat vague will let

Grant reach his own conclusion—that Sefton abducted us both. He does seem to decide that's what happened, which means he won't develop any suspicions about how Allison and I reached Fallenmouth.

"Allison's alone with that crazy guy?" Willow says once I've finished my story. "We have to go get her."

"I know. But I don't have a ruddy clue how to do that."

Grant picks up the papers I'd dropped on the ground and holds them out to me. "Maybe this will help. I found these in what's left of the Stanford University library. Heard some of the creatures talking about how their leader was fascinated with quantum physics and thought maybe I'd find something useful in these papers. I didn't."

I take the documents. "How far is Stanford from here?"

"About three hundred miles."

"You walked that far?"

Grant chuckles. "No. I found an abandoned boat, and that got me most of the way. I walked the last ten miles and decided to make camp here. Still don't know where I'm going, just that I needed to get away from LA. It's truly apocalyptic down there."

"As is Fort Worth, Texas."

"London too," Willow says. She looks at me and bites her lip. "Can't we get back to Allison the way we got sent here? You know, like, poof."

She makes a hand gesture that seems like an attempt to emulate an explosion and makes a matching noise. That must not be what she meant since we were not thrown here by an explosion. But I don't understand how a detonation sound indicates "poofing."

"Unfortunately," I say, "I can't reproduce the 'poof' that brought us here."

Grant pokes at the coals in the fire with the toe of his boot, triggering tiny sparks that float into the air. "Sounds like you need a portal."

I freeze, my gaze glued to him. "Portal? I thought you didn't learn anything from those papers."

"No, I said I didn't find anything useful in them. But I learned a lot." He stands and kicks sand onto the fire, dousing most of the coals. "Knowing how to open a portal isn't the same thing as being able to do it, though. I've tried. Guess you need some kind of hoodoo inside you already for that to work."

"What makes you think Willow or I have that 'hoodoo'?"

"Look, man, I don't like to comment on other people's looks. I'm one hundred percent committed to accepting everyone the way they are, even those creatures." Grant folds his arms over his chest. "Come on, you can't deny you aren't an average guy. It's obvious from the way you look and the way you growl. You've got some Echo blood in you, right?"

Bloody hell. How did he figure that out? This man is cleverer than I'd assumed, and now he knows my secret.

"I'm not judging," Grant says. "You look human, mostly, but no mundane man I've ever seen has muscles like yours or that animalistic quality. You also seem to know an awful lot about the Echo and the creatures that come from there. Most of us have been dealing with the creatures for less than a week, but you seem awfully knowledgeable about them."

Why should I lie? If he wanted to kill me, he could've fired his only bullet at me, square between the eyes.

"Yes," I admit. "I do have Echo blood in me. I was a mundane man until the architect of the apocalypse turned me into a beast and threw me into the hell world he had created. I lived in the Echo for five years."

"Thanks for sharing."

He doesn't sound sarcastic. I think he is genuinely thanking me for telling him about myself. Grant behaves nothing like any copper I've ever met. A deputy sheriff who behaves like a hippie? I can't fathom that. But nothing makes sense anymore, so I need to stop assuming I understand other people.

Grant claps his hands together. "Okay. Let's make you a portal so you can rescue the girl."

Chapter Twenty-Eight

Dax

I LEVER MY BODY OFF THE GROUND AND FOLD MY ARMS OVER MY chest. "You say you know nothing about quantum physics, yet you're implying you can open a portal. Have you been toying with me?"

"No, I don't roll that way. I say what I mean and do what I say."

"Then how do you know—"

"Don't *know* anything. That word suggests certainty, and I've got none of that." Grant raises his hands in a placating gesture. "Relax. I'm not a spy for the creatures or for whoever created the apocalypse. But I have seen things."

"Such as?"

"When I was getting the hell outta Dodge—Los Angeles, I mean—I had to stop and hide in a trashed convenience store. A big bunch of those creatures had swarmed the street." Grant shoves his hands into his trouser pockets, his features pinched. "They were doing things I'd rather not describe in front of a minor."

Yes, I can imagine. The creatures I've met had no qualms about performing lewd acts out in the open.

"I don't care about the creatures' antics," I tell him. "You can skip that bit."

"Well, after a while, they all stopped moving and went real quiet. Every single one of them turned in the same direction like they were waiting for something or someone." Grant shakes his head. "It was the damnedest thing. A hole opened up in the air, at ground level, and I could see another place through that hole. This happened before I read all those physics papers. The creatures just stood there, seeming almost awed, while a man walked out of that opening—a portal, I realized later."

Every muscle in my body tenses because I know that man's identity. But I need to be certain. "What did this man look like?"

"Blond hair. Blue eyes. Fit, but not the way you are. He walked with a slight limp too."

Sefton. Grant had witnessed my brother exiting a portal. But I need to know more. "What did the man do next?"

"He started talking to the creatures, but I couldn't hear what he said. They seemed to be entranced by him, so I kinda figured he's their god." Grant tips his head to the side, eying me with curiosity. "You said one man created the apocalypse and the creatures. Was it the blond guy?"

"Yes."

Grant sighs, and his shoulders slump. "Sorry, I can't tell you more about what happened that day. The creator guy and his pet monsters walked off down the street. And I scrammed in the opposite direction. I should've stayed to find out what they were doing, but I, uh…chickened out."

"I doubt that. You reacted as anyone would have under the same circumstances. There was nothing you could've done to stop them, and if they'd seen you, they would have killed you."

He shrugs and stares down at the sand.

"Tell me what you've learned about portals," I say. "Anything you know could be helpful."

"The math of it all is way too complicated for me, but some of the papers I found seemed to be aimed at a more general audience. I'm no expert, but here's what I think it means." He crouches and picks up a small stick, using it like a pen while he draws figures in the sand to illustrate his points. "To create a portal, you need a wormhole. That's basically a tunnel through space, with a mouth at either end. Even if you could find a wormhole, you probably can't just walk through it, because the structure is very unstable. You need exotic matter to hold it open."

"Would magic qualify as exotic?"

"No idea." He scrapes the stick across the drawing he'd made, erasing it. "But I'm guessing the creator guy didn't search the universe for exotic matter. Magic seems like the best bet for tapping into a wormhole."

How bizarre that we no longer doubt the existence of magic. Last week, I laughed at my brother when he suggested such things exist. Now, I'm calmly discussing how magic and theoretical physics converge to create a portal.

Grant rises and studies me again. "If you're really from the Echo, maybe *you* could be the exotic matter."

If I knew how Sefton had generated enough of that material to hold a wormhole open, perhaps I could use the same method. But he failed to share that information. He would have needed an external source, I imagine, since he is not from the Echo and has not altered his essential makeup the way he changed me.

Perhaps I am exotic matter.

"How do I create a portal?" I ask. "Assuming my body contains that sort of material."

"I think that's where magic comes into it. You need to find and lasso a wormhole."

"Brilliant. Where do I find a unicorn I can ride into the wormhole?" Perhaps I did snarl those words. I hadn't meant to, but this discussion is making my head hurt. "Sorry. I have no bloody clue how to lasso anything, much less a hypothetical tunnel through space."

"You're doing this to find your girl, right?"

Not sure if Allison would agree that she's my girl, but Grant doesn't need to know that. "Yes, I need to get back to Allison."

"Maybe what you should do is focus on her and let everything else go. If you're connected to exotic matter, I guess it's possible you'll find a portal that way."

"Your words don't inspire confidence. Maybe? Possible? You guess?"

He shrugs. "This is all new territory—for everyone."

"I know, you're right. If I'm going to try this, I should move away from you and Willow. In case I cock it up and create a black hole instead of a wormhole."

Grant chuckles. "If you do that, we're all toast no matter where we're standing."

When I glance at Willow, she doesn't seem frightened. After witnessing the start of an apocalypse and being tormented by humans and creatures alike, I suspect the girl has developed a thick skin. She'd been terrified when that winged beast attacked us, but she recovered from that quickly. She's as brave as Allison, and as clever too, but she shouldn't be left alone.

"If I succeed in creating a portal," I say to the girl, "you'll be here alone with Grant. Are you all right with that?"

"Sure. He's cool."

"I'll take care of her," Grant says. "You have my word."

From his tone and his expression, I know he means that.

Willow hops up on her tiptoes to kiss my cheek. "Go help Allison. I'll be fine."

I march across the sand, staying as far away from the wooded cliff as possible, and edge around an outcropping so I'm out of sight of Grant and Willow. This is the best I can do. Whether anything can protect them if I make a terrible mistake, I have no idea. But I must try. This is more than a quest to reunite with the woman I love. She and I have a connection to the Echo and to the magics my brother crafted, a link that might help us stop the alchemy of worlds.

I freeze, barely noticing the wavelets that lap around my feet. Did I just think... Yes, I did. I've known Allison for such a short time, and yet I know what I feel, know it with a conviction that sinks deep into my soul. I am in love with Allison.

Could she ever feel that way about me? After the things I've done, the answer must be no.

Forget about everything else. Focus on Allison.

I shut my eyes and picture her face, her smile, the way she looked at me when we made love the other night. I hear her voice whispering "you are not a beast" and feel her arms wrapped around me. Pressure bears down on me from everywhere and nowhere as a prickling sensation sweeps over my body.

The pressure releases with such suddenness that I stumble sideways and bump into an object. I should open my eyes, but I feel like I can't move even the smallest muscles.

Arms wrap around me. A familiar scent envelops me, and familiar lips press against mine.

I pry my lids open and gaze straight into Allison's eyes.

She grins at me. "You're here."

"Yes, I—" Something incredible happens to me, something I haven't experienced in years. I grin at her like an idiot and laugh too. "It worked. I found you."

She throws her arms around my neck and kisses me.

"Uh, just FYI, you guys aren't alone."

Grant's voice jerks me back to reality. I keep one arm around Allison as I turn toward him. Willow stands beside Grant, and they can't be more than six feet from me. When I'd left them, they were much further away, out of my sight.

It's magic, you bloody moron. Line of sight doesn't matter.

Allison breaks away from me to rush over to Willow and give the girl a firm hug. Then she notices our other guest, and her brows wrinkle. "Who are you?"

"Grant Larson," he says, offering his hand to Allison. "I met Dax and Willow on the beach yesterday."

"Beach?" Allison turns her attention to me. "Where did you end up?"

"The Lost Coast," I tell her. "It's in Northern California."

But now we're in the bedroom where Allison has been sleeping.

Grant seems a bit confused as he walks up to the window and gazes out at the estate. "Where exactly are we now?"

"England," I say. "This is Fallenmouth Manor, my ancestral home."

"Really? Are you royalty or something?"

"I am the Earl of Fallenmouth. Not that titles matter anymore." My attention swerves back to Allison. "Where is Sefton? If he has hurt you in the slightest, even a tiny scratch—"

"He hasn't. Sefton had to go check on some outpost of the Echo, though I have no clue what that means." She grasps my hands. "But he did tell me everything about those boxes."

"What do you mean?"

"Sefton explained to me how he created the Echo and the alchemy of worlds, and I think I know how to stop him—now that you're here."

"Me? I know nothing about that."

She clasps my face in her hands. "We are two elements of the Tria Prima, the original alchemical reaction that started everything."

"What?" If I sound baffled, that's because I am. Clearly, I've missed a lot during my brief time away from her.

"I'll explain everything," she says. "Should your new friend be included in the discussion?"

"Yes. Grant is trustworthy, and he helped me figure out how to get back to you."

"I'm glad he did." She gives me a quick, soft kiss. "But we'd better get to the explaining before Sefton comes back."

We all sit down on the bed, Grant and I on one side while the girls occupy the other side, and Allison fills us in on everything that happened while we were apart. When she tells us that she can now open the boxes in the cellar, I have to interrupt.

"How did you manage that?" I ask.

"Opening the boxes?" She bites her lip and glances at Willow and Grant. "That's something we should discuss in private, just you and me."

"Why?"

She seizes my hand and drags me to the opposite side of the room, in the corner near the window. Then she speaks in a hushed voice. "We have, um, a sort of shared power."

"What sort? I don't understand."

She raises onto her tiptoes to whisper in my ear, "Sex."

"I don't think it's appropriate to shag right now."

Allison snorts, apparently trying not to laugh at me. "I didn't mean I want to do that right now. But when we have sex, it kind of amps up my Echo power."

"Oh. Well, that's, ah…interesting."

She leads me back to the bed and continues discussing what she learned from Sefton.

I have trouble focusing on what she's saying. Sex with me gives her more power? That's barmy. I can't help wondering if she means that when we're in the throes, she feels more connected to me and—No, I will not finish that thought. She can't love me. Should I tell her how I feel? Not yet. That conversation can wait until later.

What a bleeding coward I've become.

After Allison finishes her recap, Grant shares his experiences and what he learned, concluding with when Willow and I stumbled onto his make-shift campsite.

"The Lost Coast was untouched?" she asks.

"Not completely," Grant says. "The land itself is intact, but at least one creature is hanging around there. The gargoyle thing tried to swoop down and grab Willow, but Dax and I thwarted that attempt."

"I wonder how many other enclaves have survived."

"We can find that out later," I say. "Right now, we need to develop a plan for stopping Sefton from destroying whatever is left of this world."

"Oh, I have a plan for that," she says. "It came to me while Sefton was explaining how awesome it is to murder millions of innocent people and start an apocalypse."

The coldest chill I've ever felt sifts through me, from my skin down to the core of my being. Suddenly, I know what she means to do. "No, Ally, you can't."

Grant raises his brows. "She can't what?"

Allison straightens and clears her throat. "I am going to kill Sefton Stainthorpe."

Like hell she will. If anyone kills my brother, it will be me.

Chapter Twenty-Nine

Allison

GRANT KEEPS HIS EYEBROWS RAISED, THOUGH HE SEEMS UNUSUALLY calm considering that I just announced my plan to murder a man. A psycho, but still, a human being. I don't want to do it, but I know the only way to stop the alchemy of worlds is to destroy the creator of the apocalypse. Sefton has gone too far down the rabbit hole for anyone to pull him out again, which leaves me with no other options.

Willow has wrapped her arms around herself, but she doesn't seem horrified by what I just said. Maybe I shouldn't have included her in our discussion, but this is an unprecedented situation—for the whole world—and even a teenager deserves to know what's at stake.

Dax has been staring at me with squinted eyes and compressed lips while a muscle in his jaw pulses. He fists and loosens his hands repeatedly while his gaze drills into mine. "You will do no such thing."

"It's the only way. Weren't you listening when I told you how Sefton created the apocalypse? The Tria Prima has to be demolished. That means I have to kill him."

"Will that make the world the way it used to be?" Willow asks.

"No, I think it's too late for that. But I'm hoping we can at least stop any further damage." I give her shoulder a squeeze. "And one day we will find a way to make things better. Might take a long time, but I know we can do it. All of us together."

I glance at the three people who are watching me. Yes, I believe that one day we won't live in hell on earth anymore. I have to believe it. Stopping the Echo from swallowing up this world is a start. The fact that at least one enclave has survived virtually untouched gives me hope.

And we desperately need that now.

Dax stalks up to me, seizes my arm, and drags me back into the corner we had retreated to earlier to have a private conversation. He backs me into the corner, penning me with his body, though he doesn't touch me. "You will not kill Sefton. I will do that. You'll be safe on the Lost Coast with Grant and Willow."

"No. I'm the catalyst, which means I need to be the one to take down Sefton. Besides, you don't know how to access those boxes."

"I am the anchor. That means I should be the one to do it."

"This is ridiculous." I let my head fall back against the wall and groan. "We're both a part of the equation—Tria Prima, the reaction that sparked the alchemy of worlds. Arguing about who gets to kill Sefton is not helpful."

"What are you saying?"

"Maybe I was wrong. Maybe we both need to be there to stop him and break the cycle."

He lifts one brow. "Maybe? That's rot. You are going to the Lost Coast with Grant and Willow. I will break the cycle."

"Give it up, Dax. I'm not letting you do this alone."

A throat-clearing from the other side of the room spurs both of us to look at Grant.

He scratches his cheek. "You were talking kinda loud right at the end there, so we heard what you said. And I have a different opinion."

"I don't give a stuff about your opinion," Dax snarls through clenched teeth.

Grant raises his hands, palms out. "Hey, man, I'm just trying to help. I'm not as useless as you seem to think."

"No one thinks you're useless," I say. "But taking out Sefton will require a real battle. His creatures will defend him, and he has powerful magics on his side. Dax and I will need to get into the cellar, which means fighting our way past a lot of insanely strong creatures."

"I was an Army Ranger before I became a deputy sheriff." Grant's expression hardens, his posture stiffens, and he suddenly looks every bit the cop slash soldier. His voice sounds rougher too, like he's summoning his inner badass right before our eyes. "I lived through all kinds of shit, way before the apocalypse hit, including deployments in Iraq and Afghanistan. I fought my way out of LA after those creatures overran the entire city and the county too. Stop acting like I need you to protect me. The truth is, you need me."

He could be right. I hadn't realized until just now that we have a real warrior on our side. With Dax and Grant on the team, we just might get this done—and maybe even survive it.

My gaze flits to the teenager in the group, then back to Dax. "What about Willow? We can't send her to the Lost Coast alone."

Willow leaps off the bed and hurries over to us. "Please don't send me away. Maybe I didn't fight in a war, and maybe I don't have magic, but I can take care of myself. That's what I had to do before I found you guys."

I grasp her shoulders. "You can't be a part of the battle. Those creatures are way too strong."

"But I can hide. Just please don't send me away."

The poor kid doesn't want to be abandoned again. I pull her into a hug. "Okay. You can stay, but you have to keep out of sight."

Dax clears his throat deliberately. "Willow might have magic, you know. She did breach Sefton's wards."

"Even if she does have powers," I say, "she needs to hide for her own protection. We don't have time to figure out what kind of magic skills she has."

"I suppose you're right." Dax walks up to Grant. "Are you sure you want to do this with us? It's quite likely we will die."

"I lost my wife and son in the first wave. Got nothing left to lose."

And Willow lost her parents. Dax's parents passed away years ago, and so did mine. We're all orphans in one way or another, but we've found a new family here in the middle of an apocalypse.

We will live or die together.

"Slight problem with the plan, though," Grant says. "We don't have any weapons. I doubt fists and teeth will do the trick with those creatures."

"There are weapons downstairs," I tell him. "Swords and knives, mostly. I did see a couple cricket bats in a closet too."

Dax bars his arms over his chest. "We need to get downstairs before we can even try to retrieve weapons."

"You'll have an opening soon." I glance at the clock on the bedside table. "Sefton said he'd be back by one o'clock, and that's only fifteen minutes away. You guys should hide."

"I will not hide. If my brother means to assault you, he will need to get through me first."

"That's sweet, Dax, but I need you and Grant to get those weapons."

He sharpens his gaze on me and virtually growls his words. "You are not to be alone with Sefton."

"Oh, you mean like I have been while you were gone. I can handle myself. You know that." Because he taught me how to defend myself. I know I can't beat the Echo creatures, but I have the skills to stop Sefton from assaulting me. "We don't have time to argue about this. Promise me you will do what I ask."

I watch him grinding his teeth while his shoulders bunch up and his nostrils flare. Yeah, he hates my plan. But it's all we've got, and the only way to stop the final phase of Sefton's global transmutation is to take life-threatening risks. Dax may not like it, but he understands we have no other options.

He slumps his shoulders. "All right. We'll do this your way."

"Good." I turn to Willow. "Sweetie, please go hide. I need to know you're safe while this goes down."

"Is anybody safe anymore?"

The answer is no, of course. "Please do this for me. Please."

She chews on her lip, eyes glistening as if she might cry. But she sucks in a breath and squares her shoulders. "Okay. I'll hide."

I give her a quick, firm hug. "Thank you."

"Where do you want me to go?"

"The three of you should fit inside that huge closet over there."

Grant and Willow head for the walk-in closet, but Dax does not move. He stares at me, though he no longer seems annoyed. I know he's been scared, not angry, but growling at me is how he shows his concern. Now, he stares at me in a different way, one that makes me stride up to him, boost myself up on my toes, and meet his gaze head-on.

I lay my hands on his chest. "I need you to believe we can do this, because if you don't, everything will fall apart. Our connection, to Tria Prima and to each other, is the only chance we've got. Do you trust me enough to believe we can get this done?"

"Of course I trust you." He pulls me close, and I swear his lower lip trembles the tiniest bit. "I've never trusted anyone more."

"I trust you too, with all my heart and soul."

He presses his lips to mine, holding that sweet kiss for several seconds. Then he takes a step backward. "I will never let you down."

Dax walks into the closet and shuts the door.

The rest is up to me.

I try to psych myself up with a mental pep talk, but I know nothing can prepare me for what's to come.

The door swings open, and Sefton hobbles across the threshold. "It's time."

A lump forms in my throat, but I will not let him see my anxiety.

He waves for me to exit the room. "The ceremony will take place downstairs, then we will consummate our union."

"What, in front of all your minions?"

"Yes. They are the witnesses." He waves his arm again, and an icy coldness colors his voice. "Come now, Allison."

I follow Sefton out of the bedroom, resisting the impulse to glance back, and let him lead me downstairs and into the sitting room where Dax, Willow, and I had shared hot cocoa last night. Half a dozen creatures have formed a semicircle around the room's periphery. My guards. If I try to run, they'll attack. Dax and Grant won't let that happen. All I need to do is hold the line until they get the weapons.

Then comes the hardest part—breaching the cellar and accessing the boxes so I can shut down the alchemy of worlds.

"Don't I get a wedding dress?" I ask, strictly as a delaying tactic. "I should at least have a veil. Don't you think?"

Sefton shoves me toward a large creature who has tiger-like eyes and whiskers too. The beast also holds a book that has a brown cover. I want to punch Sefton for shoving me, but I need to play along for now. So I take my position in front of the book-holding creature while Sefton comes up beside me.

"Is this guy our minister?" I ask.

"He is the officiant. And that book is not a bible, but an alchemical manuscript I nicked from the Getty Research Institute just before the transmutation began." He smirks, lifting his chin. "Being able to summon portals is quite handy for committing thievery."

"Yeah, you're so damn clever. I'm in awe."

He seizes my arm, forcing me to turn so we face each other. "Sarcasm will do you no good."

"Do you even care if I enjoy you screwing me? Or have you always been a sexual predator?"

"You will enjoy it because I will make certain of that with a spell."

I swallow hard, resisting the urge to lash out at the bastard. *Not yet.*

"When we make love," he says, "it will be more than sex. We shall replicate the moment of creation, when the world was born."

Sefton nods to the beastly officiant.

The creature begins to chant in what sounds like Latin. He wraps up his spiel, holding the book to his chest.

And Sefton grasps my upper arms. "Time to consummate."

Magics unfurl around me, their slippery tongues invisible yet palpable, coiling around me and unleashing electric shocks that sink deep inside me. My sex tingles, growing wet little by little. *No, no, oh God no.* This can't be happening. The tingling spreads throughout my body, forcing me to feel a desire that turns my stomach. I must act before the magics take control and I can't save myself.

I raise my arms, bend my knee, and swing my calf up between Sefton's legs.

The breath explodes out of him. His eyes widen, and he tips forward.

Before he can react, I thrust a palm out and up, ramming it into his nose.

The madman cries out, stumbling backward.

I can't wait any longer. Dax and Grant must have found the weapons by now, so I suck in a deep breath and summon the magics. A portal opens behind me.

"No!" Sefton bellows, his face crimson, his eyes wild.

I step backward through the portal and watch the opening telescope shut just as Sefton staggers toward me with his teeth bared. He thrusts out an arm as if to hold the portal open, or maybe grab my neck to wring it, but I hit him with another groin kick that sends him tumbling to the floor while cradling his privates.

The portal closes, and darkness envelops me.

I can feel the magics zinging in the air around me. How much power do I have left? One way to find out. I wish for the overhead bulb to come on, and it flickers to life. Wan light illuminates the cellar, showing me that I'm standing halfway across the space, facing the collection of spooky boxes. I hurry to the shelves and trail my fingers over the tops of the boxes in hopes I'll sense which one I need to accomplish my task. I shut my eyes, focusing on one thought.

Show me how to stop the alchemy of worlds.

The thought repeats in my mind over and over, almost like a prayer. I suppose I am praying—for the power and wherewithal to end the worst of the horrors one man unleashed.

Click. Click.

My lids fly open, and I scan the shelves. Two boxes have sprung open.

Noises erupt upstairs. The pounding of feet. The shouts of male voices. The metallic clang of blades connecting. The inhuman roars of Echo creatures.

I force myself to block out the melee upstairs and focus on my task. Spreading my arms, I lay one hand inside a box to my right and settle the other palm within a box to my left, with two closed boxes directly in front of me. Magic slithers into me, cool and electric, winding its way through my veins to spread into my entire body. From head to toe, hairs lift and goosebumps pebble my skin.

Yes, almost there, almost.

A portal opens right beside me.

Willow stumbles out, whipping her head left and right as if she's confused. The portal closes. "Holy cow! I did it."

I have no time to consider the ramifications of what she has done. I need to focus on the boxes. Symbols light up on each box in a rotating sequence. The power within me rises and expands, tingling down my arms and into my hands.

Peripherally, I see Willow staring wide-eyed at the boxes.

The sounds of the battle upstairs grow louder.

"Stop this now!" Sefton roars from behind me. But his enraged cry crumbles into wheezing.

He must have opened a portal to get here, and the action drained him. That gives me an opening. I summon everything I have to ramp up the energy in the boxes and funnel it into me.

Willow clamps her hand around my forearm. A surge of power rushes into me from her.

Someone tumbles down the cellar stairs. Though I hear Sefton shouting, my awareness of his angry words has retreated into the recesses of my mind. Only the boxes matter. Only the power they have. Only what I can command them to do.

A scuffle erupts behind me.

"Hurry!" Willow says. "That guy looks really mad."

With a suddenness that steals my breath, the flow of magic stops. I have what I need, and I know how to do it. I raise my arms high and release the magics.

My head falls back, my body stiff and immobile, as the power I'd consumed floods out of me and straight up through the house into the sky. I don't need to see the sky to know what happened. I can feel the change in every cell in my body, the seismic shift that first slows the alchemical reaction and then grinds it to a halt.

Silence yawns around me in the pitch darkness.

The overhead light flickers on again, but I'm breathing too hard to speak or move. Willow still has her hand on my arm, though she gapes at me like I've turned into a human-size light bulb. I'm not glowing, though.

"Wow, Allison," she says, her tone as awed as her expression. "You stopped it, didn't you?"

"I think so. With help from you and Dax."

Though I hadn't consciously taken power from them, I had experienced an invigorating sensation of feeling them both inside me, more so with Dax than with Willow. Only now that we've completed our task do I understand what I felt. Dax has been a part of me since before we ever met, thanks to the Tria Prima, and we will remain connected in a deep and irrevocable way. Willow holds the Echo power inside her too, though not as deeply as Dax and I feel it. She is a part of me too. The alchemical reaction that created the Echo and started the apocalypse bound her to me, which makes me wonder if others out there share the same power and the same link to the Tria Prima.

"Allison, you faithless bitch."

The harshness in Sefton's voice spurs me to whirl around and face him. He stands a few yards away with every muscle in his body bunched up, his entire demeanor electrified by a fury that warps his face into a hideous mask. He clenches his fists so hard that his hands tremble.

Sefton takes one step toward me, his teeth clamped shut and his lips peeled back. Sweat trickles down his temples. "You tricked me, Allison. But you've done worse than that. You have stolen my power."

"It's over, Sefton. The alchemical reaction has ground to a halt." I can't explain how I know that or exactly how I did it—or rather, how I, Dax, and Willow did it. "The alchemy of worlds is over, and I disentangled you from Dax and me. No more quantum connection. You've lost."

"Stopping the process won't reverse what has already been done."

"I know, but it's a start." I glance up at the ceiling, where I can still hear the noises of the battle going on upstairs. "We will find a way to reverse everything you've done. Maybe the world won't be exactly what it was before, but it can be a good place again."

He glares at me for a moment, then his demeanor abruptly shifts. His body relaxes, and a bizarre calmness sweeps over him. "I'm afraid I can't let that happen. You and Dax are bound to me forever, and I will use you to restart the alchemical process. Now that I know you and the girl share the power of the Echo, I can amplify the process by draining that energy from every human who possesses those magics. Thank you for pointing that out to me."

How did he know? I thought he just got here a minute ago.

Sefton chuckles, but it's a dark sound. "You didn't notice when I opened a portal to get here? Took a significant amount of energy to do that while you were siphoning off my power. But I succeeded, and I saw the two of you sharing the energy of the vessels."

Oh shit. I must kill him before he tells anyone else what he knows. With a burst of power that makes my head throb, I conjure a weapon. Since I don't want to steal anything Dax and Grant might be using, the weapon I now hold in my hand is a fencing foil.

A foil is a dangerous weapon, Dax had told me.

Sefton laughs. "You mean to fight me with that flimsy blade?"

I rush forward and slash the foil toward his throat.

He scuffles backward and trips over…the corpse of a creature that lies in the corner, shrouded in darkness until Sefton moved and I could see that body at last. The creature's weapon—a carving knife—is still clutched in the dead beast's hand.

Sefton grabs the knife and lunges toward me.

I slice the foil across his throat. Blood trickles from the wound, but it's not a deadly blow. Dax told me a foil can kill if the blade breaks.

Just as Sefton staggers forward, stabbing his knife at me, I duck sideways and jam the tip of my foil into the earthen floor, then stomp my foot down on it. The blade snaps. I roll out of the way as he jabs at me again. Springing to my feet, I slash the jagged tip of my foil at his neck.

He pulls back, and the blade misses him.

Before I can strike out again, he thrusts his knife into my chest.

Willow screams.

I crumple to the floor and fumble with the hilt of the blade that's sunk deep into me—into my heart. Blood stains my shirt, spreading inexorably outward as the life pours out of me. I feel it happening. I know I'm dying.

My lids slide shut, and the world vanishes.

CHAPTER THIRTY

Dax

SEVEN CREATURES LIE DEAD ON THE FLOOR IN THE EXERCISE ROOM, THE foyer, and the hallway. Grant and I have battled our way through the house, with the former deputy wielding a cutlass while I commandeered the broadsword. Five more creatures continue the fight, but we keep making headway toward the cellar.

A scream reverberates through the house.

Not Allison. It sounds like Willow.

"We have to get to the cellar now," I shout to Grant. "Something's wrong."

Grant glances at me, nodding once. His expression of grim determination becomes more intense and deadlier as he swings his cutlass toward the nearest creature. His blade slices the beast's head off. While the head rolls across the floor, Grant rams his cutlass into another creature's belly and yanks it upward, gutting the monster.

I dispatch two more creatures, but Grant gets the last one.

And we run for the cellar.

The door hangs open, the darkness below broken only by the wan glow of a single bulb. Down there, someone sobs.

"I warned her," Sefton hisses. His face has taken on a grey pallor. "She should have obeyed me."

A rage like none I've ever experienced before descends on me, hot and feral and unstoppable, because I know what has happened. I feel it before I see it and pound down the stairs, leaping over a dead creature, roaring as I punch my brother in the chest hard enough to send him flying into the wall.

I fall to my knees beside Allison. The broadsword tumbles from my hand.

Willow crouches across from me while tears stream down her cheeks and sobs rack her body.

Allison is pale and covered in blood. I check for a pulse but can't feel anything. My hand trembles as I lay my palm on her cheek. She can't be dead. We haven't come this far and stopped the alchemy of worlds together for everything to end this way.

Sefton starts laughing.

I turn my head toward him slowly, my fingers curling into my palms while my pulse surges in my ears.

He keeps laughing. He points a quivering finger at Allison. "You lose again."

My focus telescopes down to Sefton alone as a cold rage infiltrates every cell of my body and the certainty of what I must do erases everything else. I see only him, hear only his manic laughter. As I rise and walk toward him, he still won't shut up. By the time I reach him, standing inches away, his eyes are watering and his cheeks are red from the strength of his laughter. He's begun to wheeze, but I spare not one millisecond of thought for his condition.

"Shut up," I say, my tone deceptively calm, "or I will silence you permanently."

My brother stops laughing, but he still wears a look of manic glee. "I took the thing you wanted most. I won."

"You murdered Allison."

Laughter splutters out of him. "Of course I did."

I take hold of his arms and lift him off the floor until his face is directly in front of mine. "You murdered her."

"Keep saying that. I love hearing it."

"Why, Sefton? Why did you do any of this? You had a good life, but you threw it away to become a monster. Our parents didn't raise you to be like that."

He huffs. "They only cared about you, the golden boy."

I stare at him while cold certainty solidifies in my gut. "You know I have to kill you now."

"Do it. Prove you are the monster I turned you into."

I shake him hard. "You are the monster, not me."

He sneers and cackles. Then something past my shoulder catches his attention. His eyes widen, and his sneer disintegrates. He struggles to get free of my grip, almost whimpering in his desperation. "No! You can't do that."

I swivel my head and…drop Sefton.

Willow crouches beside Allison with a palm flat on Allison's chest, over her heart, and her other hand inside a box that lies on the floor beside her. Silvery light emanates from Willow's palms and spreads outward to encompass Allison's body.

Sefton and I both stand paralyzed, our gazes locked on whatever the girl is doing. I sense energy crackling through me, drawing from the magics my brother had instilled in me, growing every second until, with a rush that sucks the air out of my lungs, the energy reels back into…Allison. I feel that's what happens.

And I feel it when her heart thuds back to life.

"No!" Sefton wails. "I'm meant to win, not you."

He rushes for the broadsword, but I snare him around the waist and haul him backward into me. Shackled by my arm, he can't escape. I lay a hand on his forehead. "I'm sorry, Sefton, but you cannot be allowed to live."

I yank my hand, snapping his neck.

Allison's chest rises on a deep breath, and Willow grins at her even while tears pour down the girl's cheeks.

I drop my brother's body and kneel beside Allison, cupping her face in one hand. "Wake up, love, we need you. I need you."

Her lids flutter open, and her shimmering eyes focus on me. Her lips curl into a soft, sweet smile. "Can't get rid of me that easily."

"Don't want to be rid of you." I touch my forehead to hers. "I love you, Ally."

"I love you too."

Once, I'd told myself she shouldn't feel that way about me. But now, I realize I am not the monster my brother convinced me I am. Allison wouldn't fall for a vicious beast, but she loves me. That's all the proof I need that, despite all my mistakes, I am nothing like the Echo creatures.

Allison pushes up onto her elbows. "This isn't a complaint, but how am I not dead?"

I nod toward the girl. "Willow saved you."

"She did what?"

The teenager hunches her shoulders and bites her lip. "Don't know how I did it. I wanted you back, so I got one of those boxes, shoved my hand into it, and wished hard for you to come back to us."

"Willow shares our Echo power," Allison says. "I realized that right before Sefton attacked me. And I also realized that might mean more people out there have the same gift."

I help her sit up and brush hair away from her face. "But I don't understand how that power could resurrect you from death."

Her brows lift a touch. "I actually died, didn't I?"

"Yes. Please don't ever do that again."

"I'll do my best." She slings an arm around my neck and kisses me. "Don't you want to know my theory for how Willow brought me back?"

The girl raises her hand. "I do."

Pulling Allison closer, I hold her while I rise to my feet, then set her down. "Tell us your theory."

"Sefton told me that he wanted to reenact the moment of creation, when the world was born." She turns slightly to see both me and Willow. "Sefton also said alchemy is the quest for eternal life. I think both of those elements gave the three of us the power to bring me back. A new creation, as in a rebirth. Eternal life, which means to cheat death. I doubt I'm immortal, though the Echo power we all share brought me back."

"But Sefton hadn't achieved either of those goals."

"He was trying, and the magics he gathered in that quest became a part of me and you, and by extension, Willow and any others who have the same power. Sefton had also ensured that you and I were entangled on a quantum level along with him. But I severed his connection to us." She hunches her shoulders. "Do you mind being bound to me? I can sever that link too if you want."

"There's no one else I'd rather be entangled with."

I'm not certain her explanation of how she managed to stop the alchemy of worlds accounts for everything, but I don't care. She came back to me. Nothing else matters.

Footfalls pound in the hallway above the cellar.

We all glance up just as Grant appears in the doorway, breathing hard. "What did I miss?"

Allison shrugs. "Oh, just me dying and being resurrected. Plus, Dax offed his brother."

"Sounds like a good result."

"What took you so bloody long?" I ask. "You were right behind me."

"Yeah, sorry," Grant says. "The creature you skewered with your broadsword didn't quite die. He bounced back and attacked me. Damn, those things are tough."

Allison leads me and Willow out of the cellar, and Grant suggests we go outside to see what effect, if any, halting the alchemy of worlds has caused. Willow sidles up to me as we pass by the corpses of Sefton's minions. I find myself wrapping an arm around the girl. I hold Allison's hand too, which leaves me with no hands free to fight, if the need should arise, but I don't care. After five years of torment, I've found peace in the middle of an apocalypse.

We stop halfway across the lawn and tip our heads back to take in the sight above us.

Fireballs and lightning streak across the sky, slamming down to penetrate the earth. The concussions of those impacts vibrate under our feet, growing stronger every second as they draw ever closer to Fallenmouth. Darkness pours out of the Echo, rushing toward the estate in a tidal wave of dark energies that will soon engulf us.

Allison grips my hand more firmly. "The alchemy of worlds hasn't stopped. We failed."

"No, I don't believe that's what is happening."

"What, then? Looks like the apocalypse all over again."

I nod toward the sky. "Look. You can see the alchemical reaction hasn't started up again in the distance. It's only here at Fallenmouth. Sefton had created wards around the estate to protect it from the chaos. Now, with him gone, the last gasp of the alchemy of worlds needs to fill in the gap."

"There's only one way to know for sure. We need to zip ourselves to various places and see if the reaction has ended."

"I agree."

And we do just that, though I grab the alchemical manuscripts Sefton had collected before we leave. We discover the books in the library, laid out on the chaise by the windows. Sefton must have put them there after we searched the house and didn't feel the need to protect them, arrogantly certain of his impending victory. They might come in handy. We check London first, then Fort Worth and several other cities around the globe. After satisfying ourselves that the reaction has ceased, we return to the Lost Coast. The four of us might be the only people living here now, but things will change. We will make certain of it, together.

My brother believed he had cursed me to eternal torment, but he never predicted the one variable neither of us could control—Allison Dahl, the woman who saved my soul and the world.

EPILOGUE

Allison

A BONFIRE CRACKLES IN FRONT OF US WHILE DAX AND I CUDDLE ON the grass nearby, his arm around me and my head on his shoulder. Not that long ago, I hated and feared him. Now, I love to cuddle up with my sexy beast and gaze at the stars or the ocean or a bonfire. Today, we're celebrating the Fourth of July—a little late. With no clocks or calendars to go by, we didn't realize until this morning that Independence Day had come and gone weeks ago. Everyone in our camp agreed that we should do something to commemorate the holiday.

Why? Because everyone who lives in our new enclave on the Lost Coast has escaped from the horrors of the alchemy of worlds. We have broken free of Sefton's vision for the world and created a community out here in the wilds. The cities are still ruled by Echo creatures, and the opening to the Echo still hangs in the sky above us, though we can't see it as long as we're outside the invisible boundaries around the cities and a good chunk of the suburbs, not to mention sections of the rural areas. Whenever a solitary creature manages to reach this enclave, we take that monster down. Everyone pitches in. Even the former nun in our group has taken up arms to help defend the community.

At first, we didn't seek out new members. They would find us, though no one could explain how they discovered our enclave. I think it's the Echo power in them. It just hasn't surfaced yet in a way that anyone can recognize. How many people harbor that power inside them? Nobody knows. These days, when we venture out into the world, we invite the lost souls we meet to join our community. Some do, some don't. We rely on our instincts to decide who to trust.

Grant has become a good friend to both me and Dax—and our adopted daughter, Willow. He still grieves for his wife and son, but I hope one day he will find someone new. Grant is such a good man that he deserves to know love again.

Seven weeks have gone by since the day Dax killed his brother and the alchemical reaction ground to a halt. We returned to Fallenmouth a few days after that and found the estate in ruins, ravaged by the apocalypse. But over the weeks since then, we've checked on other areas around the globe. The alchemy of worlds has clearly ended for good, though the consequences of what Sefton did haven't been erased. One day, we will undo the damage. I believe that with all my heart and soul.

Grant ducks into his tent and emerges holding a plastic bag. He waves it in the air. "Look what I found today. Who wants toasted marshmallows?"

Willow jumps up and down. "Me! Yes!"

That's right. We hunt for more than essential supplies when we head out into the post-apocalyptic world. Allowing ourselves to enjoy the occasional treat makes living out here seem less like escaping from danger and more like coming home.

As much as I love toasted marshmallows, I have something to tell Dax—alone. So I lift my head to whisper into his ear, "Grab the lantern and let's go for a walk."

"Now?"

"Yes. Please."

He retrieves our oil lantern from our tent and takes my hand as we amble away from the group, into the woods. We stop just inside the canopy of trees.

"What is it?" he asks.

Yeah, he knows me well enough to realize I need to say something. "Well, it's, um…"

"Relax, Ally. You can tell me anything."

"When we were in LA today, in that pharmacy, I grabbed something. While you and Grant were hunting for medicine and food."

"What did you take?"

"A home pregnancy test."

He goes perfectly still, his eyes glimmering in the lantern light.

I take a breath and just say it. "I'm pregnant, Dax."

The lantern drops to the ground, and his mouth falls open.

"Are you okay with this development?" I ask. "It's a lot to process, I know. We're living in a post-apocalyptic world, which isn't the ideal place to raise a child."

He wraps his arms around me, tugging me close. "We can do this, Ally, I know we can. All that matters is our family—you, me, Willow, and our baby."

"I'm so glad you feel that way, because I want our baby so much."

"And I do too."

We wander back to the bonfire and share our news with everyone. I cry. Willow cries. Even Dax gets a little choked up. This will be the first baby born in our new community.

That night, we make love in our tent, slowly, sensually, celebrating our impending parenthood the best way we know how. Willow has her own tent, as any teenage girl should. That means Dax and I can spend all night reveling in the love that saved us both and made this baby.

A month later, a newcomer arrives. The raven-haired beauty catches Grant's eye, though he won't admit to that. So he does what any red-blooded man would. He ignores her. I know Grant can't admit he's attracted to Erin yet, not until he has more distance from the loss of his family. That might take years. Of course, the pace of life during the Echo has changed things for everyone. Time seems more precious, every day more meaningful.

Dax and I have become the unofficial leaders of this ragtag group. Everyone expects us to have a plan to undo the apocalypse, but we are not experts on the topic. Not long after we settled here, Grant asked if he could study the alchemical manuscripts Sefton had stolen from the Getty Institute and that Dax had rescued from Fallenmouth before the Echo ravaged it. Grant isn't a scientist or a philosopher, but he has become engrossed in understanding those books.

One day, we will find a way to restore the world. I believe that. I feel the truth of it. Someone in our community is destined to uncover the secrets of the Echo. Will it be Grant? Who knows. But it will happen.

If a beastly man from the Echo can win the heart of a librarian, anything is possible.

The apocalypse isn't over yet.

**Grant Larson returns in *Echo Dominion*,
book two of the Echo Power Trilogy.**

ANNA DURAND IS A BESTSELLING, MULTI-AWARD-WINNING AUTHOR OF contemporary and paranormal romance. Her books have earned bestseller status on every major retailer and wonderful reviews from readers around the world. But that's the boring spiel. Here are some really cool things you want to know about Anna!

Born on Lackland Air Force Base in Texas, Anna grew up moving here, there, and everywhere thanks to her dad's job as an instructor pilot. She's lived in Texas (twice), Mississippi, California (twice), Michigan (twice), and Alaska—and now Ohio.

As for her writing, Anna has always made up stories in her head, but she didn't write them down until her teen years. Those first awful books went into the trash can a few years later, though she learned a lot from those stories. Eventually, she would pen her first romance novel, the paranormal romance *Willpower*, and she's never looked back since.

Want even more details about Anna? Get access to her extended bio when you subscribe to her newsletter and download the free bonus ebook, *Hot Scots Confidential*. You'll also get hot deleted scenes, character interviews, fun facts, and more!

VISIT ANNADURAND.COM TO SIGN UP.